Autumn Nightmare

Published by:
Powder River Publishing LLC
1014 Black Mountain Road
Thermopolis, Wyoming 82443

www.powderriverpublishing.com

Table of Contents

Dedication

This book is dedicated to:

To the family that saw something in me I did not. Especially my husband and hero, Scott.

John's ever supportive Mom, Jane.

Special thanks to Captain Sean VanSyckle. For serving this country when it isn't popular and for helping shape this book.

PROLOGUE

She didn't understand how he knew where to go; didn't care really. It was a fleeting thing, that moment of curiosity. Swallowed up by the darkness inside, almost as quickly as thought.

It was a living thing, that darkness, a seething, squirming thing smothering any light that may have once been a part of him. It was hungry. Hungry for more, for everything.

She figured that was how he knew where to go now though. Well, maybe it was the smell too. That miasma of desperation, hate, anger, hopelessness that hung in the very air of this part of Chicago.

Too many years of gang fighting, drug dealing, drug use, murder, and prostitution, tainted the brick and wood of the buildings and soaked into the broken pavement like water in sand. Blood, semen and puke was the ink used for this terrible illustration. Boarded up windows, burned out cars, used needles were the stories told.

Craziness. The nectar of his dreams, if the black, fetid thoughts in his seething mind could be called dreams. Her nightmare.

So, here she was, hunting with him. There was something specific he was looking for. Something that was expected of him as well. When his hunger was satisfied he had to return with a gift.

Again the darkness pushed away thought, nudged his hunger. He relaxed tight muscles, took a deep breath and let his sinuses and senses filter out the distracting scents to the one he needed.

There. Behind the barred up grocery store that probably got robbed twice a week. Just there, around the corner. The girl was already dead, though the heart still beat. The effects of meth were as unforgiving as his hunger. That was ok. He didn't need the girl to be responsive.

The girl did manage to lift a hand weakly, a plea in her eyes that quickly changed to terror. Slowly the eyes showed nothing as blood pooled over the iris. The killer didn't even pause in his pursuit of temporary satisfaction.

When he was done he stood up and stepped back. In the darkness the victim's blood merely looked like darker shadows but she knew what would be found in the light of day. And what would not.

He found a relatively clean piece of cloth that could have been a tattered shirt and wiped dripping hands and face. Stooping; he picked through the shredded remains, looking for the prize he'd been sent for. Finding it, he gently wrapped it in the black velvet cloth he'd been given for that purpose and walked away, not caring that his footprints were like finger paintings on the alley floor.

Jane sat up, sweating, crying. Oh, my God! What had just happened? What had she just seen? Where were her cards?

Chapter 1

Zoey Abero looked at herself in the mirror. She briefly thought about taking a selfie, but she wasn't sixteen anymore. She pouted into the mirror. Her lips could convey many things. The expression might be disappointment, or it might be a playful tease saying want to see what else these lips are capable of? Continuing her self-examination Zoey noted that she didn't look bad for twenty-seven.

Her breasts didn't sag, they were still firm, some people might even call them perky. Her freshly shaved legs were long and athletic. She spent the little free time she had off work taking care of herself, which equated to miles of running through the safer parts of the Windy City.

She knew she should eat healthier, junk food was a weakness, but what the hell. You only got one life to live, she could at least indulge herself when it came to food, right. Right!

Checking the mirror a second time, she smiled. She had her daddy's eyes? Dominant genes and all that. Her father was Hungarian and always claimed that he was a demigod descended to earth to court her mother. She knew they glimmered as if they spilled out mischievous dust crystals. The color was commented on by anyone who took the time to actually look at them. They had been called golden, amber, and even tiger eye by many, though they were not striped. She knew they were the object of much envy by some of her female colleagues.

Her hair, she inherited from her mother. To call it simply brunette would be an unfair injustice to her French heritage. The color of her hair was Noisette. Black espresso with a drop or two of cream shaded with hazelnut.

Then Zoey's smile turned into a frown. The snow was a

thick curtain as it came down harder every Moment. Chicago in the winter. Her headlights barely cut a foot out, she reduced her speed. It didn't help. Tires spinning on ice, not getting traction. She was sliding. She tried turning into the slide to correct the action and regain control, but it wasn't happening. Time seemed to slow down as the lights of the semi blinded her.

When she woke up in the hospital, she was told that the collision sent her car through the guard rail. She was lucky to be alive. The first responders saved her life. They needed to work fast or she would have bled out after the piece of windshield went into her neck. That piece of glass had become this long dark reddish brown puckered ugly mark that ran from her throat up her face ending below her right eye.

She refused to get plastic surgery to alter her appearance. She knew that one's physical appearance was only cosmetic. A person's spirit, personality, and non-physical attributes truly defined who a person was, but the scar still made her feel self-conscience. If any man couldn't appreciate her for her mind and laughter then he wasn't worth a pot to piss in anyway.

The scar made Zoey feel ugly though, and that is when insecurity reared its dragon-like head dripping with slime from the swamp it came from. She knew that her parents would have many things to say along the lines of how proud they were of her, that she had a career. They would say that the scar was just a reminder of the car crash she survived. That was true. But her parents were biased. Parents loved you unconditionally, they were not a man she wanted to ravish her with masculine abandon to the point of exhaustion.

Yeah right. As if that was ever going to happen. Zoey pulled on her favorite pair of grey slacks. She spent the money to have these pants tailored to fit her correctly. They accented her derriere, but more importantly they were comfortable and professional at the same time. Win, win.

Next, the pink brassiere. The one that fit properly, did its job, and hurt the least. Once that was in place Zoey looked through her blouses trying to decide which to wear. She picked the grey silk one that went with her pants.

In the middle of brushing her teeth the music on her Spotify stopped. The music interrupted by the phone ringing. Who called at five A.M.?

Zoey fumbled for her phone, and the toothbrush flew out of her hand splattering her mirror with gunk. Her hand knocked the phone off the edge of the sink onto the floor.

"Niquer! Too early for this. Need coffee, " Zoey swore. Retrieving the phone Zoey smeared the screen with white and blue toothpaste, but she managed to accept the call with the swipe, and a few more curses in French. It was such a beautiful language, even the swearing sounded sexy.

Unceremoniously spitting, she answered the phone, "Hello."

"Abero?" The gruff voice inquired. She thought she recognized that voice.

"This is she," Zoey confirmed.

"Detective Victor Kingsley here. I've got something you've got to see."

Chapter 2

Jake heard the phone ringing as he stepped out of the shower. Grabbing a towel he swiped at his short blond hair even as he reached for the offensive piece of equipment. He glanced at the raven-haired beauty in his bed to make sure she was sleeping. Flashes of the steamy night of sex they had shared tempted him mightily to put the phone back down. But no. She was sexy as hell and hot in bed for a fact, but she couldn't hold a candle to the adrenaline rush of work and that's what this call was about, only Detective Victor Kingsley had the "Hawaii Five O" ringtone. The office had "Magnum PI."

"Corde," he answered with his standard greeting.

"Marquette and Wolcott, can't miss the cars."

"Shit. That's forty minutes from here."

"Well, hurry up, Cinderella you are not." Kingsley sniped.

Coffee pot on automatic had some hot brew ready for him in the kitchen. He was tucking his shirt in and pouring some of the life-giving liquid into an igloo cup when Alissa shuffled out of the bedroom wearing one of his shirts. That wasn't sexy to him, it was irritating. It meant more laundry.

It meant she would rather rummage through his drawers than get dressed in her own clothes. If they were a steady couple or something it might be different but he didn't really even plan to get to know her better. He already knew more than he wanted to. She was a nail biter, a teeth grinder and she made yum noises when she ate. It was all too much for his nerves.

More sharply than he probably should have, he said, "Get dressed sweetheart, I gotta go."

"I can lock up." She yawned and stretched. He could tell it wasn't real. She was trying to exert her sexual power and make him forget his purpose for the day.

"No, sorry. Hurry up." Cold day in hell anyone was left alone in his apartment. Even colder day when someone had power of any kind over him.

Once he had her disgruntled butt in a cab he got into his vehicle and headed for one of the worst crime spots in his beloved Windy City. "Siri," he told his car "Call the office."

"Calling Office."

"Corde Brothers Investigations."

"Hey beautiful. Just got a call from Lieutenant Kingsley of the Chicago Bureau of investigations. Have you seen it on the news?"

"No but one of Matt's buddies called, it's a pretty nasty business baby. Some girl was murdered in West Englewood. Help them boys in blue figure this out and I'll love you forever."

"You will anyway. You married my carbon copy so you must think I'm hot. I keep trying to get him to play the 'twin switch' on you for one night but he refuses."

"Because he is brilliant enough to know I would figure it out within seconds and kill him for it. You are too much of an adrenaline junkie to care about the danger you court. You have premature frown lines between those hazel eyes."

"Chameleon."

"And," she continued as though he hadn't said a thing, "your lips are thicker."

"More kissable you mean."

"You are more serious."

"Intense."

"Meaner."

"Honestly concise."

That earned a snort of derision.

"Peggy?"

"What?"

"You forgot built like Adonis."

"I forgot humble too, see the trend?"

Jake burst out laughing. Peggy was a special light in the family. Loving, kind, honest, funny. Jake was secretly jealous of Luke's damn good fortune. She was an amazing addition to the family.

He would never find his own Peggy. He accepted that. He

was too average. Six foot tall, dishwater blond hair, hazel eyes, wide mouth with full lips, stubborn chin, square jaw.

Decent hands, long fingered and clean, trimmed short nails. Tight ass and slim waist. He had nice shoulders, wide and strong but lots of guys did. Still, nothing spectacular. His mind was sharp. High I.Q. But as soon as he opened his mouth he showed his true colors. Angry, dark, distrusting, cynical, skeptical and sarcastic.

While he and Luke were identical twins, Luke's physique was more suave, slimmer. Probably because Jake worked out more in the weight room. Alex was built like a pro football player, while Matt was the perfect combination of brawn and good looks.

Jake had started his own detective agency after only one year on the police force because he couldn't play nice with others for more than a hot second. Except his brothers Luke, Alexander, and Mathew. But they loved him. Mom said they had to.

Mom was God's right hand on earth. Everything she said came straight from heaven and her boys acted accordingly. Jane Corde was not a force one battled against.

His thoughts switched gears between heartbeats as he came to a roadblock with six police cars staggered around the intersection. Victor hadn't lied. He parked and got out of his Mustang, flashing his identification fifty times to reach the detective through the crowd. He could see Victor talking to a hot little number. A reporter probably.

Chapter 3

"I told you Victor, I understand, now will you let me have a look?" Zoey asked.

"One second, Abero, I get you want to get to work but there are a couple of things I want to go over. First, you need to steel yourself. This is more than we have run across in quite some time. Gruesome.

I would also appreciate it if you would let me introduce you to someone I asked to join us. Jake, Zoey Abero is our medical examiner. Zoey, Jake Corde, a top notch investigator. I hope you two can work together." Victor introduced them.

"Hey," Jake said, and nodded his head instead of offering his hand for a shake.

"Hey," Zoey shot back coldly. Inwardly she winced, was he too good to shake her hand? What was up with that?

"What have we got?" Jake asked Victor.

"A true nightmare or I wouldn't have called you," Victor said.

"I get it," Jake returned.

"Don't say I didn't warn you," Victor stepped aside sweeping his hand indicating that the two proceed to look at the scene. Zoey watched Corde walk forward. His pants fit him extremely well. What a nice ass, it practically screamed grab me, I'm firm. Too bad his personality wasn't as great as that view. Damn! She pulled her mind back to the work at hand, knowing that time was of the essence.

The crime scene before her, graphic beyond description locked in her memory. Victor calling the scene a nightmare didn't begin to do it justice, nightmare was too soft a word. This macabre picture would have been a horror writer's wet dream and still make them wake up screaming.

She swallowed convulsively, took a few shallow breaths and looked at the scene edges rather than straight on. It was a technique she had learned long ago. The human psyche can get used to anything if given time to adjust, foreknowledge if you will. By looking at the blood spatters, the bent knees, the foot with the missing shoe, the mind is able to move ahead without shock.

Blood splattered the street and sides of the buildings. Blood pooled in every crack the street provided in a five-foot area around the victim. How much blood did a human body hold? She knew the answer ranged from 1.2 to 1.5 gallons, and that amount was outside of the corpse. The cadaver, or what remained of it, appeared as if it had been shredded, ripped apart like someone caught in a war zone.

"Teeth," Zoey said almost inaudibly.

"You think an animal did this?" The consultant Corde asked.

"Your hearing is acute. I whispered, and I don't know. I just don't know," Zoey admitted.

Corde pointed to something laying on the ground a foot away from the body. Zoey's eyes followed his finger. She got one of her flashes of intuition as soon as her eyes fell on the piece of fabric that Corde pointed out. Unfortunately, the image didn't show her who or what had dropped the blood drenched remnant of a shirt onto the street. It never did. Her talent was as unreliable as it was helpful most of the time.

"Victor, bag that for evidence. It might have a hair follicle or skin cell sample. Get it to forensics a.s.a.p. for analysis," Corde said.

Wearing gloves, Victor carefully picked up the soaked item, placed it in a bag, sealed the bag, and handed it to Zoey.

"I'm forensics, remember?" She curtly told Corde. His eyes were a stormy sea of serious green, and stern grey. They were all business and more intense eyes than she'd ever seen before. On any other day but this one, those eyes might have been captivating. Today they were haunted by the scene before them.

He looked away from her and in fact stepped back a few paces and set his jaw. Zoey couldn't help but watch him. Obviously he took care of himself because he was cut! How much free time did he have to work out?

Zoey returned her eyes to the victim. The projector in her mind brought another image.

The victim's hand was outstretched as though pleading for mercy. Blackness. What the fuck? What kind of twisted psyche could have allowed someone to murder another person in this manner?

Shooting someone, stabbing someone, but this. This Zoey couldn't begin to comprehend.

There seemed to be no logical thought behind the act. Maybe the 'no thought behind the act' would be a topic to revisit later. Corde moved closer to the remains and knelt. Then he snapped his head up and studied the surrounding buildings. His body tensed, his eyes shifting back and forth.

Zoey couldn't help herself before she blurted. "What?"

"Nothing," Corde answered.

"Bullshit!" Zoey followed Corde's example and squatted near the corpse to examine details more closely.

"She was dissected and..." Zoey gasped.

"Then eaten!" They said simultaneously, still staring at the mutilated cadaver.

"Her entire jaw is missing. That will make dental identification difficult," Zoey noted.

"Ripped it right off of her skull! What could do THAT!" Corde asked.

"That is the sixty-four-million-dollar question isn't it," Zoey said, rising from her squat.

"That it is," Corde affirmed as he too stood. "Want to get a drink?"

"I need to get to the lab," Zoey said, holding up the evidence bag.

Chapter 4

Once she had all of her Personal Protection Equipment on, Zoey carefully opened the evidence bag that Victor handed her. After two years as a professional Forensic Medical Examiner the smell of blood should have been something that Zoey had become used to, but she hadn't. Despite the face mask as soon as she opened the bag the tangy metallic scent entered her sinuses.

The smell of blood didn't bother her, but reminded her constantly of why she did the work she did. It wasn't her job to catch killers; that is what the police did, but it didn't mean that she couldn't do her best to assist the world to stop evil. She wasn't altruistic, but if she could aid the Police Department or whatever agency required her services so much the better. She also had more mundane work, people who weren't murdered, but died from accidents or natural causes.

She needed to work on this first piece of evidence before the rest of her team got the body here. How long that might take depended on any number of factors. The first thing Zoey did with a pair of forceps is remove the bloodstained article and place it on her sterilized microscope to look at the blood, and work on identifying the blood type of the victim.

She also needed to identify if there happened to be any other liquids on the tattered piece of shirt, such as sweat, semen, vaginal secretions, and so forth. Was only one person's blood on the evidence? She started working. Looking at blood through a microscope fascinated Zoey. Platelets and cells.

"Come on, get a match already," she muttered to herself, "What is taking you so long?" Oh shit, she reminded herself to look for trace amounts of drugs to see if they were interfering with the process. Sure enough there it was, Methadone. Okay, she told herself, and adjusted her instrumentation accordingly. And Type O it was. Not surprising as it was the most common blood type and also therefore the most frustrating as it meant the largest population of people to work with, made it harder to narrow down a positive I.D. for Jane Doe.

Zoey now looked through the microscope for trace amounts of any substance other than blood. Just as she began her stomach growled like a cornered animal. Damn, what time was it anyway? She hadn't eaten anything yet.

She couldn't leave with the body coming in soon. But, it had been a very intense morning, and eating something was not against the rules, right? Right! So how about some takeout? She went to her office and dug out a menu from her favorite breakfast place.

"Biscuits and gravy, along with three pancakes smothered in blueberry syrup," she ordered over the phone for delivery. "And an English muffin, cream cheese, and strawberry jam. You have my card number, the delivery guys know how to get here. Add a $10 tip."

Zoey stared at her computer screen impatiently waiting for the delivery. Her phone rang.
"Hey Kell, what's up?" She asked.

"We are almost there, meet us at the door?" the woman warrior said.

"On my way," Zoey said, ending the call.

It was a short elevator ride up and ten steps to the back door where incoming bodies were brought through for processing. The evidence for this one was in quite a few bags stacked in crates. It took all hands to carry everything to the morgue.

The cold autopsy room was noisier than television portrayed. The air conditioning unit that regulates the room, the ventilation exhaust, the hum of the computer, the squeak of wheels on trolleys, so many things made noise down here. All of it was white noise once you started work.

They put the bags on the tables. They waited for Zoey to give the go ahead, which she did. Then they began opening the bags. Her assistant had magically managed to get everything else ready in the few seconds she had been back. She really appreciated Kellesha. The woman worked hard and showed real initiative at the right moments and deference when she should. The perfect combination. Zoey would be very disappointed when Kell finished her internship.

"Lieutenant," Zoey nodded to the man in the dark gray suit.

"Doc. How long will this take?" Victor asked.

"You know better than to ask me. I have no way of knowing what I am going to run into. The blood brought back from the scene is being analyzed as we speak, the cloth gone over with infinite care. The lab techs are top notch. I can tell you type O blood laced with Meth. We will call you as soon as we have the other results."

"As soon as you have dental impressions, finger prints, anything I can use to identify the...are you sure of gender?"

"Yes. Female. I can even tell you the time of death was around one in the morning."

The detective nodded then turned and left the room. No nonsense about that guy. He probably folded his dirty clothes before putting them in the hamper. Still, he was a good cop, a good man.

She watched him go then turned to her team, and the work before them.

The task ended up being more like a jigsaw puzzle than an autopsy. Whoever...whatever had done this had used such force that the rib bones had shattered. Some of the rendered flesh was clean cut, some raggedly torn.

Zoey dispersed the rest of her team, all but Kellesha. Her warrior woman intern remained and assisted as instructed. This needed to be treated with even more than normal care.

"Let's cover her up for a minute. My back could use a bit of a rest. Come into my office and have coffee with me?" Zoey suggested.

Kell gave her a look, then shrugged. "You're the boss."

"Coffee break," Zoey affirmed. They went to her office a few doors away, poured cups of Java, and sat at the small round table.

"I know you, you didn't need a break this early. What is bothering you?" Kell opened.

"Thought we should chat," Zoey responded. Kell nearly spit her coffee out repressing laughter.

"Chat? What do you want to know about?"

"What are you going to do when you finish your internship?"

"Find a man, get married, have 2.5 kids, all that?"

"Don't believe it for a second." Zoey said.

"Honestly, I don't know. I haven't thought about where I see myself five years from now. I'm trying to focus on my school work," Kell admitted.

"I'm not that far removed from it, if you ever need help with some of the medical terms or anything else for that matter," Zoey offered.

"Thanks, Boss."

They both laughed.

Finishing her coffee, Zoey said, "Work the desk for an hour, I'll get back to Jane Doe."

"On it."

Zoey returned to the autopsy room. Once all of the missing organs had been noted, Kellesha's return was right on time to get everything catalogued and the remains put back in the best anatomical order she could manage, she closed up. If not for Kellesha's help she would have been bent over that body for an extra three or four hours. The logging in of the various and assorted injuries alone took hours. Never had she encountered such a difficult autopsy.

Suddenly the images flashing through her mind made her flesh crawl and her blood run cold. This killer was more than a man, worse than a man. His actions were not of hate or anger but hunger and direction. He worked alone, but not.

Her confusion angered and frightened her. The very fact that she couldn't find answers right away was frustrating. But there were upper jaw impressions and a few fingerprints for identification so there was a positive.

The other side of that positive coin was that she suspected the woman was a homeless prostitute. She could have a record but did it have her real name or her street name? It would be a

wonderful thing if they could find a family for her, give her a proper send off.

Completing that autopsy, she dismissed Kellesha, and went to work on other less complicated autopsies. Zoey didn't watch the clock, she just worked. Three more done.

Sighing, she stretched side to side then backwards to work out the kinks. It was getting late. She had been at it all day and she noticed the take out delivery boxes of food sitting on her desk and shook her head. As much as she loved to eat it seemed like she would be less careless.

She tossed the boxes into the garbage, took off her lab coat and walked through the door. Kellesha was gone already. The lab was empty except for the corpses laying in their coolers.

The guards wandering outside were the only living things around here. She saw one turn the corner as she stepped outside and turned to lock the door. Her mind on her task she didn't hear the steps approaching.

She had just armed the security system when she heard a cough behind her. Whirling around her gaze fell on the consultant from this morning who was too good to shake her hand. Her heart skipped a beat. She noted the butterflies in her belly and pushed them down. No. Dammit.

Chapter 5

0700

    No ordinary day starts out in such a horrible manner. Who shreds a human being, eats their fill, then leaves with a mandible as a trophy? What happened to popcorn for a midnight snack?

    The world was going to hell in a handbasket. Bunch of crazies out there now. Was a time when Tommy guns and Godfathers ruled the streets. Oh for the good ol' days!

    Jake spun the wheel of his Mustang, turning into the small parking lot next to the family owned and run business. Only two of his brothers were in today. Alexander's candy apple red corvette was nowhere to be seen.

    That was nothing new though. Alex was always off on the long distance jaunts, courting international sources, more big money cases, or both. He was probably in England or Switzerland or something. Alex liked to travel, meet new people. He said he gained culture, whatever that meant. There was plenty of culture right here in Chicago.

    But Matt and Luke were in. He felt a wash of relief. Only his brothers and Peggy, and Mom of course, knew exactly why he was such a successful investigator. They would not doubt him, nor laugh when he told them about his morning.

    Peggy was at her desk, phone to her ear as usual when he entered. One look at his face and she was ending the call though. He turned the closed sign and indicated the conference room.

    Every morning this room was swept for spy devices. They hadn't found anything in years but some of their cases were supremely sensitive so the extra care was not only necessary but the right thing to do. The windowless room had no floor or ceiling crawl space. The walls were lined with top of the line soundproofing and all of the power sources were fed by a small generator that sat in the corner. Cut the power to the building and this room would still be viable.

Peggy must have pushed her magic panic button because Jake no more than sat down with a dram of ginger brandy when little brother Mathew walked in, followed closely by Jake's twin, Luke. Peggy came in last with a tray of bagels and cream cheese and an armful of folders. She was ever hopeful that her endless pile of folders would get worked through in these meetings. But she was doomed to disappointment today.

She pulled the door shut tight behind her, placed her hand into a recess in the wall for a finger prick blood identification and stared straight ahead for a retina scan. That done she turned and placed the tray on the table and sat down.

No one would enter this room now, until Peggy herself opened the door. No one would leave it either. Everyone settled in then looked over at Jake.

Taking a deep breath Jake described the crime scene in vivid detail, sparing no one. A murder so heinous deserved the bald truth. When he finished he glanced at his sister-in-law apologetically. She was pale, but otherwise showed no sign of weakness. "And?" Luke's voice drew his attention. Luke, always the good man. Kind and gentle. When Luke was in the room Jake felt grounded, in control, less...angry.

Throwing back the brandy Jake looked his brother right in the eye. "I saw this building blowing up. Mom, bloody in the street. I saw Victor Kingsley staring up sightlessly. I saw Doctor Abero and I standing next to each other. More, so much more! Too much, too timeless. I am struggling to process it all. I saw a cops badge. A red car but I can't make out the model. I saw a little girl crying. I saw myself hunted, all of you hunted."

He poured another brandy and tossed that back as easily as the first, missing the look that the others shared. Jake was a "my body is my temple" kind of guy. In the gym three times a week, jogging every day he was the most health conscious of them all. Except for coffee. And now, apparently ginger brandy.

Jake was the rock. The big brother who always stepped up and did the things that needed done. It was a shock to see the guy who had a "one beer" rule down liquor like it was water from the fountain of youth.

So they sat up straighter and waited. Jake was rattled. He was worried even. It was the right strategy. Jake dropped his bombshell.

"Peggy, cancel all activity, even if it means giving money back. Then go home and pack for an extended vacation. Luke, get her out of this city. Go to Vegas or Monte Carlo. I don't care. Just go."

He turned to Matt without missing a beat. "Go get Mom. Take her to Grams and Gramps in Hawaii or Vegas with Luke. Whatever. Just go. I have this..." he curls his fingers and gestures in circles around his midriff, "...awful feeling Mom is in danger. I don't want her anywhere near here with her damn cards. My visions are mystic enough for now. This is far, far from over. And it's going to get worse. I feel it to my very bones. Nefarious."

"But what about you?" Peggy asked, already knowing the answer.

"I'm in it. It's too late. I have to stop this monster. Call Alex. Tell him what's going on but don't worry, we have it under control. Tell him to travel Europe. Have fun."

"We aren't leaving." Mathew the most obstinate of them almost visibly digging in his heels.

"The hell you say!!" Jake roared, coming around the table. "You go get Mom out of this goddamn city little brother! I am as serious as a heart attack. Our girls have to be your first priority. I've been to the crime scene. I'm a part of it now. Do as I ask! Do what we both know I can't. Please."

The brothers talked about money next. Jake knew his brothers would know what to do in this situation, but he wanted to go over protocols anyway. This part was very important. Everyone agreed to the set procedures.

They would make some calls and put a hold on all of their credit cards and bank accounts. It would take Mom to reactivate everything. It was perhaps over-kill but it kept anyone from messing around with you financially.

Each brother had their own hidden stash, that was one of the protocols that had been set up when the company was started.

They had taken the first amount of profit from the company and each set some aside in case they needed it in the future. He had enough money to last a while before he had to break into his real stash.

Jake would need to stop at a supermarket and buy a burner phone. This was how he would communicate with the world from now on. Each brother would kill their phones and do the same. They took on clients who drew some powerful enemies. It was never a bad time to watch your back and prepare for the worst.

Proper previous planning prevents piss poor performance or something like that. Thank you, Mom.

"Fuck." Luke muttered angrily even as he ushered his wife toward the door. It was a bad situation when Jake used his angry voice at the baby of the family.

Jake gave Peggy an encouraging smile as she looked at him worriedly over her husband's shoulder. "I will get those files when I come back this evening. Just leave them on my desk, love. I promise."

She obviously wasn't reassured by his words, but she nodded acceptance and opened the door to allow egress. Jake gave Matt a pat on the back. "Thanks Matt. I'm sorry, I know Mom can be tough."

"I can handle Mom." Matt rolled his eyes. "What I really don't appreciate is my big brother trying to Lone Ranger it."

"As soon as I get a better picture of what's going on, I will call you first Matt."

After watching his family slowly make their way out of the building and off to their own tasks Jake went to his apartment, putting everything important to him in a lock box, storing it in the small building that was the office of Corde Brothers Investigations. It was secured with protocols put in place for just this kind of eventuality.

With the button on his key fob sheets of steel slid over windows and doors. Iron bars then fell into place. Mechanical locks could be heard slamming home and cameras came on, giving full on views of all four sides and the roof. The scene was being fed to a bank of computer screens far off site, viewed by a loyal friend who did not exist in the real world.

The only way in would be with a court order or a shit ton of semtex. Both of which leave behind a paper trail no self-respecting criminal wants. Hopefully it didn't come to that though, Jake rather liked the building and its contents.

If they needed to contact each other they would call a friend of a friend of a friend who would pass on the new phone number and only that. No messages. It was cumbersome but kept the bad guys from tapping phones.

From the store Jake went to a hotel and checked in. He stayed there for an hour then snuck out the bathroom window, just in case he was already being watched. From there he walked down a couple of blocks to a car dealership and rented a beater. He knew in his bones everyone connected to this case was in danger. Detective Victor had to be warned as well. But his first priority was the mysterious Zoey Abero. The Medical Examiner's office was halfway across town but he was determined to get there before it closed. He needed to talk to Miss Abero before she left work. She too needed to take precautions.

Corde started the rental. What a disappointment, it didn't even remotely sound like the low growl of the Mustang. Oh well, he knew his pony stuck out like a sore thumb, this was much more discrete. For safety, it needed to be that way.

He turned on the radio. It came on with the current pop station, after he heard the first few notes of the song, he turned it off again. Silence sounded better than the W-Sex station of the day. Fuck, could this day get any worse? Don't answer that Corde, he told himself, knowing that it could.

Chapter 6

Driving to the M.E.'s office was a nightmare. Damn Chicago rush hour traffic anyway. Corde pounded on the steering wheel in frustration.

"Fuck! Fuck! Fuck!" He turned the radio back on. After listening to the three songs they had in rotation twice, he decided that his opinion of it hadn't changed. Stopped behind a line of cars, he flipped through the stations. He found a classic rock station. Better.

At last traffic started moving again. Slowly, but movement was movement. It meant progress. An hour and a half later he arrived in the M.E.'s parking lot. Now the question happened to be if Miss Abero was still in the office.

She started her day at the crime scene, and that was well over thirteen hours ago. When he got there, he no more than got out of the rental when he noticed the guards walking their beat. She was gone already. He got back in and slammed his door so hard the other windows rattled in their tracks.

He should have come here first dammit. He should have warned her at the scene of his suspicions. But how could he explain what he knew?

With no idea where she lived he had two choices, he could go back to the office and use his sources to find her or he could get Victor to call her.

He looked at his phone. 8 P.M. There were two other cars in the lot, could one of them be hers? One of the cars was a newer silver Audi, that must have cost a pretty penny. The other car, a light metallic green electric Renault Twingo. Both of the cars were worth noting.

He again debated calling Victor. Not yet, that would be a last resort, he wasn't a private investigator for nothing. He got out of the piece of shit, and looked inside the two cars. The Audi's floor was littered with fast food wrappers. Not a healthy diet.

The interior of the Renault was pristine, did anyone drive this car?

With his inspection of the parking lot complete, Jake headed toward the building. He made it halfway across the lot when the door opened. He stopped in his tracks, watching.

Abero turned and locked the door, then armed a security system. He didn't want to scare her, so he faked a cough. She turned around. She really was a stunning woman.

"I thought we might share some thoughts on this case, Miss Abero," he opened.

"The guy who is afraid to shake a girl's hand?" Zoey said blandly.

"I could buy dinner to start?" Jake offered.

"I'm starved. A slave to my stomach, so I'll agree, but I can buy my own meal," Zoey said.

"Have it your way," Jake said.

"Where are we going?" Zoey needed to know.

"That Tavern by Millenium Park is the closest," Corde said.

"I'll follow you," Zoey said. Jake thought about insisting they ride in his rental, but decided that he better spill his guts a little, and earn her trust before asking her to ditch her car.

"I'm driving that," Jake pointed.

"The city is paying you well I can see," Zoey quipped, and instantly regretted the judgemental way that sounded.

"Sure do," Jake retorted. Who did she think she was? Damn the rental, he should have taken the Mustang despite the danger it presented.

"Are you the Audi or the Renault?" He asked.

"Stalking me I see," Zoey said.

"I'm a private investigator, it goes with the job. There are only two cars in the parking lot," Jake smiled.

"Point taken," Zoey said, heading for her car.

Jake watched her walk to the Renault. A cute little car, it fit her. He knew that with the kind of money a M.E. made she could have afforded the Audi, but instead she had a smaller environmentally safe car. Not his choice for a vehicle, it wasn't a Mustang, didn't have a V-8.

Jake got back into his unsophisticated, unsexy rental, started it up, and headed out of the parking lot. Zoey followed him closely, and he drove more carefully than normal, he didn't want her to lose him.

Even the classic rock on the radio irritated him. What a day! He turned off the radio, and concentrated on driving to The Billy Goat. She didn't lose him. Good. Jake pulled into a parking slot, shut the car down, and slammed the door without bothering to lock it. Zoey parked two slots over, and got out of her car.

There were those amazing red lips, what did she do? Apply fresh lipstick while driving over here? Well, it didn't matter, he wanted her to do more things with those lips than pout. He locked those thoughts away for a moment. Okay Jake get a fucking hold of yourself and play the gentelman. Should he hold the door or not hold the door in this day and age? Fuck!

Well it isn't like he hadn't fucked up before numerous times, so why not. He walked up to the door and held it open. Call the act a professional courtesy, if nothing else. Zoey walked past him into The Billy Goat. She smelled absolutely delicious, which made him think that this actually wasn't his favorite restaurant, it wasn't exactly healthy. However, his brothers liked this place, it celebrated Chicago. The Goat just happened to be the first place he thought of in the vicinity.

Jake looked around, the place wasn't overly crowded, but he knew they were going to discuss sensitive material. He headed for a table in the most secluded spot of the restaurant, so they had the least chance of being overheard.

The waiter came over. He must be a college kid, Jake thought. He had intentionally mussed brownish hair, two days worth of stubble, and glasses that screamed, 'I have to keep studying so I can get out of this restaurant job'.

His name tag read Colton. There have been a slew of Coltons in the last few years. Where once it may have been an exotic name, now it was commonplace. Why was Jake thinking about that, well he couldn't keep the investigator out of himself. There were however better things to investigate than Colton, still he would try not to come off as an ass.

Colton handed them menus. Zoey did in fact read the menu, and Jake found her facial expressions fascinating. She clearly thought that some items must taste good, because she actually smiled while reading a menu. They both ordered cheeseburgers, this place was known for them. Colton disappeared.

Now they could talk shop.

Zoey looked at him. That is when he noticed her eyes, really noticed them. What incredible eyes! Completely, utterly unique. Holy wow Batman. Jake could not help or stop himself from just staring. He didn't even care if it seemed rude, let her comment on it.

Those eyes! Never in his 32 years had he looked at eyes that color. Jake had so many thoughts go through his head at once that he tried to reign them in, or at least slow them down. In his line of work danger was often present and real. He had been in a few shoot outs, and he would never forget them, real life wasn't the movies, that danger had been real, he could have been killed, but these eyes said danger on a whole different level. They didn't intimidate him, but they did call for caution.

The eyes also seemed to be spilling out a joke all the time, and he admitted to himself that he wouldn't mind looking into those eyes a long time, maybe even a lifetime, but he knew in his line of work he wasn't marriage material. Arousal didn't even come close to how he might feel, falling into those eyes and finding the person inside her mind, the non-physical part of what made Abero, Zoey.

Chapter 7

"You asked me to talk about the case, so talk," Zoey said. Her voice was musical too, some man was one lucky son of a bitch to have her.

"Tell me your scientific findings, and I'll tell you some of my investigator hunches," Jake countered.

"You go first, I'm still eating this second cheeseburger."

"Where to start. I don't even know where to start. Let me say this. We are dealing with a killer that is not going to stop until he is dead. I am struggling with the trophy taking aspect. I don't know why yet.

And call me crazy, but I don't think Victor, you, or myself are safe. I think we might easily become targets," there; he had laid some of his cards on the table.

"I agree for the most part. I don't think he is wholly human anymore. The way the body was shredded, no human in their right mind does that.

Add to that, the fact that the mandible was literally ripped from the face, the strength needed for that kind of thing is incredible. I don't even know the math off the top of my head. There were other things missing. Part of the kidney, the pancreas, the bladder of all things...ew." She took the last bite of burger and delicately wiped her fingers and those red red lips.

He couldn't help but notice there wasn't any lipstick on the napkin. No way! Could those lips naturally be that color? Like a red delicious apple just...ok, enough for the love of God.

"So what are we talking about here? A Sasquatch?" he asked her.

"Just a sec." She instructed him, as she waved Colton back over. "Is that carrot cake I saw on the counter when I came in?" She asked. Colton nodded. "Could you fetch me a piece? And one to go as well." She turned back to an astonished Jake. "What! I haven't eaten all day and I love carrot cake."

"Eat all you want." He shrugged.

"I will. No, not a Sasquatch, what's the matter with you? But someone extra strong. Maybe enhanced? Steroids? Into bodybuilding. That kind of thing."

He couldn't help it. His brat side came out. "A hairless Sasquatch?"

She laughed. "Ok, for the sake of the child in you, let's call him a hairless squatch."

That comment amused Jake.

The cake was set in front of her with a flourish and Colton removed their dirty dishes. She smiled up at him. He blushed and scurried away. Jake felt his groin tighten and nearly groaned at his own weakness. God forgive him this woman was going to make him insane.

"Alright, now you can tell me how you know so much about the killer." She stared at him over the forkful of carrot cake. Do not watch her eat that damn cake. Pretend your coffee is ultra interesting. He sighed, staring down at his cup.

"You will laugh me out of this dive."

"I won't. I am very open minded. Spill."

"I get flashes of knowledge. Pictures of what will be sometimes but mostly I see clues like a number, car, house, street. Very rarely, but occasionally, I can make out a face, or a personal item that belongs to someone. I don't know where it comes from so don't ask. I know it is reliable. I have trusted it for years now."

"Good, that's good. Thank you for sharing that. I know what it's like to have no one believe you." She fiddled with her fork, staring past his right ear for a Moment then her eyes swung to him and he felt gut-punched for a second.

"I get images, feelings, sometimes a stray thought. It is horrible. I can't really control it. Mostly I focus hard on the subject at hand and it all comes flooding in. So random and chaotic that I have to piece it together like a puzzle. The intensity can give me migraines at times."

Thinking of a puzzle, he placed a piece, and his understanding of the picture that was Zoey became clearer. Like him, she had visions. They shared this bizarre trait, which happened to be both helpful and frustrating when it came to their work. She was the same as he, essentially. The differences were semantics. He didn't know what to say.

"Do you ever feel like you are drowning in hate?" He asked.

"Sure, but I'm good at what I do. My parents remind me that there is light in the world."

"Yeah. Me too. Three brothers, a Mom, sister in law, one set of grandparents." He volunteered. She now knew more about him than the woman he had had in his bed just this morning. What was going on with him? When had he become such a chatty cathy? He could just hear his brothers making kissy noises and fluttering their eyelashes.

"Where do you go?" She asked.

"Pardon?"

"When your eyes turn grey and you become still as a statue. Where do you go in your head?"

"My eyes change color?"

"You're such a girl." She laughed at him.

"Are you done stuffing your face? We need to discuss safety, security. You should go to a safe house, get off this case right now. I really cannot stress...why are you looking at me like that?"

"Because you're an idiot. I am not leaving the case nor am I going into hiding. Detective Victor needs both of us with this one. You are right, it isn't over and it is only going to get bigger and bigger. Victor has to have someone watch his back as much as we need him to watch ours. Our next priority is to find him and have a chat."

"I knew the moment I laid eyes on you that you were going to be trouble."

"Wow, that was so smooth I nearly missed it. You completely changed the subject. Nicely done."

"Thank you. Stay out of my head, tiny one. You already know more than I wanted to impart."

"Fine. I'm calling Victor. We might as well get this over. The sooner we make plans the sooner we can move forward and catch a bad guy or three."

"I like catching bad guys."

She had the phone to her ear but managed a shrugging gesture that possibly meant agreement. He wasn't sure. She was an expressive woman. He liked that.

"Hey Officer Kingsley, how goes it? You wanna meet the PI and I so we can talk? No? Oh, wonderful idea. I don't mind getting drunk on a Tuesday. We'll be there in ten, twenty. Depends on the piece of shit the old guy is driving. No, no Mustang. K. See ya." She hung up and frowned at him. "You have a Mustang and are driving a...what the heck is that rust bucket?"

Chapter 8

2100

The place Victor had picked out was considered a 'cop bar' because of the number of badges that frequented the place at shift changes. Zoey had been there several times and didn't need to follow the private investigator. She wanted to drive her own vehicle. She drove toward the bar near the police station. The drive would give her time to consider this new intrusion into her well planned and scheduled life.

Jake Corde, she found him irritating and attractive at the same time. What a strange mix. She realized that although he indeed had a very adept brain in his head, when he spoke he said the strangest stuff. Sasquatch indeed!

Yet, he was certainly a specimen of a man. What a hunk! To have those hands massage her, to have those arms hold her. Who was she kidding? The butterflies were still fluttering around in her stomach as if they were frollicling through a summerday. At least now thank all the powers that be, she had some food in her stomach too. Those hazel eyes of his did turn gray when his mind went someplace. Most likely he was unaware of the details because he hadn't studied himself when his mind went places.

They both had extraordinary talents. She actually found it very honorable of him to share that with her. Most people didn't divulge that kind of information with anyone, or if they did, it had to be someone very close to them. He still irked her though, with his macho crap about her going into a safe house or whatever.

2105

Zoey had her phone plugged into her car, and it played one of her playlists. She liked this particular playlist because it was dark and powerful, stirring her emotions as little else could. The lyrics, the music itself. She also loved her car. It was French, and that reminded her of her Mom. She smiled thinking about the woman.

She always thought that her mother was strict and not very nice. Now that she lived on her own, she could not ever express to her mother what a good parent she had been, and how well she had raised her. Teaching her right from wrong, how to respect people and property, how to do mundane chores, skills that one needed.

Looking back on her childhood she realized that where she thought her Mom to be a stern jerk, she had only been that way out of love and concern for her daughter, and she had also taught Zoey to appreciate music, fine clothing, and coffee. Oh it was past time for more coffee. She pulled into the bar parking lot, and entered the establishment.

Victor and Jake waved her over when they saw her come in. Jake had beat her here, even driving that piece of crap he had climbed into at the Medical Examiner's office. Zoey vowed that next time they had to be at a similar meeting, she would drive her car like she stole it, and beat him to the location. Not that she had a competitive spirit, she had an ultra competitive spirit, that is how she made it through Med-School. Push, push, push.

In front of Victor sat a Modelo beer. He always drank Modelo. Zoey couldn't stand beer, any kind of beer. An appreciation for fine wine, she learned from her father.

Jake had a tall glass of water in front of him. Zoey wondered what he was thinking? She liked the personal stance he was taking by drinking water. It showed a man who didn't suffer peer pressure. She took her seat and waited for one of the men to speak before she opened her mouth. Before they said anything a waiter came to the table.

"What can I get you?" He asked.

"Coffee, strong coffee, with French Vanilla or caramel creamer or both if you have them, and lots of sugar," Zoey answered.

"Coming right up. For you, it's on the house," the waiter said.

"Don't even," Zoey warned the men. "I'm already beyond tired and I'm driving."

"We have more important things to discuss," Victor said. Jake's grim visage said he wasn't going to make any smart ass remark.

"What have you got Abero?" Victor asked.

"The results are not back yet. I know that I'm just a lab rat to you gendarme's, but I have a gut feeling that we are dealing with a serial killer here, not a random act of violence, and just wanted to convey that message to you, to at least keep the Force alert to that possibility," she explained.

"What grounds do you have for the idea?" Victor wanted to know.

"I don't have scientific grounds, call this one a hunch if you must. I just want everyone to be cautious and proceed as if that might be a possibility. I get my hunch from the shape the remains were in. There were organs missing, which might be blackmarket, and the mandible was removed perhaps as a trophy, and when killers take trophies, they want more, just like big game hunters with their stuffed heads all over their houses," Zoey said.

"Good observation," Victor complimented. Victor never complimented, how many beers had he consumed? "Corde, what have you got?"

"I agree with Abero. I think we are dealing with a serial killer. In addition to that, my gut feeling is that we might all be in danger, like the next targets," Jake answered.

"What leads you to that conclusion?" Victor asked.

"Honestly, that crime scene "felt" like a beginning to more carnage to come, and I want us to shut that shit down faster than cars on the Autobahn," Jake said.

"I appreciate that both of you aren't taking the case lightly. I have already gotten some heat for bringing Corde on, "without just cause, we don't have unlimited resources you know. Yahda, Yahda, but I'll deal with that. Corde, don't make me regret bringing you on," Victor said.

"Have I let you down in the past?"Corde said.

"Not once. That's why I called you," Victor lifted his beer and took a large pull. "Which reminds me, we have a task force meeting on this case at eight thirty tomorrow morning. I expect you both to be there," Victor stated.

"I need you to add something to that meeting's agenda Victor. I can't stress enough that this case has me spooked. That is not a normal occurrence, could you work on additional safety protocols. I even think that maybe we need a safe house?" Jake said.

"I'll see what I can do, but the brass are cracking down on the budget," Victor said, clearly unhappy with that situation. "It could take weeks to push the paper through."

"Do you want me to finance it, and screw the paperwork?" Jake asked.

"Let me get back to you," Victor said.

After finishing her coffee Zoey got to her feet, to establish she was leaving. "If we are meeting in the morning, then this is all moot." She gestured at the three of them and the table. "I have a shower and pillow calling my name." Bidding the men good night, Zoey drove home. Long hours were not a new experience for her, but she felt like a sponge that all of the water had been squeezed out of, but in this case what had been squeezed out, happened to be her energy.

She opened her wine fridge, which chilled all of her wine to 14 degrees celsius or 57.2 degrees fahrenheit. The proper temperature to drink wine. She pulled out a bottle of Babits 5 Puttonyos Tokaji Aszu, and carefully opened it. She let it breathe, studying her collection of glasses.

"My Little Constellation. You only live once! Drink the wine like you are happy to be alive. Taste the truth of the grapes!" How many times had her father said that? He only called her 'my little constellation' when they were tasting wines; otherwise he shortened Zoey to Zo. Remembering her father's saying she selected her large glass. Why the fuck not, to say it had been a rough day would have been the understatement of the decade. She poured the wine into the glass and held it up to the light. Then she took a sip and luxuriated in the flavor. There was no other wine in the world like this one. It tasted like a first kiss.

"A votre sante," Zoey said. She bluetoothed her phone to her speakers, and turned the volume up. The stormy brooding and frenzied music of Tchaikovsky's "Marche Slav" filled up her unwinding mind.

After her glass of Tokaji was empty Zoey undressed and crawled under her covers. The meeting was at eight thirty but her day started long before that. She thought that sleep would claim her in seconds but it didn't. Visions of the crime scene flashed over and over.

"Stop already!" Zoey screamed and got up. She poured a second glass of wine, emptying the bottle into the large glass. She changed the music to her Imagine Dragons playlist. Again she thought about Jake Corde.

He had seemed so somber at the job site. But over dinner he had talked about Sasquatch. Then with Victor, back to Mr. Sober Face. How was a girl supposed to read a guy who switches his face like that? So serious. Was he like that all the time? Did he know how to have fun? All work and no play...

Zoey picked out her outfit for the next day. Setting the alarm on her phone, she climbed under the covers a second time. This time she fell asleep thinking of walking through vineyards in late autumn.

Chapter 9

0000

    No one paid attention to the stray dog that yipped suddenly and ran, tail between its legs. And no one saw the shadowy figure that made its way in the dark as though born to it. He was at his destination so fast even if someone had noticed they would have questioned the validity of their eyesight.

    There was a small panel in the back of the garage, hidden by a row of six foot tall Burning Bushes. Straight across from the poor excuse for a door in spitting distance was the neighbors fence. The space between the back of the house and the fence could technically be called an alley, but was more like a bike path.

    The point was easy access even without a key, which he had thanks to past visits and a lock-smith. The garage was clean and sparse, the way a non-mechanically inclined man's garage is. James was not a grease and engine kind of guy at all. James was weak.

    You had to love careless people. The key ring that hung on the hook near the telephone. Spare keys, easily stolen, copied and replaced without anyone the wiser. He had full access to every room in the house that had a lock.

    He removed his shoes and gently placed them by the door. No inadvertent squeaks or thumps. When he stood up he sniffed the air. They had had fried chicken for dinner, the smell lingered in spite of the dozens of candles Katie kept lit during the day.

    She had candles for every occasion from relaxing lavender to appetizing blue-berry. It was an insult to the sinuses even four hours after being snuffed out. He would light one of the offensive things when he made his exit. A tribute to Katie.

    The house was as quiet as a house can be situated as it was only a few blocks from the O'hare Airport. It wasn't the total black of dark either. Street lights, the occasional car, and a night light in the bathroom actually provided more than enough lambency for the task he came here to do.

He had been here before, many times. James and Katie would be shocked to hear it of course, he had never been invited after all. The fact remained, he knew the house layout well. He had installed cameras and listening devices back when he finally felt confident James was the one.

Now, well, in the living room he switched some throw pillows around and opened a magazine on the stand. He took a great deal of pleasure messing with Katie's compulsive neatness. He carefully moved one curtain just enough to cause a wrinkle at the bottom so the line was off center. Petty he knew, and didn't care.

The kitchen was his favorite room. Food. He opened the ever-humming fridge and winced. Apple juice. He preferred the V8 splash she sometimes bought but intruders were like beggars right? Can't be choosers. He barely contained a bark of laughter. He cracked himself up sometimes.

A tall glass of apple juice, and a chicken sandwich made from leftover supper. Perfect for a hungry man who worked so late into the night. He pulled out a chair and sat down at the dining room table.

One bite of the sandwich and he was transported on a wave of flavor. Katie might be a controlling, sanctimonious harpy but that girl could cook like a five star chef. He ate the sandwich with reverent bites chewing slowly. It was important to drink the juice in little sips so as not to ruin the wonderful sandwich.

As he ate his midnight snack he listened to the loud refrigerator and grinned. The noise added to the ambiance somehow. Finally, forced to admit the food was gone he downed the juice and stood up to continue on his mission, leaving the mess behind for Katie to wonder about in the morning.

For the umpteenth time he examined each picture hanging on the wall, each knick-knack and brick-a-brack he came to. It was part of his ritual, this attention to someone else's belongings. He liked knowing that they were ignorant of the fact that his prints were all over their stuff and that it had happened while they slept. But more than that, he wanted, no, needed to know what the residents touched and how often.

It was dark enough here that he had to go in close. That four year old Amy was adorable. He would have to tuck her in before he left. Maybe someday he would adopt her, when her Mommy was dead.

Six year old Donald was the first bedroom door he came to. He peeked in but did not linger. Little Donny was a precocious child with more common sense than was comfortable for adults to witness. The man would avoid his room for now. It was obvious that someday the boy would have to die with his Mommy, but not today.

The man berated himself. He was getting ahead of himself. Stay on point. The adrenaline was making him excitable. He took a few moments to calm down as he passed little Amy's room and stood in the doorway of the master bedroom.

The sleeping couple seemed so content, so comfortable laying there under the hand-made quilt. Katie again. That woman irked the hell out of him. She thought she was a regular Susie homemaker! Her ego must be enormous. Always so perfect in everything she did.

If only she knew what James had told him. He took a deep breath to calm his racing heart. It was almost too exciting to think about James killing his chubby, mouthy wife.

He quietly moved to Katie's side of the bed. He moved her glasses ten inches further away, turned the lamp switch away, shut off her alarm. He kicked one slipper under the bed and very carefully tucked the blanket in as tight as he could up to mid-mattress.

He loved the thrill of this. The sneaking, pushing the limit. If she woke up things would change for him in a hurry. But he couldn't help it. He was still a child in his heart. He just loved fucking with her. Yeah, that's what it was that drove him, the kid inside. Well that and watching his video later. That was too much fun.

His self-imposed time limit was almost up. He went around the foot of the bed, to the softly snoring James. Bending at the waist he put his thin lips close to the mans' ear.

James' eyes opened but he didn't move. The man left the

room.

Quietly he opened Amy's door and walked in. He bent down and kissed the pretty little girl on the forehead. With one finger he pushed a stray lock of curly blond hair off her cheek. Then he put his lips to the pink radio on her stand.

In the next room James glanced over at the baby monitor on the dresser. The light flashed green as a whisper came through.

"Time to come out and play, my friend…"

Chapter 10

Wednesday 0500

Jake didn't bother having the hotel give him a wake up call, he woke up every day at five without setting an alarm. Even the days he was trying to sleep in when five A.M. hit, it was go time. He could have set an alarm on his phone, you could do everything on your phone, but again there was no need.

He threw off the covers, pulled on his sweatpants and sweatshirt. He stretched, then started his workout routine with the easy part, five sets of ten sit ups. Then he did five sets of ten pushups. From there he moved into the crunches. They were the hardest and the most beneficial. When he made it through his crunches it was time for the road. Needed to work on cardiovascular.

Jake slid his room key into the credit card slot built into his phone case, put his ear buds in, and started running. A piece with a good drum beat came on and got him moving faster. He ran faster and faster. He began to feel the burn in his legs, that was a good thing. Endorphins flooded into his bloodstream, the rush, the natural high. No drugs or alcohol needed. Exercise was a good thing, but there was a meeting to get to this morning.

Checking the time, Jake decided to return to his hotel room. Six meant he had two hours to shower and make his way to the precinct. Once in his hotel room Jake checked the time on his phone. Doing good on time.

In the bathroom, Jake turned on the water and let it heat up while he stripped off his clothes. He knew it wouldn't be as nice as the shower at his place, but what could he expect from a hotel? All that aside, he stepped under the pounding hot water, and washed.

Finished with the mundane act he shut off the water and reached for a towel. His curse filled the bathroom, echoing around as though in an empty theater. How was a man supposed to dry himself properly with scrap cloth? He would not forget the one that took up half his bag again, he thought as he eyed said luggage sitting on the bed.

Standing in front of the mirror Corde carefully, and meticulously shaved. He brushed his teeth, and put on deodorant. He brushed his hair. Then he got dressed in a pale green dress shirt, and Khakis. He cinched his belt, and slipped on his black S.A.S. walking shoes. He might have time to grab something healthy to eat before the meeting, depending on traffic.

At 0815 Jake walked into the conference room. Two people were in the room. One was an aide setting up the computer for visuals and the other was Zoey Abero. How did she beat him here? He debated sitting next to her, thought again, and sat across the table from her, so he could look at her.

"You're early," Jake commented.

"This meeting is interrupting my work day, I should be at the office," Zoey said and took a sip from her Starbucks cup. Jake looked and once again there wasn't a lipstick stain, yet her lips remained vibrant. Damn hot!

The officers of this small task force began shuffling in. Two of them looked ragged, perhaps they were just coming off third shift, that would make sense. Two of them looked fresh, they must be the first shift. Jake wondered who was getting short-changed by Victor's new task force, pulling guys in from different shifts like that. Eventually, the man of the hour entered followed by a tall suit. Who was this guy?

The impeccable man's suit appeared to be of Italian make, it probably ran $1200. The suit did make an impression; charcoal with alternating silver and muted black pinstripes. His grey belt at first glance passed as unnoteworthy, but Jake glimpsed that the silver buckle had engravings on it. His shoes were clean, no dirt or scuff marks, highly polished. His tie, with a Double-Windsor knot, was red and silver, and perfectly fit the colors in the suit. Was he F.B.I.?

"Morning. Let's start with introductions," Victor nodded at the man.

"If you don't know me, I'm Stephen Abernathy, the department psychologist. I just wanted to let you all know that some of the madness you ladies and gentlemen encounter can be rather overwhelming.

I know you are all good at your jobs. I am not here to tell you how to do those, but I am also good at what I do, should you ever feel that you need to talk, all visits to me are completely confidential, and without any department repercussions or retaliation. I hold normal office hours. I will leave some of my business cards. My personal cell phone number is on them, you may text instead of calling, or email me," the man said. Stephen Abernathy, apparently liked to hear himself talk. Verbal vomit, mental masterbation. He placed his cards on the table and left.

Jake watched Victor nod at Zoey and followed suit, after all Victor had given him a free pass to do so. Medium length mahogany hair, framed her face with her stunning red lips, and those unforgettable golden eyes.

"If you are new and haven't worked with me, I'm Chicago's Medical Examiner. Call me Abero not Ishmael," Zoey said. The literary reference was lost on the officers as they didn't chuckle.

The officer seated clockwise looked nervous. Young and green, full of energy and bright eyed. "Anderson, the rookie," he said.

Jake mentaly nodded that he had been correct in his assumption. Now it was his turn to introduce himself. He disliked these sort of ordeals, it was a good time to make a joke.

"Corde. I'm the dick," he said. That earned laughter. Score one point for Corde, Abero zero. Once the laughter abated the next man spoke.

"Jackson, homicide." Said the officer, built like he could survive a nuclear blast, and outlive the cockroaches.

"His driver and gunman, he can't do either for shit. I'm Sanchez, homicide." said the last member of the seated officers."

Fuck you!" Jackson said to Sanchez.

"Knock it off, you two. Let's get rolling," Victor said, moving to the back of the room to operate the computer. He put the first image up. Jake had the crime scene memorized, this photo had a yellow circle around the missing jaw. It didn't hurt to revisit anything that was important.

Victor went through a number of more images of the crime scene. He was thorough but not long winded.   Jake respected that. Victor opened up the floor for discussion when the door to the room opened.

"We got a fresh one!"

Chapter 11

Jake took note of the crowd pushing the perimeter of the crime scene. He made sure someone was taking pictures of the faces. It was a well known fact that murderers often hovered near the scene of their act to watch things unfold.

Zoey Abero was two steps ahead of him and her abrupt halt brought him to attention. Over her head he caught sight of what she was looking at. His stomach rolled as he heard someone retching. A bystander.

Angry, he turned to a police officer, "Get them back further!"

"Jake! Jake over here!" His eyes followed the sound of the too familiar voice. What the hell?

"Let him through!" Jake ordered, then, as his brother got closer; "By all that's holy Mathew, I'm going to create my very own crime scene right here. Talk fast before I lose control and beat the shit out of you."

"Chill brother, that would piss Mom off no end. She's on a plane." Matt grinned like a Momma's boy, which he was.

Jake snarled. That grin bought the youngest Corde brother a free pass nine out of ten times. That curly, soft looking long hair, those chocolate eyes, and that damn grin. But not this time. No sir.

"Get your ass back to Mom!" Jake demanded.

"Your people are staring at us." Matt jacked his chin out, indicating the task force who stood around the scene. They weren't exactly staring, but curious looks were being cast his way. "We can talk when you are done here. I'll watch your back. Oh fuuuuck, that's nasty." He was looking at the mess the killer had left behind. "Get moving big brother."

Jake growled in frustration, turned and trudged to where Zoey crouched at the edge of the massive blood pool. This was a

nicer part of Chicago, fewer cracks in the ground, no dirt to absorb the liquid, nothing to stop the flow. Jake noticed the set of
footprints leaving the site of human carnage.

He took care to examine each foot step until they faded to
nothing ten or so paces away. Pretty distinctive prints. The killer
didn't give a damn what information he was leaving behind.

Bare feet, mens or a large woman. Not too heavy though,
maybe 170. A scar on the left heel. A crooked toe on the same
foot.

He fell to one knee as flashes came to him in crashing
waves of detail. He felt Matt's presence at his back. The comfort
that gave him probably should have been a little embarrassing.
But it wasn't. That was the Corde brothers greatest strength, that
bond. He didn't fight the images. The throb in his temples less-
ened.

The girl was a dancer, walking alone on this street. A black
sedan sped by her, license plate J-- ---9. A shop owner turned his
sign. A kid on a skateboard, the lettering on his backpack said
"Cowabunga!" A cop got into his squad car.

"She should have been safe here, on this street. So many
people. Lights everywhere. Cameras everywhere. Someone saw
something." He stood up, rubbed his temples before sliding his
sunglasses over his suddenly burning eyes. "The son of a bitch
didn't even care if there were witnesses."

Matt quietly followed him and stood facing the crowd. He
was determined to watch for any danger to one of the most important people in his world. He knew Jake was born to fix things.
He was the caretaker of all and sundry. But even Jake needed
back-up sometimes and he wasn't going to let his brother bully
him into leaving. Not this time.

The forensics team worked a path to what remained of the
body. Zoey, kneeling on two folded pieces of plastic bent over the
mess. There would be no sewing this corpse back together. The
skin had been rendered to threads the width of a string of yarn.
She heard someone come up behind her and was grateful for the
waft of clean scent. She knew who it was before he spoke. That
irritated her almost as much as the next words out of his mouth.

"Jesus, he took her fucking legs."

"Congratulations Captain Observant. I would have never noticed on my own." She snapped.

Jake bit back the grin that trembled on his lips. "Someone needs more coffee. No, sugar! Are you diabetic Dr. Abero?" Not bothering to turn her head to look at him she sighed. "You're an idiot. No wonder you were a terrible police officer."

Jake frowned down at her then knelt on his heels to say next to her ear; "I was an awesome cop."

Zoey remained still, her breath caught in her throat. It was too nice, having him so close. Still, work to do. Blood all around her, a body torn apart and partially consumed in front of her. Work. Her job.

The blood spatter team was going to have a field day with this one. There were spots of blood as far away as the yellow line on the road and as high as the awning that undoubtedly stopped it from flying up to the second floor windows. The black, red, gooey, sticky blood ran down every surface, coated everything.

Stuck intermittently among all of the blood, like maca- bre glitter was brain matter, hair, the pulverized remains of soft organs, and strings of skin and intestines. It was a gory mass of death. Proof, if anyone needed proof, that evil was real and right here in their front yard.

She heard someone talking in the background, "Christ there's a hand on the hood of that car. Tony, don't miss the ear stuck to that parking meter. Careful everyone this is chaos."

She had thought the last scene was violent. This one was ten fold. Unlike Jake, she could not withstand the onslaught of images that came to her. She fell back against him.

Jake put his hands on her hips to hold her steady as she knelt there, shaking like a leaf in the wind. He knew what was happening, knew too she would not take it well if he interfered in any way. She would want to weather this storm as much on her own as possible.

The dancer had been pretty in her pink and white tutu. Her outfit had been no kind of impediment, tearing easily in his rough hands. Too thin to even soak up blood like a decent rag would.

Blindsided. He had come up from behind this time. He didn't need to see them die. There was no emotion involved, no fascination with death. He was just hungry. Hungry for the violence, the blood and the flesh he consumed.

The only true thought in the virulent mass of darkness was of hunger and legs. There were no other signs of intelligence or even a modicum of humanity. Just black as thick tar and the ravening.

But he was a man. Strong beyond belief. Fast too. Not efficient, though. God no, not that.

She finally pulled away from Jake with a muttered thanks and stood up. "He's about six foot three. Hairy. His hands had hair on the backs. Not a lot, but more than usual. He is mindless. At least when he's doing this. Savage yet unemotional, like what you would see with an enraged grizzly."

"Not a hairless Sasquatch after all."

"Be serious!"

"He's careless too." Jake whispered in her ear. "He left witnesses. Not a word to anyone Zoey. I am going to find the witnesses, try to make them safe."

"Who's that?" Zoey asked, nodding at Matt.

"Dr. Abero, this is my little brother Matt. Matt, this is Dr. Zoey Abero, the Medical Examiner," Jake quickly introduced the two.

She nodded. "Good luck"

He grinned as he turned and walked away. "I'm too good to need luck, Doctor. Just watch me catch this guy."

And there was the arrogance she had heard that Victor and other members of the police force talked about. Just when she was starting to like the guy. It was sad, really.

Chapter 12

The Glasgow International Airport, once known as the Abbotsinch Airport prided itself on being kept clean, and overall it had good lighting. Alex had wandered the Celtic Store, which specialized in sportswear, which made him think of his brother Jake.

Always the fitness nut, that one. His brother needed to learn to loosen up. His brother needed to learn that we only live once, and we should enjoy life. Maybe Jake needed to travel abroad, get out of the city of Chicago, and see the world. Chicago was a great city, but it was just one city in the world. It didn't have above ground cemeteries like New Orleans. It didn't have the Tower of London. It didn't have a Blarney Castle, or The Vatican.

Alex walked into the Sanderling, and took a seat at the bar. He ordered a White Russian. Sipping the drink, he enjoyed the creamy coffee flavored alcohol. They didn't make the drink strong enough for his taste, but a bar needed to make money somehow, not that airport prices weren't already inflated to the umpteenth degree. When he finished his drink he walked back to the waiting area next to the gate the plane should arrive at. Waiting.

Alexander Corde didn't do waiting well. It allowed his thoughts to jump around in all sorts of directions not relevant to his task at hand. He missed his Vette. He missed unlimited ice cubes without sounding like 'A Greedy American'.

He should have brought a book. What was the last book he'd read anyway? His Mom insisted that he read a book by some guy named Thor or something? Brad Thor. He hadn't read it. Marissa, an old highschool girlfriend with hip length flowing auburn hair wanted him to read some book relating to her nerd game Dungeons and Dragons, he hadn't. Matt recommended The Devil in the White City by Erik Larson, some history shit about Chicago. Again, he hadn't. Right now he would have killed to have any of those books to absorb the agonizing wait.

His mother's flight from America should have taken seven hours, and the monitors on the wall said it was 'On Time', so why hadn't it landed? Calm down, he told himself. Maybe there had been a longer than normal layover, and the monitors didn't reflect that. Maybe he needed another White Russian, no he was driving.

Alex didn't plan on staying in Scotland long, if his mother wanted to catch any of the tourist attractions like Loch Ness they would make a day or so out of it, and then he planned to take his mother to Italy so she could meet Ilaria. As long as Mother was going to be outside the U.S., he might as well kill two birds with one stone. Ilaria could cook traditional Italian food like nobody's business. If the saying 'the way to a man's heart was through his stomach,' Ilaria not only had found Alex's heart, but burrowed in there and set up a house filled with children, grandchildren, two dogs, and a cat.

Little Ilaria. A smile formed on Alex's face just thinking about her. She rocked his world. Not only could her cooking rival Gordon Ramsay, but her mind put Tesla to shame, and her body! An amazing woman. He would be happy to explore all her mysteries for many lifetimes. She could take her coat, and throw it on his floor every day.

What would Mother think of little Ilaria? He hoped she liked her. Knowing Mom, she wouldn't say anything, at least right away. She would slowly form the most interesting, comprehensive opinion. Then in confidence she would tell him her thoughts, good, bad, and otherwise. A bridge to be crossed later. He looked at the monitor. It now read the plane was arriving in ten minutes. He double checked that he sat at the correct terminal, that the arrival gate hadn't changed. All of his worrying for nothing, but could you blame a son for worrying about his mother? No.

The passengers began disembarking. First came the folks that needed mobility assistance. Next came ragged looking business people that had flown First Class. Then the Coach passengers. Mom always flew coach even though they could have afforded to put her in first class. She said, 'Do I look snooty to you? Why spend all that extra money for comforts I don't need?' That was

Mom, and there she was now walking into Scotland.

"Mom!" He hugged her.

"Alex. You're glowing," Mom greeted. Alex momentarily ignored the comment although he knew she was already prompting. Damn, she could read him so well, even now.

"Let's get your baggage and get out of here," Alex said.

"Can we eat something?"

" As soon as we are out of the airport. Do you have a desire to see the sights of Scotland?"

"Was there another agenda?"

"Not necessarily," Alex evaded. His mother knew better.

"I see," she said.

"Why did Matt send you to me?" Alex asked as they waited at the baggage carousel. The silver movers started rotating, looking like a flattened escalator. Alex grabbed his mother's bag when she pointed it out.

"Jake is being Jake, I'll tell you more in the car," she said. Alex walked her out to his black crossover SEAT Tarraco. His mother raised an eyebrow.

"I know. I know, not the Corvette. This is unobtrusive, it blends well. Come on. It will be a more comfortable ride for you, than a sports car," Alex said, stowing her luggage.

"Your brothers would be proud of you," his Mom beamed.

"Thanks Mom, let's get something to eat."

Chapter 13

1000 Chicago

Zoey exited the facilities, and began pulling on her Personal Protection Equipment. Clearly these remains were in a mess, but they might also have more valuable information than the last victim. They might contain a hair follicle from the killer's hands that she'd seen in her vision which could lead to identifying him. She walked into the office.

She stood surveying her domain with maternal pride. It had taken her years to get things set up the way she liked them. The new equipment had been hard won. Proving herself every day, a balancing act. Nodding with satisfaction, she turned to Kellesha.

"Kell, will you assemble the team?"

"On it boss," the intern said with a smile.

Zoey returned to the morgue. She stood still listening to the hum of white noise thinking about her vision at the crime scene. The missing legs, another sick trophy. A mandible, and legs. It didn't have to be the same trophy every time, that meant something.

Her crew had the bags on three separate tables. Tags indicated the different parts. "Let's open them up, and put them in a semblance of an anatomically correct position," Zoey instructed. The group worked quickly and efficiently. Zoey felt proud of her team. It had taken her two years of work to get them to work this way, but now they moved as a well oiled machine.

Once the remains were laid out, the cadre exited the room, and left Zoey alone. She looked at the cadaver. She hadn't known the victim, but her family and maybe even a lover would mourn her. A young vibrant life taken out of the world.

Death made her think about war. The death that war brought was pointless. Well, Zoey couldn't change the world, but she could do her work. She refocused her mind on the job at hand.

Zoey started circling her table, walking around the body. She looked up to make sure the recorder, hanging above the table, was recording. "Doctor Zoey Abero 1027, Case subject number two. Female, between seventeen and twenty years of age. Time of death 0200 hours, Central Standard Time. Teeth intact, will be sent for dental identification. Hair color blonde. Eye color blue. Estimated weight 48.534 kilograms. Estimated height 173.736 centimeters."

She needed to give a cause of death, but she couldn't say 'being eaten', she would need to think about how to word that in the written report. Cannibalism had to be in there of course, but she hated that term too. There were no synonyms she could think of either, she would have to Google it. Fuck this unthinking monster.

After a few hours of bending over the table in front of her, Zoey called a short halt. She needed some caffeine and a stretch. Her team needed a break too. Starbucks called her name from down the street.

Arching her back and eyeballing the group looking at her expectantly she smiled. "Let's take a few. I'm walking down to get a real latte. Anyone care to join me?"

Everyone agreed quickly, getting the cadaver into the safety of the refrigerated cabinets and shoving dirty grubs and gloves in the appropriate containers. They were like a bunch of little kids, chatting and laughing as they made their way down the drab hallway to the outer doors.

The autumn air was refreshing, blowing the cobwebs out of the mind, even in the middle of Chicago. A walk had been a great idea. Everyone chatted amiably behind as they followed her the three long blocks to their favorite coffee shop. There was that welcoming green and white sign.

At Starbucks, Zoey ordered a grande Hazelnut Bianco Latte, then waited as the others ordered their mixed bag of favorites. A Venti Java chip frappuccino here, a grande Pike Place roast there. She picked up the bill, the privilege of being the boss. She decided they would take their time going back to give them all a chance to socialize for just a few moments longer.

The sunshine of the day, and mild autumn temperature made for a nice day for the other denizens of Chi-town, but soon, Zoey's mind returned to the darkness of death and human re-mains. Walking back to the office, her mind lingered over the case even as she enjoyed the easy banter the others shared around her.

The coffee tasted good, and warmed her insides from the chill of these murders. The building, though well ventilated, was still a building and still had that used air smell, compared to the outdoors. It was almost sad to leave the sunshine for the LED lights. But, you couldn't have a morgue in the middle of the street. Zoey laughed thinking about the gawkers. Good Lord, she couldn't concentrate on work that way.

Time to get back to work. Time to catalogue. Suiting up in her lab uniform, she pulled Jane Doe out of her drawer and metic-ulously started the process of entering verbal data into the record-er. Later they would have to write the report.

Hours later Zoey stretched. Damn this killer anyway. Who the fuck did he think he was? She still didn't have a better word for Cannibalism. Fucker! Enough.

Zoey pushed Jane back into her metal cavern and pulled out a new drawer. This was John Doe, an unrelated victim to the Nightmare Case. Zoey looked at the deceased. Wow, this one was going to be easy in comparison to the Jane Doe Ballerina.

She started working. One done. And onto the next, and the next. Four more after that.

It was a sad fact that, thanks to gangs and drugs she didn't need to worry about job security. Three of these guys were drive-by shootings. Pretty simple to see what took their lives. Bullets. A few more hours passed during the work, now it was definitely getting to be time for wine though. Wine!

Chapter 14

0900 Still Wednesday

Jake gestured to Matt and the two left the crime scene. Taking the sidewalk down a block and a half until they came to the store window Jake recognized from his vision. The sign was turned to Open. Jake pushed inward and gave a crooked smile as the bell above the door jingled.

He stopped and looked up at the brass noise maker; a single bell, simple and unadorned. it suited the small bookstore he stood in.

"Welcome. You smile. Do you like the doorbell's tintinnabulation? It is a welcoming sound, is it not?"

Jake grinned at the diminutive fellow who balanced on a rolling ladder, a book in one hand, the ladder rail in the other. He could only assume the ten dollar word meant noise or something like that.

"It is."

Behind him Matt was moving off to examine books on a shelf near the door, his nerdiness showing in the sudden glow of pleasure on his handsome face. Matt was the unabashed book worm in the family. His love of the written word was rivaled only by Webster and Wikipedia.

Jake stepped forward. "I'm not sure you heard. There was a murder last night."

"I saw the police cars. I assumed it was something bad because of the sheer numbers." The elderly gentleman backed down the ladder and came forward, a frown marred his forehead.

Jake stuck out a long fingered hand. "Jake Corde, private investigator. I am assisting the police. I wonder if we could talk for a few minutes?"

The hand that shook Jake's was small, warm, and frail. "I am called Edwin Lovington. We can talk there." He gestured to an alcove that housed four huge, overstuffed chairs, a fake fireplace, two coffee tables, and a coffee stand with a coffee maker and cups. "Would you care for a cup of coffee?"

"I would love some, black, thank you." Jake smiled. He sat on the edge of a chair, afraid he would be lost in the comfort and hominess of the tiny room, if he sat back.

Matt shook his head from his post by the door. Jake noticed the sign was turned to closed now and the door lock was engaged. He threw a crooked grin of recognition at his brother. No interruptions.

"Ah, thank you." Jake accepted the aromatic brew and decided to sit back after all. Matt could come save him if he started sinking out of sight. "Someone mentioned that you often stay open late. How late, if you don't mind?"

"Oh, sometimes I forget to turn the closed sign. Friends will stop by and we will get caught up discussing a favorite piece of work. I have been known to still be open at midnight."

Mr. Lovington's slow, soft speech coupled with his small stature gave the impression of a kind, gentle old man. His hands cradled the coffee cup steadily as he curled up in his chair like a kid digging in for a nap. His gaze was direct and open, his lips slightly parted. No sweat, eye tick or other outward signs of nervousness or deception.

"Is that what happened last night?"

"No. Last night I got caught up with cataloguing and shelving a new shipment of books. I was very excited. Tolkien, Martin, Williams. Makes me smile just thinking about it."

"Did you see a boy on a skateboard?"

"Oh my yes. Ryan Schoemaker. I pay him cash for his help, when a shipment comes in. He is my ladder man, and my muscle. I can't lift the boxes like I once could."

"What time did Ryan leave last night?"

"Well, I'm not sure. After eleven." The old man frowned. "Oh, don't even think it!" He exclaimed. "Ryan is a good soul. He would never hurt anyone."

Jake's smile was reassuring. "Of course not. No, I just want to talk to him as a possible witness. Did you see anyone as you were locking up or when you left for home?"

"I live above my shop. No, I'm afraid my eyesight is rather poor. My spectacles are for reading, you see. I suppose I should go get those bifocal lenses Ryan keeps talking about, but I can't justify the cost, you understand."

"I sure do. Any medical expense is ridiculously high."

"Indeed."

"Do you have Ryan's address?"

"Oh, no. I pay cash so there's no need for an address. But he rides that skateboard of his everywhere. And he stops by every third Tuesday of the month to see if I need his help with a new shipment. Such a considerate boy."

"So you did not see anything suspicious last night?"

"Lord no." He shook his head then hesitated just a tic.

"What?" Jake prompted.

"Well, nothing suspicious that I saw, but that little ballerina girl didn't come by. She always stops for a cup of tea and a little light reading. Poetry usually. Around eleven."

"What direction does she come from?"

"Well, I believe her dance school is a bit up the way. I guess that would be north? She lives four blocks down that way." He gestured in the opposite direction. "The apartment building across from the gas station. I overheard her telling Ryan one night."

"Ryan knows her?"

"Well, yes. They are of an age you know."

"No, sir, I did not know. Does she stop every night?"

"No. Every other night."

"And you are sure last night was an every other?"

"Yes, quite certain."

"And you don't have Ryan's address?"

"Oh, no. But I have his cell number."

Jake closed his eyes and counted to ten. He couldn't blame the old guy really. After all, he hadn't actually asked for a phone number, just the address. Still, he sent up a small prayer for deliverance from dreamers and book worms.

"If you could give me that number please?" He asked gently as he finished his coffee and pushed his way out of the plush chair.

"I don't want him in trouble."

Oh my Gawd. It is illegal to shoot old people. It is illegal to shoot old people.

"He isn't in trouble with the police, Mr. Lovington. But if he witnessed the murder, he may be in danger. I need to find him quickly."

"Oh. Well he's probably at his sister's house. Their grand-mother lives there. Ryan stays with her every morning from six to ten when the nurse comes in for the day." The shopkeeper made it to the service counter and reached under it, coming up with a well-worn address book. "Hold on one second while I write this down."

"Greatly appreciated." Jake nodded then all but snatched the yellow post-it out of the man's arthritic fingers. "You have been extremely kind and cooperative. Thank you so much."

"Any time young man. Come back for a book sometime. I bet you would enjoy some Koontz."

"That place is amazing! The old guy was delusional, though. Imagine him thinking you actually crack open a book. Koontz!" Matt laughed so hard he stumbled. "I will definitely return one day. I can't believe I've never heard of it before. The smell! Did you catch that wonderful smell? I thought book stores smelled musty, like moldy books!"

"He had incense burning somewhere."

"The ambiance!"

Jake stopped and waited for Mathew to do the same.

"What? What!?" Matt asked defensively. "I can't appreci-ate a bookstore?"

"No. We are investigating a murder."

"And that precludes literature? They aren't mutually exclu-sive, brother dear."

"Ok. Whatever, just be still for a moment."

Jake got out his phone and dialled Victor's number and waited for it to ring twice before gesturing to Matt to head back toward the crime scene. "Hey, Detective, there is a bookstore a block and a half from the crime scene. Little old man. Says he saw nothing. Just letting you know. I don't know. I have a bad feeling about this. Yeah, I've got a couple of leads. Heading to one now. Listen, there was a patrolman in the area last night. And a black sedan, license J-- ---9 Ok. Yes! I know it's only a partial. I think there was tape or something over the rest. I'm going to get my brother Alex on it too. Great. Later."

His rental was parked less than a block away from the bookstore and they came up on it just as he was dialing Alex's number. He unlocked the door, pushed the button to let Matt in and settled himself behind the wheel.

"Hey Alex. I have a partial. The plate was deliberately covered. J-- ---9. Yes, I have been told the odds already. Thanks. He's killed two so far. Yeah, my instincts are telling me he is far from done. Appreciate the help brother. Talk to you later."

Hanging up, his mind was already on the next lead. This was the worst part of the job. Chasing down the possibilities. Fishing. It took patience, due diligence. Not one of his virtues.

"Mom sent me back." Matt said as he eyed his oldest sibling. "She said that her cards saw you surrounded by death and danger. She said going to Alex was her best choice and that Luke couldn't leave Peggy, who is pregnant."

"What? How does that woman know these things? Did Peggy tell her?"

"Her cards man. It's always her cards. I doubt Peggy knows yet. Anyway, I'm all you have you poor schmuck. She wouldn't take no. And she said if you send me away she will come home and post an article in the paper."

Jake heaved a mixed sigh of frustration and resignation. "She is going to drive me crazy." He told his brother as he called the number Mr. Lovington gave him and listened for a second.

"Hello?"

"Ryan?"

"Yes."

"This is Jake Corde. I got your number from the bookstore owner. Mr. Lovington. I am a private investigator, is there any way we can meet?"

"For what?"

"A girl was murdered last night.'

"I didn't do it!"

"No. I know. But you might have seen the killer without realizing it."

"Uh, no. I...wait, what girl?"

"Can we meet?"

"Was it Shai Craig?"

"We haven't been able to identify her yet. I really need to talk to you Ryan. Can we meet? The mall or your house. Wherever you feel safe? The police department?"

"I can't leave right now."

"We can come there. Really, the sooner the better Ryan. I'm honestly worried for your safety. The sooner we catch the perp the better, and you might be able to help."

There was a hesitation then Ryan sighed, "Fine. I'm at my sisters' house."

Jake repeated the address back to him and got his car moving.

Chapter 15

1100 Wednesday

Everything about Ryan Shoemaker was stringy. From the tiny little braids in his unidentifiable color of hair to his long, gangly limbs. Standing in the middle of his sister's living room, he looked awkward and uncomfortable in his own skin. His hands were crammed into his pockets, his knit, beaked cap was pulled low over his eyes, and his jeans looked painted on his skinny legs in a very uncomplimentary fashion.

He was at that stage, that age of teenagehood that just breathing was an invitation to disaster. Jake remembered the stage well. Just walking through a room resulted in broken knick knacks and knocked over drinking glasses.

"It's ok kid." Jake gestured at the couch. "Have a seat. I just want to pick your brain."

Ryan frowned, then in a mad rush of words asked, "My friend, Shai, didn't show up last night. Was it her? The murdered girl?"

"Did you try calling her?"

"I did. Voice mail."

"Well, keep trying. How late did you stay at the bookstore last night?"

"Eleven fifteen."

"Exactly?"

"Yes. I remember because I was watching out for Shai. If she doesn't show by eleven fifteen, then I know she isn't going to make it. I finished the last box of books and hung out until I knew she wasn't going to make it. Then I headed home."

"So you looked out the window a lot?"

The boy blushed and nodded.

"Can you remember everything you saw between ten thirty and when you got home?"

Ryan's eyebrows rose out of sight. "Uh, well, probably not, but I can try."

"Let's try an exercise that sometimes helps me. Sit down. Relax. Close your eyes. breathe gently. You are on your skateboard."

"It's the easiest way to get around." He sounded defensive.

"I get it. No judgement. Let's not get distracted. You are on your way to the bookstore..."

"At seven. Right after dinner. It's the only time my Mom lets me out so late. Mr. Lovington pays me well. It gives Mom an extra hundred bucks a month."

"Ok. You get to the store. Help the old man move and stock the books..."

"I break down the boxes and take them out back to the dumpster at about five to eleven." Ryan's eyes pop open. "There's a black car, four doors. I don't know the make, cars aren't my thing. It was parked near the end of the alley. Lights off."

Jake made a mental note that it could be the same car he saw in his vision. "Was there anyone inside?"

"Yes. One person. Behind the wheel. I figured he was waiting for one of the coffee shop waitresses, or one of the girls from the dress shop. He was impatient. He drummed his fingers on the steering wheel. Not following a song beat, you know?"

Jake nodded. "Did you see a face?"

"No. Back of the head."

"Plate?"

"No, there wasn't enough light. I'm sorry."

"Did anyone join him before you went back inside?"

"No."

"Okay. How about out the front? Did you notice anything off or different when you glanced out the windows?"

Ryan shook his head. "Too many cars. It's always changing. The stores close between nine and eleven. I didn't really start looking until ten thirty or so. Shai has dance class every evening from eight to ten. She hangs out for a while with the girls then walks home."

"Ok. So what else do you remember seeing?"

"There is a police car that parks down the street, in front of the coffee shop. The officer always gets a cup of coffee and sits there for a bit. It's a great place to sit because the traffic light is right there and he catches folks running red lights sometimes."

"Good. You are doing great."

"No. That's it. So lame. I just see the same old thing every day. I didn't realize how much I don't see."

"Well, don't beat yourself up over it. You are young and untrained." Jake stood up and dug a card out of his wallet. "Listen Ryan, do me a couple of favors ok? I want you to call me if you think of anything, no matter how small you think it is. Don't tell anyone about the black car alright? This is important. Don't even tell the police unless I am with them. I will make sure the information you have shared gets to the right ears and only those ears."

"You think that guy was the killer and he saw me?"

"No. But I think if you blab about seeing that, the killer might wonder what else you saw. So better safe than sorry. If you need me, call me, I'll come right away."

Ryan nodded. Jake gave his shoulder a comforting squeeze and left. Matt came from around the side of the house.

"Hope we don't have to guard this logistical nightmare. There's more holes than a sieve. Five doors, one slider and seventeen windows, just on the first floor. Who needs seventeen windows? Shouldn't you save a little wall space for pictures or something?"

Jake grinned. His brother's quick mind asked questions about everything, in a manner that was easy and humorous rather than intrusive or irritating. It made him an interesting companion. And, he was a security genius. Bonus!!

"I hope not, too." Jake grimaced.

Matt shook his head. "Wow. Your positive energy is really uplifting brother mine. I feel like my own life is in great hands."

"Fool."

"Are we going to check his Mom's house just in case?"

"Not now. I want to touch base with Zoey first. Then I

think we get a guy to tail Ryan. Keep an eye on him. Maybe the bookstore too. Christ. I wish my flashes weren't so vague."

"Zoey? The medical examiner?"

"Yeah."

"What's up with that?"

"What?"

"She's hot. You bangin' her?"

"What the hell Mathew?! No, I'm not."

Matt's eyes sparkled and he bit back a grin. "Mom's cards strike again."

"What?"

"Nothing. So, is she good at her job?"

"Very. And, she's like me."

"Visions?"

"Yes. It's like we see different aspects of the crime. She sees things from the perpetrators view sort of. I see the outer perimeter. The witnesses, the dangers."

"That's crazy awesome! What a team!"

Jake shook his head. Trust Matt to find a silver lining. Always sunshine.

"So, why aren't you banging her?"

"For God's sake Matt! I just met her."

"Right. So, you're a scaredy cat?"

"Are you ten?"

"You are a chicken! Ha!" Matt slapped his knee in triumph. "Big bad Jake, afraid of an itty bitty girl."

"I think you're adopted." Jake snarled as he got in the car and slammed his door a little harder than necessary.

"It's only noon. Let's go change hotels, get Burke and Erik on the horn. Then we can do food and figure out our next move. Give your Zoey time to do her thing." Matt suggested as he climbed into the passenger seat, "And Mom said you and Luke were found in a cow pile."

Jake and Matt checked into some shithole hotel. It was inexpensive by Chicago standards, but they didn't need the Taj Mahal. It would work for now, they might change hotels again in a day or two, you could never be too safe.

Unzipping one of his duffle bags, Jake took out his gun. He checked the weapon over, made sure it was clean, loaded, and that the safety was on. With his inspection complete he holstered the Remington 1911 R1.45, and put on his shoulder harness. He dug a light windbreaker out of a different duffel bag, and put it on. Concealment.

Jake took out his phone, and got his databases working on looking up Shai Craig. Then he thought more about the interview with Ryan. A black four door car. He called Alex again. "Yes brother, I have more work for you. Don't swear at me. We run a company, in case you've forgotten. Now run the damn plate for me, please. Thanks."

Ryan said the man drummed his fingers on the steering wheel that might mean something? 'Not following a song's beat.' Impatient, definitely meant something. Then there was the cop car to consider. A cop that close to the murder happening, and yet the officer didn't see a thing?

Next Jake dialed Burke and Erik. "Jake here. Got an assignment for you. I need you to keep an eye on a kid that may be in danger. 24 hour surveillance. Yes. I'll text you the details. Start now. The kid Ryan rides his skateboard everywhere. Thanks. Later."

"Last I heard, investigations were completed in the real world, not on one's phone. Speaking of the real world, breakfast?" Matt broke into Jake's thoughts.

"Where do you want to eat?" He asked Matt.

"Anywhere, I'm starving."

"Not helpful. Your ribs aren't showing, you're not starving."

"My rumbling stomach doesn't care."

Even when Matt irritated him, Jake couldn't help the grin at his brother's over-the-top drama. A healthy breakfast? Matt didn't care where they went so long as he got something to eat.

"Wildberry Pancakes & Cafe it is. I'll drive."

"You always drive," Matt said.

"I'm the older brother. Driver picks the music, the passenger shuts their cakehole."

"No wonder you haven't got a girlfriend."

"I do have a girl, she was wearing my t-shirt the other morning."

Driving to eat, Jake couldn't help thinking about Zoey. Damn Matt, 'was he bangin' her' indeed! Zoey, so vibrant, full of energy. Her eyes! Her lips, her skin, her hair, her every-damn-thing. Not even the dark red scar that ran down her face was able to detract from her attractiveness. Focus on the road, he chided himself.

Even though the restaurant was busy, the pretty blonde hostess seated them quickly. The waitress arrived a little slower. She flipped over her ordering pad to a new page, and then greeted them with a smile.

"Good morning. How may I get you started?"

"Can we still get breakfast?" Matt wanted to know.

"Of course."

"Then I will take a large orange juice,"

"And for you?"

"Same," Jake said.

"Are you ready to order, or do you need a few minutes?"

"Eggs Benedict on top of the Corned Beef Hash, and one of the blueberry pancakes," Matt beamed at the waitress.

"And for you?" She nodded at Jake.

"Turkey bacon, egg whites, wheat toast."

"Easy enough. I'll be back with your O.J."

Once their food arrived, they dug in. Jake didn't know when they would eat again, but breakfast was the best meal of the day, even at noon. It fortified you for the day. Breakfast ensured that you at least ate one healthy meal.

Jake couldn't help the sigh that escaped him as he settled in, relaxing just a mite. His thoughts were racing all over the place and he was struggling to put things in order. He looked up from his water to find Matt frowning at him.

"What's up Jake?"

"Things are moving way too fast. I feel as though I finally get a firm grip on some detail and swoosh! In comes another to mess me up."

Matt smiled his charming 'I've got a secret' smile at Jake.

"You always do this when there are too many changes in your life. You met a new woman who has shaken you up, you closed everything up tight, sent your family away, and sin of all sins, you put your car in storage. It will be ok Jake. You got this."

Jake wasn't so sure about all that but he did miss his Mustang. Since he couldn't drive his baby, maybe they should switch cars? Nothing that stuck out but a small upgrade from the P.O.S. Any upgrade would be welcome. Yes, they should do that.

"So, what's next?" Matt asked.

"Next, we get a different car. I'll think of the next steps along the way."

"You are going to see Zoey, when?"

"Matt, leave it alone!"

"Okay. Fine. Then, how can I help?"

"What kind of car would you like to drive?" Matt couldn't believe Jake had offered him the option to drive.

"I don't know?"

"Get your mind working on that, I'll pay the bill."
They rented a silver Nissan Sentra. Jake allowed Matt to drive as he worked on his phone. Directing Matt to the first murder scene, he brought him up to date on the details of the beginning of the case. After revisiting the scene, they had lunch in a nearby restaurant. The food wasn't up to Jake's health standards, but at least his brother wouldn't complain that he was starving.

The rest of the day felt like beating one's head against one brick wall, and then finding a new wall and repeating the process. Sooner or later his hard head was bound to give. Frustrated didn't begin to describe Jake's mood. He vowed to himself that he would try very hard not to slam the Sentra's doors, none of this was the car's fault. The car was a very nice upgrade. That had been a good safe decision, and yet it didn't get him any closer to catching the killer.

Chapter 16

Checking her phone for the time, it read 1323. Definitely lunch time. She entered the bathroom and took off her Personal Protection Equipment. She hung up her lab coat, properly discarded her gloves and thoroughly washed her hands. She exited the lavatory, and left the morgue.

Stepping outside she quickly put on her sunglasses, sunlight differed from human made light. Brighter, and warming at the same time. The wind caressed her hair like a lover's fingers pushing through her mane. Most of the time she didn't notice how cold the morgue was as she focused on her work, the outside world temperature was a welcome change. Today she even noticed the leaves cracking and clattering as the wind swept them down the street.

She set out walking. A few blocks later she arrived at her favorite lunch spot. They had a deck that allowed for outside seating. She decided that outside seemed what the day called for. Beautiful and warm enough, it deserved to be lived in.

As she waited for the waitstaff, her mind dwelled on the case. To reiterate herself to herself, she thought again about the killer's hairy hands. They were his murder weapon, and he may have unknowingly left clues behind that would help catch him. She optimistically hoped that science would allow that to happen.

"Miss?" The waitress interrupted her thoughts.

"I'd like an order of mot-sticks with ranch and marinara. The reuben, with no sauerkraut, on the marbled Rye, with extra Thousand Island. A load of fries with extra, extra ketchup. I'd like a piece of the tiramisu cheesecake, you may bring it with the meal, and a glass of Louis Martini Cabernet Sauvignon by Napa Valley," Zoey rattled off.

"I take it, you've been here before," the waitress said, scribbling down the order.

"A few times," Zoey admitted.

The waitress zipped away to place her order. Hopefully she would bring the wine before the meal. She did. "Thank you," she told the waitress.

"Anything else, before your meal is up?"

"A glass of ice water with lemon."

"Right away."

The dark sauvignon looked like deep purple blood in the glass. Zoey checked her reflection in the glass, and laughed at her sunglasses. She felt good to be alive, scar included.

Zoey took a sip of the cabernet. Delicate balance, a hint of plum, rich, velvet on the tongue. Drinking on a Wednesday. You only live once. Not that her work wasn't a constant reminder of that fact. Life, laughter, and wine.

Unwillingly Zoey's mind brought her back to the crime scene, but her thoughts were not about the crime scene itself, but the scent of arrogant Jake Corde. The pleasant clean smell of him. At the crime scene her nose may have smelled him, but not registered it perfectly as she came out of her vision. And he had touched her too. Mind you, it was a steadying gesture only, but he had put his hands on her hips.

Maybe she should have asked for his phone number for work purposes of course, not that she couldn't look it up online. But whatever. He had won out with the officers at the meeting with his crude humor. Jerk.

Her meal arrived. Zoey set to, like a man who had been shattered by a divorce after seventeen years of marriage, not feeding himself right, so when he eats it looks like he hasn't eaten in weeks. Zoey ate a little slower, to savor the flavors. Mot-sticks gone, and half the reuben. Maybe she would save the second half. Now for the cheesecake. Nothing like a good tiramisu cheesecake. Creamy, chocolatey, just perfect.

"May I bring you another wine, or anything else?" The waitress asked, appearing out of nowhere.

"Umm, yes. Sex with a handsome hunk. And a to-go box, I guess," Zoey answered.

"Can't help with that first request," the waitress laughed, "but I'll get that to-go box," the waitress disappeared again.

Eaten. The victims had been eaten for the love of all things! So his hands were not his only weapon, his teeth were another. Tearing teeth. A wild hunger. Fucking savage!

'When I get back to the office, I better do some work on the other deceased in their drawers', Zoey thought. This wasn't the only case she had to work on, it just happened to be the most engrossing at the moment. Her other cadavers, she didn't think had been eaten.

Zoey paid the bill, and headed back to the office.

After many hours, Zoey checked her phone. 2102. Time to call it a night. Zoey alarmed the office door and walked to her car. Darkness claimed the land like a wraith. Shadows within shadows. The moon hung, a gossamer wedding dress covered in cobwebs.

Zoey got into her car, plugged her phone in, and found one of her upbeat playlists. This one featured some heavy metal that a friend of hers in med school introduced her to. She didn't know the groups or the song titles, but it had a heavy beat. Good driving music. She cranked up the volume and merged into traffic.

When she got home Zoey threw her keys on the table. Here she was at her place, and she felt lonely. Being a work-aholic might be good for the pocket book, but it sucked on the social life. She didn't even have any friends to call. She debated binge watching some mindless show, but decided against it. What did she have in her wine cooler?

There was a late harvest riesling, but she wasn't in the mood for that right now. She kept digging. Ah-ha! The LVE French Sparkling Rose. It had red currant flavors and light bubbles. That would do nicely. She withdrew the bottle, closed the cooler, and began uncorking the bottle.

She poured some into her second favorite glass, which wasn't as large as last night's glass, but much prettier. She held the glass up and admired the light pink color of this vintage. She put her nose to the glass, and inhaled the aroma, then she took a sip. Effervescent wine. Just the thing she needed.

Maybe she should call her mother? When had she called last, at least a month ago. She dug out her phone, found Mom, and punched send.

"Hi, Maman. Yes I'm fine. No, I don't have a boyfriend yet, but thanks for asking. Oh, you know me, work, work, work. Yes, of course I'm eating," Zoey laughed. "I have a French mother, you know. No, it hasn't snowed here yet. Thank the stars, I'm not ready for that white merde yet. I wish I could say yes to that question, but I haven't had much time for reading. I promise I will check that out. Send me a text with the title of the book. Okay, you take care of yourself. Love you too."

Zoey ended the call and poured another glass of wine. She picked out her outfit for tomorrow. She set the alarm clock feature on her phone. She put on Dvorak's symphony From "The New World", and crawled into bed.

The phone rang.

Chapter 17

2300

Back at the motel, Matt drifted toward sleep. Jake waited until he heard snoring. Good, his brother was out. The T.V. droned on, but Jake wasn't paying attention to it. His mind ran through details about the case.

He needed to catch this killer quickly. What was he missing? Maybe Zoey could help? A different perspective. Jake had no problem utilizing any and all resources available to him. The goal was to solve the case. Fuck it, he dialed her number.

He knew there was no reason this couldn't wait until morning. He also knew he wanted to see her, smell her scent, be around her, she was more intoxicating than ginger brandy. He glanced over at Matt. Without intruders who would later make unwanted comments.

"Hello?" Zoey answered, sounding groggy. Damn, her husky voice turned him on.

"Corde here, meet me in the M.E. parking lot," he said, striving to sound all business.

"Do you know what time it is?" Zoey said, irritated.

"And, the killer is still out there. I'm driving a silver Sentra now," Jake said.

"Give me half an hour pending traffic," Zoey said, sounding more awake, and more irritated. But she was complying. Jake wouldn't lie to himself, he wanted to have her. Have her, this way, and that way, and all ways possible. He got in the rental and drove to the M.E. Office. One car in the lot, security guard.

While Jake waited, he distracted himself with the Sentra's control panel. He wanted to listen to his playlist so he plugged his phone into the jack. He would never tell anyone but he kind of liked this car. It wasn't his pony, but it had great traction and a tight wheel. On the way here he had driven it like he'd stolen it and it's performance was quite acceptable.

Ten more minutes passed. He couldn't remember ever waiting on a woman like this. It only took a moment to decide she was worth it. So worth it.

At last the Renault pulled in, and parked next to him. Zoey rolled down her window. Jake followed suit.

"You want to sit in our cars, go in your building, go somewhere for coffee?" He asked.

"Why don't you get in my car? No other ears at a coffee shop, H.I.P.A.A., and all that jazz. Let me just clear the seat off," Zoey answered. Jake rolled up the window, killed the engine, and walked around to her passenger door. She unlocked it for him, and he climbed in, surprised the fit wasn't as tight as he imagined.

He closed the car door as gently as he could out of respect for her property. The car smelled like her. She clearly didn't smoke, and didn't have air fresheners in the vehicle. The car was immaculate, other than the few items she'd moved to allow him to sit down.

Jake felt a little like Ryan may have felt, the proverbial bull in the china shop, and he tried not to touch anything for fear of breaking it. And nervous as hell. Christ he hadn't felt like this since he had asked Amanda Jacobs to Prom. In hindsight he realized he might have been better off in the morning daylight with Mathew watching his back, that's how much this woman threw him.

"You called the meeting, what have you got?" Zoey asked. Jake met her eyes. Her distinctive golden eyes.

"Nothing extremely helpful yet unfortunately. I called the meeting hoping you might give me an angle to explore," Jake said. He grasped at whatever plausible explanation he could come up with. Half truth's were ok.

"You're the dick, isn't that your job," Zoey burst out with.

"I've been looking for the hairless Squatch, but..."

Zoey's laughter cut Jake off. At least that was good, a potentially hostile discussion, defused. Of course her throaty, musical tones had the power to shake his self-control further.

"You keep looking for Bigfoot, and watch me catch our

killer," Zoey grinned. Those lips were going to be the death of him. He was so focused on the red heart shaped lips that he nearly missed her comment.

"What are you going to catch him with, your bone saw or your scalpel?"

"I'm going to catch him with my brain. What are you going to catch him with?"

I'm going to catch him with you at my side, Jake thought. Now to do that first he needed to catch Zoey Abero. She was the fish he didn't want to let get away. Oh if Matt saw him now.

"Let's start by discussing our visions, and how they might assist us," Jake offered.

"In case it hasn't occurred to you, I don't talk about my visions with random people. My visions are a very private thing," Zoey confessed.

"Intelligent. I don't either. We are not random people, we are two professionals working a case together," Jake said.

"Touche! In that case, we might as well build a bonfire and dance around it naked," Zoey said.

"As stunningly wonderful as that sounds, and I am more than willing to participate, we might have to get out of the city for that. Lucky for us though I hear Bigfoot frequents forests," Jake said, understanding that her comment was sarcasm.

"I checked my newsfeed, it said there was a hairless Squatch sighting in Michigan."

"Shall we take a road trip? We could do that naked too."

"You are such an idiot." Her lips quivered, a sure indicator she was fighting laughter.

"I've been called worse. I shouldn't have to remind you that out of the two of us sitting in this car, you are the doctor," Jake said, smiling softly.

He studied her face. The scar was the only blemish on the otherwise smooth, beautiful face. He couldn't help wondering what story that scar told. Her hair looked good, he wanted to run his fingers in that silky mane, experience every single sensation that celebrated her sexuality. Suddenly her vehicle was too hot. He glanced at the dash. Time to shut that thought down. He switched back to their visions.

"My visions help me see periphery things, like the outsides of the picture. I see the edges, I don't see what is in the middle. Do you see the middle of the picture?"

"I do," Zoey divulged.

"It has been pointed out to me by another intelligent person that we might make a good team, if we put those skills together. Both of our visions combined, give a more coherent picture," Jake said. No matter how Zoey answered, Jake was going to have to give Matt that point.

She didn't say anything. Jake waited. What might she be thinking about? He wondered if she could hear his pounding heart; it probably sounded like a jack-hammer on speed. He want-ed to rub his sternum in an effort to calm the traitorous thing.

Jake's phone rang. For fuck's sake. It was Matt calling. He answered.

"Corde Brothers Investigators."

"Where are you? I got up to take a leak, and you were gone," Matt shouted.

"I'm fine, thanks for asking. My apologies, I'm in a business meeting. Can I call you back later?" Matt hung up. Jake knew his brother was pissed. He would get over it.

"Never stops ringing," Jake apologized to Zoey. "I put a tail on two of the witnesses. I'm worried about their safety. I haven't figured out why I saw those particular people, truth be told, but it can't be anything good. They really didn't have much, though the boy did see someone in a car in the alley about a block from the crime scene." He informed her, trying to give her some breathing room, to show her he was not a bad guy and that he was willing to share what he knew.

"That was good thinking. I'm sure Victor will appreciate the help. Since the latest suicide by cop killings, the police are not viewed favorably," she nodded.

She was quiet for so long Jake finally decided to call it a night. It was obvious this was going no further. "Look, I don't know how this will end, but I do know the sooner the better and the only way to reach that conclusion is by making it happen. By pooling resources and watching each other's backs. I realize you are a rogue warrior but sometimes even heroes need sidekicks, ya know?"

"Can you give me some time to process how we might put our visions to work on solving the case, and I'll get back to you?" Zoey asked.

"Fair enough," Jake admitted, opening the car door.

"Have a good night Detective," Zoey said, studying his face.

I haven't had a good night since I first laid eyes on you Doctor Abero, Jake thought. He didn't foresee that changing in the near future. What he said aloud was, "You too Doctor."

Chapter 18

0100 Thursday

Zoey pulled her car out onto Flournoy Street. A confused frown marred her forehead. What the hell? What had the entire meeting meant?

Why couldn't this have waited until morning? Better question, why hadn't she told him to fuck off? She wasn't normally very nice to people who woke her up out of a sound sleep. This late night, clandestine, pointlessness could have absolutely been done over coffee at the police station.

Yet here she was, driving home after answering his demand complacently. He was turning her into a pushover. A sheep. She sighed. Always honest with herself Zoey was forced to admit she wanted to see him again. That and only that was why she was on the Chicago roads in the middle of the night.

The memory of his strong hands on her waist, his scent filling her senses, made her belly flutter. The memory of it for God's sake! He was a potent drug. The effect he had on her libido was distracting and addicting. It was also damned inconvenient. Where was her will power?

No stranger to sexual frustration, Zoey was never-the-less overwhelmed by the strength of the need that shot through her at the mere thought of his clean man scent. Oh my Gawd! That was it! He had been turned on right next to her, in her passenger seat!

Jake wanted her.

She recognized the 'call of the wild' like any red blooded heterosexual woman would. And she recognized her body's response to it! She understood biology and chemistry quite, quite well. The truth was unrelenting. The conclusion, undeniable.

But Jake Corde? Her mind struggled. Really? She sighed again as she pulled into her building's parking lot.

An arrogant private detective. She wasn't sure if it was indicative of the sad state of her sex life or the bad karma she'd managed to accumulate over the years. Didn't really matter, did it? She never fell for the doctors and lawyers. No, not her.

Much to her chagrin, she realized she had a soft spot for guys who had hero complexes. The ones who loved dangerous occupations like policemen, firemen, and apparently, private detectives. Men who lived with the possibility of violent death every day. Great. She huffed as she came to her door.

As she pushed the key into the lock, she fumbled a little, and took note of her shaking hands. Curious, she did not feel cold. In her apartment she tossed her keys onto the hall table and hung her coat on the corner tree. Without bothering to turn on any lights she went into the kitchen for a drink of water then made her way to her bedroom.

The curtains filtered the city lights, casting the room in soft relief. Still no indoor lights. She liked the semi-dark. It was relaxing to her.

Sitting on her bed she removed her shoes then stood and shucked the rest of her clothing to her black panties. She caught her own image vaguely in the shadowed shine of the floor length mirror a few feet away. She wondered how attractive she would be to men if not for the scar?

Her fingers traced the scar down to the column below her chin. She cupped the side of her neck, felt the warmth, she had nice hands. She traced the muscles, the tendons of her throat. Her thoughts drifted to Jake and it took no imagination to see his hands on her breasts, gently rolling and tugging at the dark nipples until the aerole's tightened. A jolt of pleasure brought her attention back to the moment and the mirror.

Fuck. Her fingers held her breasts lovingly. She watched, red lips slightly parted, as one hand slid down, pushing under the black lace that hid her mound.

There was no sin in needing release right? Right. It was a natural occurrence. No harm. Still, it was a guilty kind of pleasure that made her shiver as one long, slim finger slid over the throbbing, hard nub at the top of her slit. Her hips jerked and she fell back on the bed, moaning slightly.

One hand gave a nipple some friction as the other pressed

a little harder even as the finger slid back and forth, slowly. She wanted the heat, the pleasure to last. Slowly she rubbed two fingers from the top down, over her soaking wet sex.

Her legs fell open further, the sensations intensifying. Her stomach contracted. Her silky thighs quivered. Slowly another swipe, another. Her mind full of Jake Corde, as her fingers pushed a little harder, stroked a little faster.

There was no more going slow. As her vaginal walls contracted on the first wave of an orgasm she couldn't help but cry out. She didn't stop stroking, demanding more from her body. Corde deserved two orgasms, no matter how tender it made her clit.

She laughed softly as the second wave washed over her from head to curling toes. If he lived up to ten percent of her expectations she would probably fall in love. It was a sobering thought.

A quick shower removed the physical evidence of her foray into self-gratification. She was exhausted. There were four hours left before she had to make an appearance at the morning meeting.

She climbed into bed naked, pulled the covers up to her chin and sighed. Maybe now she could manage to not throw herself at Jake like a sex starved maniac. Maybe.

0150

He took his hand from his softening penis and wiped it on a shirt hanging in the back of the closet. He tucked and buttoned himself back into a semblance of decency. Waiting patiently for her breathing to slow he forced his own to do the same. That had been one hot fucking moment.

At last he deemed it safe to leave the closet. Carefully pushing the door out he silently closed it and tread softly over to her bed. Gazing down at her with a new appreciation for the brunette.

His eyes gleamed in the muted light. She was beautiful, even with the scar. Maybe even because of it.

Who would have guessed there was such a naughty little sex

toy under all those proper clothes and lab coats? Not him. He was glad for it, to be sure. Not even Katie gave him so much pleasure. He remembered his disappointment when he had gotten here to find Zoey gone, short lived as it was keen. He had barely opened her fridge door when he heard the key in the lock. Good thing she hadn't looked in the closet.

Now staring down at her he smiled a little. 'Oh sweet Zoey, you just bought yourself some extra time. You were next, now you are last. I have to think about you some more. Do I want those busy, capable, naughty hands, or something else entirely? I think I want you to live long enough to repeat that little performance.' He whispered above her.

Abruptly he turned and walked to the hallway, stopping to grab the shoes he had left under the hall table. Tonight was as perfect as it could get. Hopefully James put on as good a show as Ms. Abero.

Chapter 19

0430 Thursday

Her phone rang before her alarm and Zoey groaned. She wasn't ready for her day to start. One eye opened to look at the digital clock on her night stand.

Four thirty?! What the hell? She would kill Jake if it was him.

Her caller I.D. saved the P.I. "Detective Victor, another one?"

"Yes. This one is clear across town, dammit. Get to Dunning, West Irving Park. We are now dealing with a serial killer. I want to solve this before the Feds get involved."

"I'll get there as soon as I can." Zoey promised, hanging up and getting right back on with her team.

When she was assured they were on their way she got dressed and ran down to her car. She double checked the trunk to make sure the extra forensic kit and lab coat were there. Bonus! Now she wouldn't have to go to the office. Dunning was a bit of a drive from her apartment. Traffic shouldn't be a nightmare if she hurried. Another hour and it would be gridlocked.

She prayed the team brought enough evidence bags this time. The last murder had emptied the van and Kellesha's extras as well. Part of her had to wonder if the very messiness of the scenes wasn't some misguided attempt at confusing or even hiding possible evidence.

If so, it was futile. Zoey and her team were the best forensic operation in Chicago, maybe the whole state, for a reason. They were meticulous and relentless in their search for the truth. They worked tirelessly for hours bagging, tagging, and logging evidence. They crawled on hands and knees where necessary. Climbed ladders, left no nook or cranny un-investigated.

The drive afforded Zoey the time to get her mind ready for the scene she would be facing. The chaos of people, noise, smell.

She wondered what body part would be missing this time.

There was a college in the area. She couldn't help thinking that it was a great hunting ground. Serial killer. He had changed the game.

Maybe he didn't care. He was so blatant it was clear he had no fear. No fear meant nothing to lose. Or, the inability to recognize consequences. Was that it? Was he somehow mentally impaired? It seemed like that might be the case.

Was he drugged up? Heroin? Drugs would explain the incredible strength. The lack of sophistication certainly backed up the theory. It would explain the darkness too. No cognition? A man of brute force with a feral need for human flesh and no thought process to teach him the benefits of secrecy and conceal-ment.

She felt the tingle that told her she was so very close to the bottom of it. So close, yet it was all intangible. She needed some hard evidence and so far there had been none. Not really anything definitive.

Three blocks from the epicenter she had to flash her badge at which point a policeman gestured for her to go through. She edged forward and eventually stopped her car in the middle of the street. Vehicles with flashing lights sat hither and yon. Yep, the chaos.

Gathering her kit and coat Zoey made her way through the press of bodies. She wasn't gentle about it. Reporters and gawk-ers made her sick. The ending of a life was not a circus act to be ooohed and ahhhed over.

Victor stood talking with the bane of her existence. Their heads down, faces grave. They both looked up as she drew closer. Victor nodded. Jake just stared.

Her pulse jacked up. She had a job to do. Another murder to solve. Post haste.

This time the killer had chosen a most unfortunate back-drop. A small dog park. Plenty of dirt to soak up the blood and dog dung, foot prints and debris that at best had nothing to do with the crime and at worst completely compromised the real evi-dence.

Damn. She shook her head and took a deep breath. That's when she noticed it. How could she not? What should have been a chest cavity was destroyed flesh and blood and gore but...no bones. No ribs, no sternum. Torn out like a piece of notebook paper.

What the hell? Shit. Why not organs? You can sell them for bundles of money. What was the killer doing? This trophy taking hadn't made sense from the very beginning.

What was she missing? Was he trying to reconstruct a skelleton? Why? The evidence said it was so, but the killer's only motive was feeding.

"What is it Doctor?" Jake's deep tones came from behind her. He must have noticed something in her body language.

"Trophies. Why is he taking trophies if he only cares about the destruction and consumption? It doesn't track, but I think he's building a skeleton."

"Really? What is the psychology of that one?"

She shrugged. "I don't know. I can't see a reason, but the truth is right there. He has taken a mandible, a ribcage, and two legs. What else could he be doing with them?"

"Fetish?"

"Most killers that take body parts are specific to that body part. They have a story for it. This guy is taking parts, helter skelter. No. There's no other explanation."

"I'll talk to Doctor Abernathy. Maybe he can give some insight." Victor said, coming up next to Jake. "It couldn't hurt, right?"

"You do that. I think I will interview the officer, what was his last name?" Jake asked.

"Palmer."

"Thanks." Jake turned to Zoey.

"What you are saying in layman's terms, correct me if I'm wrong, is that a serial killer would take the same body part as a trophy every time he kills because it fits a story he has, is that correct?"

"Yes. This killer is not following that pattern," Zoey said.

"And this leads you to believe that the killer is building a skeleton?" Jake asked, trying to follow the mental leap.

"I just work with the facts. I'm not saying absolutely that the killer is building a skeleton. If that is the case, I want to stop him before his project is complete, I can tell you that for free."

Zoey squatted closer to the corpse, studying the once human remains. Suddenly she planted both of her palms on the ground. She trembled. The hunger was so invasive, so pervasive it made her stomach roil.

Again, the victim hadn't stood a chance. The killer hit so hard, so fast she was dying before she could feel fear, opening her throat with his teeth. The shock on her face seemed frozen in time, burned into Zoey's psyche like a brand.

"Abero, you alright?" Victor asked.

"I'm fine Victor," Zoey answered through clenched teeth.

"What did you see?" Jake asked.

"Fuck you Corde," Zoey raised her voice.

"I see you two are getting along handsomely, working as a team to solve this case," Victor didn't do sarcasm well, but he was trying to make a point.

"I'm sorry Zoey," Jake began.

"Fuck off Detective," Zoey flatly said.

"Testy, testy," Jake said.

"Maybe if people didn't keep me up at night asking asinine questions that could wait," Zoey said.

"Abero, I'm going to talk with Stephen. I'll let you and your team complete your work here," Victor said.

"Appreciate that," Zoey told Victor. "I'll touch base with results as soon as I have them." She watched him walk away from the crime scene. Still in her crouching position; Zoey directed her team into action.

"I'm going to do a quick walk around then go talk to Palmer. If you need anything, give me a call." Jake told her.

"Ok."

The victim had been a college student. Maybe a grad student, studying Behavioral Psych, or Business Administration. The books were strewn around the area, ruined by dew and blood. It didn't matter now. Red hair in a ponytail. Maybe she'd been walking home from a four hour class that ran from 2000 to 0000? She could have been going to visit a tutor, or heading to the campus pub? Again, it didn't matter now.

Zoey studied the corpse. Another mess, another nightmare autopsy in front of her. Fucking Bastard. She needed to stop this mayhem. This wonton slaughter.

The whole rib cage including the sternum. Like the previous crime scenes her limbs were flung in a radius around her head and torso. Her intestines were spilling out of her body over her shoulders looking like a ghastly angel's wings.

Why the different bones, if he wasn't building a skeleton? Corde was right about one thing, they didn't need the psychologist's input to solve this case. He would come up with some cock and bull theory that wouldn't be helpful in any way. Most likely get the regular officers thinking along incorrect lines, and skewing their judgement. They didn't need that right now. They needed everyone sharp. They needed science to work its wonders. Facts which lead to answers and apprehension, so they could end the escalation.

The team was efficiently bagging and tagging. Zoey rose from her position. Coffee. She definitely needed about three or more shots of espresso and chocolate. Oodles of chocolate. It was going to be another long day.

"C'est la vie."

Chapter 20

Jakes investigation of the area around the murder turned up nothing but vague snatches of shadowy bushes and a dark sedan parked near the exit to the park. No witnesses. No real clues. He didn't think this was a failure of his visions though. Simply nothing to follow.

After an hour of aimlessly wandering around he gestured to Matt and the two of them left the scene. He couldn't help feeling disappointed and a little powerless at the moment. He could use a win right now. Maybe Palmer would be a more fruitful path.

The nineteenth district parking lot was packed by the time Jake and Matt pulled in. Shift changes were always like this. The two men split up once they were inside the building, too much area to cover, too little time. The break room or lockers would be where to look first.

Turns out Jake never made it to the break room. He asked the first cop he came to if he knew Palmer's whereabouts and was pointed to the hub of all police stations, the war room.

When the officer he was talking to shouted "Palmer" the big guy turned. Jake strode right up to him and stuck out his palm. "Officer Palmer, my name is Jake Corde. I was wondering if you could spare a few minutes?"

Palmer was just what you might expect of a beat cop. An ex-military man, tall, strong, good looking if he wiped the bitterness off his mug. Giant chip on his shoulder. It was more than obvious he already knew who Jake was by reputation if nothing else. His pale blue eyes narrowed and his lip curled up.

"Victor is too good to come talk to me himself?" He asked belligerently.

Jake shrugged, "Probably. Look, I don't have time for bullshit. Let's cut to the chase. You were on Lawrence Avenue around the time of the murder. Can you recall seeing anything out of the ordinary?"

"How do you know where I was?"

"Witnesses. Did you see a black sedan? Did you see the victim walking home? I was told she dances often and that street is her chosen path home."

Suddenly the cops face crumpled. "No. I didn't see anything. I don't know how I missed it all! How did he kill that sweet little girl right there on my beat? None of those folks are ever going to trust me again."

"How long did you sit there?" Jake nearly growled. Nothing worse than a man in the throes of self pity.

"2130 to 2230. Then I moved four blocks down. Black sedans are fairly commonplace so I probably saw one, but if it wasn't doing anything suspicious to draw my attention I looked right by it, no doubt."

"Did the stores close at their normal times? Did the usual people do their everyday routine as far as you could tell?"

"Yes, except Mr. Lovington. That old guy never follows a routine. His only consistency is his inconsistency. The kid Ryan stayed with Lovington until after I left, from then, I couldn't say." Jake heaved a sigh. This guy was useless. "Keep your back safe officer Palmer. He's not done killing and I have a feeling potential witnesses are in peril."

Palmer nodded. "That poor girl…"

"Another in Dunning, this morning."

"I heard."

"Well, you know the drill." Jake handed the cop a card. "Call me if you remember anything."

"Sure thing." The man hesitated. "I'm sorry about the attitude. I'm frustrated and angry. I tried to take it out on you."

"Hey, I get it. Really." Jake gave a single, sharp nod and turned on his heel. He had no intention of playing nice for ten minutes just so the guy would feel better about his shitty attitude and shittier policing. He had a killer to catch. Right after he found his wandering brother.

Back in the car Jake gave the steering wheel a hard slap. "I don't get it! Only Ryan saw anything remotely off! Why did my

visions give me such complete dead ends? This has never happened before."

"Just because you can't make the connection yet doesn't
mean there isn't one." Matt said quietly. "You are far too intuitive Jake. You'll get it. Why don't you mull over it all and let me
drive?"

"The guy is taking trophies, to build a skeleton according
to Zoey Abero, which indicates a thought process, reasoning if
you will. The murder scenes are nighmarish chaos and destruction, indicating an abandon, a lack of thought. Zoey felt like the
killer was pure dark, no thoughts of consequence or caring, and
yet there was the bone collecting, indicating a focus, or purpose,
besides feasting," Jake started the car distractedly.

"Your visions of the first murder were vague. The second
one gave you much clearer information. Maybe because she was
found quickly, so you got there faster. Who knows?"

"Wait! There it is!"

"What?" Matt looked around.

"The guy doesn't make sense. There's something there.
Something..."

Matt watched his brother with a small smile on his full
mouth. Jake was a fascinating man when his wheels were turning. He took leaps of faith when he needed to but the majority of
Jake's success was pure intelligence and due diligence.

"Christ! I gotta call the detective and Zoey!" No sooner
said than done.

"Jake! I'm up to my elbows in...."

"Listen Zoey, I have you on speakerphone. Two killers.
There are two of them. I know you're only seeing evidence of one
but think Zoey! Think about the whole thing!"

"Calm down Jake. I was thinking along those lines already.
It brings the picture into focus a little better doesn't it?" Zoey's
voice was music to Jake's ears, even when she was up to her elbows in gore.

"Yes! A master and a puppet! Somehow the one who wants
the body parts for a skeleton controls the guy who does the actual
killing and eating." He shook his head. "It's so simple! But, even

if we catch the killer, we will have a hard time getting to his con-
troller."

"True."

"You need to take precautions, Zoey. I have to call Victor
now. Watch your back." He hung up.

"Matt, can you call Willy in to watch her?"

Victor also answered quickly and his expletive filled side
of the conversation made Jake's eyebrows go up in amazement.
He hadn't known the detective had it in him. "Are you sure?" He
finally calmed down enough to ask.

"Zoey agrees with me. It makes perfect sense. The guy that
actually does the deed is being manipulated by someone. It explains the organization behind the trophies that have purpose and
the chaos of the destruction."

"That complicates things considerably."

"I agree. You get a chance to talk to Doctor Stephenson?"

"No. And it's Abernathy. But I left a message so I'm sure
I'll get the chance today. How did the Palmer interview go?"

"It went. Nothing new to add. I was just telling Abero to
be alert. What are the chances you could convince her to change
residences until this blows over?"

"Next to none. She isn't my bestie. We have a reasonable
work relationship. She won't listen to me any better than she
obviously did you."

"I figured. Ok. Well, what she doesn't know can't hurt
her. I'm putting one of my guys on her. Just so you know."

"Ok. It's your funeral."

"Such caring. I'm touched."

"Don't be, it wasn't on purpose. See you later."

"Take care, Victor."

Hanging up he finally pulled out of the parking lot and went
straight to the ME's office. They would sit in the parking lot there
until their man showed up to watch over Zoey. He felt so strongly
about her protection he wondered exactly how attached he had become in so short a time? How much of his worry was professional
courtesy and how much personal?

In the end it didn't matter, the goal was the same. Keep

her safe. Nothing wrong with that, no matter what reasoning stood behind the act of protection.

If he honestly felt like their lives were in danger, then he should do what he thought was right. Which is to watch over her. She could get mad and beat him up later. He had broad shoulders, he could take it.

Chapter 21

0900

Victor Kingsley looked at his watch. A Seiko two tone stainless steel Solar watch. It didn't have a digital readout, and didn't show military time. Victor had been a cop for so long his mind automatically worked on military time. He liked his watch. The Seiko had stopped running the day his wife died, and he hadn't replaced the battery. The timepiece was a reminder. Old-fashioned, like he himself. He was pushing sixty.

Victor walked into his office and sat down at his computer. He sifted through the emails, marking them in order of priority. Briefly thinking about lunch, he knew he needed a cup of coffee, if nothing else. He thought about calling Abero, when his own cell phone rang.

"Kingsley," he answered.

"Hello. Stephen Abernathy; returning your call," the psychologist greeted.

"I wanted to pick your brain," Victor stated.

"Shall we grab lunch?"

"That would be time efficient. Where?"

"How does Everyone's Fav sound?"

"Perfect."

"Meet you there at noon?" Victor hung up.

Work kept him occupied for the rest of the morning and he was about to leave for lunch when his phone rang again. He ignored it. He better go to lunch before he fell prey to the stupid thing consuming all his time.

The Italian restaurant happened to be one of Victor's favorite places to eat. He got a table for two, and waited for Stephen. Victor looked at the menu to kill the time. A few minutes later Dr. Abernathy arrived. They placed their orders. Victor went with the chicken parmigiana while Stephen picked the eggplant parmigiana. While they waited for their food to arrive they started conversing.

"Why might a serial killer take different trophies instead of the same one over and over from his victims?" Victor asked.

"Is this the case?" Stephen asked.

"Would I be probing your mind, or asking you questions for no reason?"

"Normally a serial killer will take something personal from their victims. Maybe a ring or necklace. Maybe a driver's license. The killer will use these items to relive the crime," the doctor answered.

"So if different body parts were taken, what would that mean?"

"As I'm sure you are aware, Bundy took heads; Jerome Brudos feet; Charles Albright eyes; and Ed Gein faces," Stephen answered.

"I know the history, but that doesn't answer my question. To reiterate, why different trophies?" Victor said.

"The mind of a serial killer is a complex question," Stephen said, shutting his eyes in thought. Their food arrived. Once the waitstaff left, Victor dug into his meal. After a few mouthfuls he resumed the conversation.

"If I knew the answer, I would not have asked for your input. I know about reliving the murders, I know about fetishes, I'm looking for the psychology behind differing trophies," he asked a third time.

"I tell you what, let me do some thinking and research along these lines, and I'll get back to you A.S.A.P.," Stephen said.

"Sounds good," Victor said, taking another forkful. He hoped the man would live up to his A.S.A.P., Victor needed the answer two days ago. They finished their meal talking about small matters within the department as a whole.

Victor left the meeting feeling more frustrated than when he initiated it. What good was the doctor if he didn't answer the question that needed to be answered? Victor told himself that he was being impatient, let the doctor do his thing. But let him do it at light speed, dammit.

Returning to his office Victor spent hours replying to

emails, arguing with his Captain about Corde and the budget again, and filling out reports. Then he went to get a coffee. With coffee in hand, he went into the conference room and started reviewing the photographs of the crime scenes.

He checked his phone for the time. 1700 hours. Crime scene photos were only so good, Victor decided he needed to revisit each of the crime scenes. It didn't help that all three of them were in different parts of town. He would start with the newest one first, and work backward.

At 2005, after battling traffic, he reached the third crime scene. Had anything crucial been missed earlier today? Why did the killer strike here? All of the victims had been young women, so there was a 'type' that the killer targeted, or at least, a gender.

The women were not all prostitutes, so this wasn't like Jack The Ripper. Did they have anything in common besides gender? Driving to the scene of the second murder Victor placed a call.

"Abero, any results?" He asked.

"I will have them within the hour," Zoey answered.

"Call me. Abero, we are going to reschedule our task force meeting to 0900."

"Nothing like last minute," Zoey laughed.

"You know how the game is played," Victor said.

"Yes I do. I'll call you soon, Detective."

Next Victor dialed Corde.

"Corde here," the consultant answered.

"We are going to have a task force meeting at 0900," Victor said.

"0900," Corde confirmed.

2213

Victor parked his police Tahoe in the alley behind the bookstore. He got out of his vehicle, and studied the narrow passageway. Too small a space for cars to pass each other going opposite directions. Not a good place for delivery trucks either. That was Chicago for you. He walked toward the coffee shop, and turned the corner to his left. Another left turn and he walked toward the store front where the second murder had been commited.

I'm getting too old for this shit, he thought. Still after close to forty years on the force he believed that crime and killers should be stopped. Brought to justice. That is what he signed up for, and he wasn't ready to retire yet. Other good officers he knew had taken early retirement, and most of them didn't know what to do with their time.

After reviewing the second and first scenes Victor thought it might be time to call it a night. The scrunched position he needed to be in to work on the laptop in his car made his back pain flare up so he stopped back at the police station where he could work more comfortably, finishing paperwork and sending Emails to the other task force members. At last he left the office for the night and drove home.

He had lived alone since his wife passed after a battle with cancer. He pulled into the building parking structure. He knew most of the cars, and who drove them. These people lived in his building. He knew that he couldn't keep everybody that lived in Chicago safe, but he could at least keep an eye out.

He shut down his vehicle. Getting out he started walking toward the elevators. Had he heard something that wasn't his own footfall? He stopped in his tracks and listened. That is when the hairs on the back of his neck started tingling. That is when his mind flew into go mode. That is when he knew that he wasn't alone.

Chapter 22

2330

Victor recognized the smell of the body spray the man wore, it was common around the station. Many men everywhere wore it, about 60% of the younger officers used the stuff. Did women actually find it appealing, or just put up with it? The spray didn't have 'class' in Victor's opinion.

Just then Victor saw movement. The movement flashed low to the ground. It wasn't dangerous though, that was Elsie's cat. She wasn't supposed to have the animal in the building, but all of her neighbors adored her, and didn't report it. Some crimes could be forgiven, and didn't warrant police intervention. The cat didn't wear body spray though.

Pretending he forgot something in his vehicle, Victor fished out his keys. He held them with one key sticking out between his index and middle finger as a makeshift weapon. Afterall, he had grown up in Chicago. He knew he could draw his service weapon, but as of yet, he didn't have enough reason to pull his gun.

His vehicle would be a more defensive position than standing out in the middle of the parking structure. He walked back toward his vehicle watching for human movement and watching the lit garage floor for shadows. He strained his ears for sounds of movement.

The detective's seasoned ears heard footsteps, but they were soft. Footsteps made by someone not wearing shoes. The sound was muted, not soles slapping concrete. Victor's mind flashed to photos of the crime scenes. Did this person's foot have a scar on it?

When he reached his vehicle, Victor spun around on his heel facing the direction he'd just walked. He couldn't see anyone. Where are you hiding? Behind a car, or that square steel support pillar?

He hoped that Abero would have some conclusive results.

He also prayed the Corde was making progress, otherwise he would hear about the blasted budget yet again. The budget was a big pain in his ass. Why was he thinking about the fucking thing when here he was potentially facing the killer in question?

Had he imagined the scent of the knock off cologne? Was his mind playing tricks on him with the sound of muted footsteps? Was this just what they used to call the jitters? Damn it, he was getting old.

But he wasn't senile yet, and the hairs on his neck rose a second time. An uncanny warning. This time adrenaline coursed through his body. No, he hadn't imagined this. There was someone else here with him in the parking garage.

This would have been a good time to have a partner with him, although he knew that wasn't normal, when you were going home for the evening. One of the benefits of having a partner was to watch each other's backs. But he didn't have a partner with him. This time he was solo. No changing that fact.

"I know you're here," Victor said loudly. He wasn't trying to strike up a conversation. He called out to buy himself time, and listen for more noise to pinpoint the person's location.

No answer, not that he'd expected one. No sound. That waft of scent said that the person had to be close though. Victor listened for breathing. He couldn't hear any.

A loud thud. Then before he could react strong hands grabbed Victor's throat and started squeezing. The killer struck from the roof of his Tahoe.

Instinctively Victor grabbed the assailant's wrists attempting to remove his hands. He dropped his keys in the process, but he wasn't going to be choked to death. Those hands didn't budge. They were incredibly strong. Superhuman vice grips. They squeezed even harder.

Victor thrashed attempting to dislodge the attacker from his Tahoe's roof. The effort failed. Victor felt his windpipe collapsing, he was being choked to death. He hated the thought that he might die this way.

If Victor went for his gun it would mean removing one of his hands. Would it be worth it? He wasn't making any progress in stopping the killer from crushing his throat. He was running out of time, he needed to save his life.

The fingers on those hands felt like iron on steroids. Victor used every ounce of his arm strength and threw his own body forward toward the ground. The killer needed to follow or release his grip. Human arms are only so long, that was physics.

The killer let go. Gasping for air, Victor fell, his body smacked into the garage floor. The killer jumped down onto his back and knocked the wind out of him again, and started punching the back of his head.

Victor heard his teeth shatter. He couldn't even feel the punches. He tasted metallic blood from where his shattered teeth cut through his facial skin. His life force. This fucker wasn't going to get any more blood out of him. Victor started throwing elbows. His left one connected. He kept throwing them faster and harder.

The killer moved off of his back. Victor rasped breath into his lungs, and coughed out a gout of blood. Then he rolled on to his back so he could use his legs to kick, and his fists to punch. The first thing he saw was the killer's bare feet. The killer circled him. Victor tried to rise off the ground but failed. His body wasn't responding the way it should. He went for his gun. Before he could unholster the weapon, the killer's knees slammed into his chest. He heard the loudest noise he'd ever heard in his life. The sound reverberated through his skull. The sound of his ribs snapping.

Agony wracked Victor's body. Then his assailant grabbed the sides of his head with those gorilla strong fingers, and began smashing his skull against the concrete. Victor started throwing punches with all his might. His blows landed, but didn't stop the attack.

Victor changed the location of his punches from the killer's arms to his groin. This didn't have to be a fair fight, this was a fight for his life. Rules didn't apply. After four of his punches connected the killer groaned and caught Victor's fists.

Those powerful hands squeezed, and crushed the bones inside Victor's hands, rendering them useless. The killer placed his hands on Victor's face covering his eyes, nose and mouth. Although he wasn't a stranger to violence what happened next Victor hadn't even thought about.

Razor sharp teeth bit into the soft skin of his neck and ripped his flesh away. The mastication noises of the cannibalism incarnate registered in Victor's ears. This monster was eating him alive.

Victor tried to knee the attacker, but the monstrous man's body was out of reach. Each time Victor's slowing heart beat, his life blood spurted out of the wound in his throat. That is when the killer spoke.

"You could not be allowed to live."

Victor thought the voice sounded familiar, but a fog blanketed his mind.

"Victor Kingsley is an intelligent man. He knows too much. Victor Kingsley will not ruin our plans. The fascinating slut Zoey will not ruin our plans. The astute detective Jake Corde will not ruin our plans. Nothing will stop our plans."

Victor's tried to say fuck you, but his vocal cords were in shreds.

The monster grabbed Victor's head again, and began bashing his skull against the floor. Thud. Crack. Thud. Crack. Thud Crack. The bastard was cracking his skull apart like a gorilla cracking a coconut.

As though sensing the dying was all but over Victor's assailant removed his hands from around Victor's throat. In one last act of incredible violence he gouged out Victor's left eye. With his remaining right eye Victor watched as his left eye slid between fleshy, wet lips.

Dying, he recognized his killer.

Chapter 23

0530 Friday

Matt checked the dozen messages Luke left on his voice-mail. The last one was said in a voice that brooked no argument and contained just a touch of panic. "Goddammit Matt, you have two hours to call me or I'm coming home." Matt sighed. Luke was such a Mom sometimes. He dialed the number.

"Why haven't you called sooner? What's going on up there? How is Jake doing?" That was how Matt was greeted.

"Wow Luke. It's been all of what 48 hours? Bored with Las Vegas already? Just relax, why don't you?"

"I swear to God, Mathew, if you don't give me some serious answers I am going to come right through this phone on you!"

"Alright, alright! Geez Louise!" Matt huffed. "Jake's very worried. His visions are driving him crazy because they are only slightly connected to the murders. We are waiting for all of the forensics to come in. So far there have been three murders all equally nasty. Body parts for trophies, plus cannibalism."

"No shit?"

"Uh, I would never joke about that bro."

"Of course not, go on."

"Not much more. There is strong indication that it's two perpetrators. One is the actual killer, the other is the collector."

"Holy crap. That's insane."

"Yeah, rare too since it's two killers."

"Like Lucas and Toole?"

"Yes, except we don't know the exact relationship."

"Okay. That's a lot to take in. You have to keep me better informed Matt. I fucking hate not being there."

"I know bro. But you have the most important job of all. Protect our next generation. We will be fine. You know Jake, no stone unturned and all that."

"You are the security genius though Matt. Make him listen.

Make him as safe as you can."

"Truthfully, Jake isn't the biggest problem. It's the Medical Examiner he has the hots for. One Miss Zoey Abero. I call her Hottie McHottie. She is his Achilles heel."

"Jake doesn't have an Achilles heel."

"He does now, bro. Dude's all tied up in knots and doesn't even know it yet. But I plan on being around when it hits him because that is going to be epic!"

Luke laughed. They all liked catching Jake in awkward Moments. He leaned back on the patio chair, relaxing a little. The murders had escalated so fast. Two killers?

He heaved a great sigh. His brothers were going to be the death of him. Not a damn one of them could stay out of trouble for more than a hot minute. Just then Peggy walked over and handed him a big fat Bahama Momma.

He smiled at his wife. She wasn't showing yet and that bikini showed off her curves in the most distracting manner. Matt was right. They were big boys. He had to concentrate on the things he could control. Like his wife's health and happiness and skimpy bikini.

The swim suit was white, and accented his wife's features in the most pleasing way. He found himself picturing Peggy when they got married, in her wedding dress. Beautiful. His wife. He wondered what their child would look like? He hoped it would be a girl and look like a mini-Peggy. Those tight black curls and mischievous brown eyes would be adorable on a toddler. The smooth mocha skin, soft to the touch. A beautiful child.

Matt's "hello" got him back in the conversation. "And how is that cute little waitress?"

"Still cute." Matt laughed. "Look, I have to go. I'll call as soon as I know more, I promise."

"Be safe little brother."

"Of course."

Matt smiled at his phone and shook his head. His brothers were going to be the death of him. He looked up as Jake put down his dumbbells. They were ten pounders, and he started lifting them up, and then slowly stretching out his arms. "This exercise

works the triceps, biceps, and pecs all at once. You should try it."
Case in point.

"Food?"

Jake rolled his eyes. "You are going to regret what you are
doing to your body some day. "Give me a half hour."

Matt gave a snort. "That's better than someday regretting
what I didn't do to it. We are all going to grow old Jake. I fully
intend to enjoy the growing."

"You and Zoey should hook up."

Matt couldn't help himself. "Love to. Give me her number."

"Fool." Jake shook his head, and disappeared into the bathroom.

"Thought so. But you could invite her to join us for breakfast. I can flirt outrageously with her and you can gauge her reaction. Maybe that would help you decide to make a move on her."
Matt shouted over the sound of the shower.

0545 Friday

In her Renault Zoey listened to music as she drove a little
southwest. The world outside remained pitch black, but the dawn
would return color to the land. She consulted Google Maps, and
started the G.P.S. Another hour passed, and at last she reached
her destination. Illinois and Michigan Canal State Trail. She
parked, and sat.

Out of the city. Here, she should be able to run more safely
than in the city. She came here to run, and now she didn't feel
like running. It was her day off. The department actually forced
her to take days off. She hated days off, she didn't know what to
do with herself when she wasn't working. Run! Exercise, keep the
body in shape. For what?

Who fucking cared what she looked like? She could be
seven hundred pounds and still be damn good at her job. Her job
didn't require that she looked good. You will feel better once you
get out of the car and start running, she told herself.

She hooked up her phone with her ear buds, and put them
in. She tucked her phone in the built-in pocket of her jacket. She

changed into her running shoes.

Exhaling a breath she hadn't realized she'd been holding, she opened her car door and got out. The cold air hit her like a blast of water, and the wind slammed into her as an unwelcome whip. She locked her car door with her key-fob.

Zoey hit the trail. As the sun rose, the light filtered into the world. The trees along the river materialized from shadowy wights into living beings of green. Some of the trees had started turning colors. Here some yellow leaves, there some brilliant red ones, further up the trail a blazing fire of orange.

It was her day and she was determined to make it a good one. She had no agenda but her own. If the department was going to force her to take a day off, then the day was hers. Selfish? The only one she needed to please was herself.

After a few fast songs, and a good pace, she slowed to a walk. Her legs were beginning to feel the burn. Sweat trickled down her neck. Zoey dug out her phone, and changed the playlist. Then she increased her speed to a run again.

Her mind wandered to her dad. What was he even doing these days? Maybe she should call him later. Was he still drinking wine? Wine. Wine sounded good. Maybe this afternoon. Maybe they could even share a glass over the phone. Maybe he would call her 'his little constellation.'

From her dad her thoughts jumped to Jake Corde. Men. Was that the common thread today? Well, thinking about men was better than thinking about death. Jake Corde, that arrogant P.I. was no closer to solving this case than she. And he was an idiot, not literally, but he was male. Albeit an extremely handsome one. His hazel eyes, and strong hands with trimmed fingernails.

She forced her mind away from Corde, and instead looked at the trees and river. She increased her speed even more by pushing herself. Push. Push. Push. That is what she did. Her heart pounded, she felt her blood coursing through her body. Her feet pounded the trail.

Her phone blipped in her ear, interrupting her music. She ignored it and kept moving. A few seconds later the phone rang again. She ignored it. What time was it anyway? She didn't care.

The phone rang a third time. WTF?

Zoey stopped running, unzipped her jacket and fished her phone out of its pocket. She looked at the caller I.D. Jake Corde. Speak of the devil. He could wait. She put the phone back, and resumed her run, but at a more maintainable pace.

Sometime later, sweat running down her spine, soaking her shirt and the waistband of her pants, Zoey returned to her car. She carefully removed her earbuds and phone. She took off her running jacket, stuffed it into her running bag. She drank a bottle of water. Her legs were trembling, a sign of a good run. She stretched, and changed shoes.

Climbing in behind her steering wheel, she plugged her phone into her car speakers. She wasn't cold, but when the sweat started drying she might get chilled, so she turned on the heater. She loved this part of the run the most. The slowing down. Should she call Jake back?

Just then her phone rang. The office. Decision made. "What's up Kellesha?"

Chapter 24

0500

Jake's phone rang just as he and Matt were throwing their canvas go bags into the trunk of the car. He tugged it out of his back pocket and checked the I.D. Chicago Police Department.

"'Lo?"

"Is this Jake Corde?"

"It is."

"Ian McCarthy here. Listen, there's been another murder."

"Address?"

"Mr. Corde, you should know, I'm the lead investigator now."

"You? Why? Where's Victor?" Something clicked in his mind and Jake stopped for a half-breath. "No."

"I'm afraid so." McCarthy gave the address and the two men broke contact.

"Skipping breakfast bro. Victor's been murdered." Jake's voice was grim as he slid behind the wheel. "This whole thing is a fucking mess."

0630

Zoey stood just inside the caution tape staring at the stream of blood that flowed out from under a car toward the drain. Why hadn't anyone stopped it yet? They shouldn't let it get in the drain.

As if walking through quicksand she stepped over to the drain. "I need this stopped, Kellesha."

The assistant turned from where she stood at the back end of a car three spots up. One look at Zoey's face convinced her to not argue. It didn't matter that the blood had stopped running hours ago. Boss wanted containment. Done deal.

"Zoey." A gentle male voice, devoid of its usual arrogance brought her attention around. Safe, strong Jake. "You want to do this together?" He asked her.

She nodded, letting him take her elbow. Side by side they walked toward the crumpled body that came into view feet first, then legs, torso. Zoey took a breath, another, steadied her mind. A professional would not make a noise.

"Fuck." Jake swore beside her.

Zoey opened her bag, put on a pair of gloves and went to work. From feet to head she caught every detail. Body temperature, head wound, bite in the neck, bruising on face and throat. Crushed windpipe, broken ribs, half eaten organs.

"He put up a fight. Bag his hands please, there's blood under his nails." She said to Kellesha. The tech would know what to do with that information.

"Why didn't he draw his gun? Why didn't the killer take the gun?" Jake looked around. "Who dusts for prints?" He pointed to the top of the Tahoe.

McCarthy glared at the very clearly defined footprint. "All the footprints we've collected were worthless and look at that. Beautiful. Somebody get over here and dust this!"

"That explains how he didn't see his attacker until it was too late." Zoey shook her head sadly. "Jumped from above."

0640

"I suppose." Jake frowned in thought. "This is all insane. Whoa there!" He grabbed the ME as she started to crumple. This time he pulled her close to him, one arm under her breasts, the other across her back.

Her eyelids half-closed; her breath rasped in her throat. The pulse at her throat fluttered. Jake could feel her heartbeat against his arm where he held her steady. He could see the beads of sweat break out on her forehead. She shook slightly.

"There was 'purpose' this time." She said softly. "He had to kill Victor. The first bite he took was before death. It was like a drug, to start eating while his victim was alive. So much darkness. No joy in the killing itself. Oh God. The look on Victor's face! He knew he was going to die. He..." her eyes popped open and looked at Jake straight on. "He knew his killer." She whispered, horrified.

Jake took a second to absorb her words. Victor knew his killer? He knew the killer! Was that why he didn't pull his gun? Caught off guard?

Jake realized his nightmares were coming true. He had known this was going to happen. Somehow the killer had found out how close Victor was to solving the case. It was only a matter of time before they decided to take out himself and probably Zoey as well.

Zoey pulled out of his arms. Ignoring everyones concerned looks, she started handing out orders like candy on Halloween. Her ability to adjust, adapt, was inspiring. Kellesha and the others jumped into action.

Jake walked around taking note of the well lit garage. The mirrors up in the corners to give a view of all the hidden areas. The security cameras on every fourth beam joist. It wasn't a high end building but it was well cared for, clean, and seemingly secure. It was the kind of place that engendered a sense of safety.

Ian McCarthy sidled up to him. "I've got Jackson and Sanchez gathering up the digitals from those cameras. If they can't burn a CD on the spot we'll take the whole damn brain. How did he not see or hear his attacker?"

"Barefoot is easy to miss, soundwise but I feel like he DID hear him. I just can't figure out why he didn't pull his gun?"
Ian shrugged. "We'll probably never know." He sighed. 'Damned shame. He was a top notch Detective."

"Yeah. He was. And I think that's what got him killed. I guess I don't have to tell you to watch your back."

The two men made their way back to the scene where Jake again eyed the car. "That is his vehicle. This is his apartment. Was he coming or going?" Jake asked McCarthy.

"I don't know yet. We will put it all together at the precinct. Are you coming?"

"Yes. Right after I see this finished." Jake waved a hand at the body being placed in a bag with Zoey's sharp eyed supervision.

"Ok. I'll see you at the station."

Jake nodded, taking up silent guard duty, nodding to Matt. Out of the corner of his eye he caught Willy moving in and out of the crowd. Jake felt some of the tension leave his shoulders.

Willy Rosen. Five feet eight inches of steel and nerves wrapped in mahogany skin. The man was one of the best in the nation, maybe the world, and he worked for Corde Investigations. An expert at gathering intel and being unseen he made the best bodyguard for people who don't want to be guarded. If Jake was seeing him, it was because Willy wanted it that way.

While he was guarding Zoey, the man would look, listen, and learn. Then he would email Jake an over-the-top detailed report. Just like the ones he got from Erik and Burke.

Jake couldn't help the small swell of pride at the people he and his brothers had working for them. They were loyal, hard-working, and dedicated to maintaining the excellence the Corde brothers demanded. To be the best, one had to have the best employees and they did.

He put his eyes back on Zoey who was walking toward the entrance, the body bagged and in transport. Where was she going? Ah yes, her car.

Jake and Matt watched Willy zip past on his CRF250F he lovingly called Asuga, right behind the Medical Examiner, before getting into their own ride and heading to the police station. There was some security video that needed watching and quite a few questions to be answered.

0648

Zoey pulled onto the street right behind the forensic van, intent on following right to the ME building door. Heart heavy, she was more determined than ever. Victor had deserved better than this. From her very first day as a medical examiner he had been professional and kind, if a little distant. She would never hear him say 'Abero' again.

She rubbed at her temple and eyebrows. Headache. Not now. She didn't have time for such silly weaknesses right now. No time.

She was going to do everything in her power to find his killer, and the one who had ordered it done. She had no doubts about a second participant now. Not actively on the scene, but orchestrating it nevertheless. They would both go down!

0653

From out of the crowd of police and gawkers a set of eyes watched the departing brothers. He hadn't wanted to start his new pet up yet. James had been doing so well. But he feared the gig was up now.

Poor Katie.

Chapter 25

1500 Friday

Hours of video and discussion later Jake left the precinct feeling sick in his gut. The camera's lenses were so dirty the best image they got was a vague outline of shadowy figures. Like looking through a thin black piece of cloth.

At one point Victor had tried to reach his gun but the fight was swift and brutal. Still, they now knew two things for sure. Victor had been arriving home, and he had heard or felt something because on the way to the apartment entrance he had stopped, turned, hesitated, then moved back toward his vehicle.

Jake had filled McCarthy and the others in on the theory he and Victor and Zoey had been kicking around, cautioning the men to keep this between them because he truly felt Victor had somehow gotten too close to the truth and that was why he lay dead on Zoey's stainless steel autopsy table.

They all agreed to pay close attention to anyone asking too many questions about the case. No-one wanted to believe a cop was responsible but they all felt confident Victor would not have discussed the case with anyone not connected to the force. That would have been unethical. Victor had epitomized being ethical.

Matt had left a few hours earlier so he could grab some sleep then relieve Willy on Zoey watch as Matt had started calling it. Jake didn't like it one bit but Matt won the fight by simply walking away. It was a page taken right out of Jake's own play book and he resented the man's audacity even while he admired him. He had great brothers, wouldn't have them any other way really. Most of the time.

A quick call had a loaner from impound pulling up to the walk where he stood. A scruffy, scrawny young fellow stepped out of the beat up white Honda Civic. He grinned at Jake's sour look.

"Hey Jake."

"Tony." Jake caught the keys tossed at him. "Really? Keys imply a motor is involved. I'm impressed. My first thought was that I was going to be Flinstoning it. Where did you find this thing, in The Stone Age?"

"Ha!" Tony gave a bark of laughter. "You funny man Jake Corde. You crack me up! Tony said `you'd bitch and I should tell you to shut your pie hole and come see your family once in a while Mr. Big Shot."

Jake grunted. "Family my ass. He's my sister-in-laws second cousin. That's so far from related we could have a beautiful wedding and two point five ugly babies and no one would bat an eye. If he was my type, that is, or if I lived in say Missouri, where they go noodling for catfish."

"Yeah, yeah. I'll tell him you said so. A beautiful ass pounding reception with beer for all. Are you giving me a ride back?"

"Sure this rust bucket will hold us both safely?"

"You've got no adventure in your soul Jake. None of you Corde boys do." He shook his head as though saddened.

An hour later Jake was sitting in the Corde Investigations parking lot staring at the building. He had to admit that the time for safety for himself was past. There was some serious work to do and it looked like he was going to need a steady location to do it in. The best place he could think of was the office. This was the family office, his brothers always surrounded him, and he felt pride in what they had built.

Moving from hotel to hotel would have been ideal because it gave him the advantage of unpredictability. Matt returning had started the decline of that advantage. The need to protect Ryan and Zoey finished it. He wanted to get a suspect board of his own going, a place to work undisturbed.

Here is where he did his best thinking, and right now that is what he needed to do. There had to be clues to find. Where had he missed something? He needed to nip this thing in the bud with the super-human efficiency that Matt worked the computer, and Luke ran the paperwork. Smoother than Alex made contacts. Even quicker than Mom reading her damn cards.

He would have to call Mom. Get her to work her magic and get the company's finances running again. Jake didn't know his mother's people, and didn't want to. All he knew was they kept the company safe from hacking and theft.

Mrs. Corde ruled that area of the business with an iron fist and a closed mouth. Corde respected that. Mom trusted them, he trusted Mom. Nuff said. Now, he needed the funds to pay the guys doing guard duty and call in some more to relieve Willy, Burke and Erik.

Matt couldn't be in the rotation, he had to coordinate, it's what he did best. Jake would leave that in Matt's hands with gladness. Who to call in? He wasn't even sure where everyone was at!

2200 Florence, Italy

The Tuscany region of Italy. Little Ilaria couldn't live in a more beautiful place for her Alex to settle down in. The countryside, Renaissance art and architecture. The Duomo with its terracotta-tiled dome engineered by Brunelleschi. The Uffizi Gallery with "The Birth of Venus."

Speaking of Venus, Jane Corde shuffled her deck. It was time. It wasn't midnight per se, not the witching hour, but the rest of the house was asleep, or at least in the bedroom for the night. She finally had some alone time. Not that she would have cared if little Ilaria saw her cards, this was Italy, but Jane relished being solitary sometimes. When one communed with The Stars it was preferable to be on one's own. She gave readings for others sometimes with the person present, but when she wished to concentrate on helping her boys, she liked to be solo.

She liked to be alone every so often, just to decompress from people. No distractions. It wasn't that she didn't like people, she did like people, but she also liked a little piece of quiet. Time to think. She could be social and she was a Leo, which meant she was The Best. But she needed to be The Best to help her boys, they were her world afterall, and she would never not be their mother. She was The Best, Yup definitely a Leo.

Jane shuffled her deck, and mentally asked the stars her

question. Then she shut her eyes and drew and placed the seven cards making up the Planetary Spread. She relaxed her breathing, cleared her head of the numerous extraneous thoughts flying around in it, and opened her eyes. She looked at the cards on the table before her.

"No it can't be? But, it is!"

The spread was identical to the reading she'd done a few days ago. The Stars were steadfast in this belief. Who was she to question them? What The Stars declared, they declared! She studied the spread again. Had she missed anything on her last interpretation?

She had asked specifically about her son Jake, but she wasn't surprised at all to see that the first card in the spread, in the moon position, the connection to family and home was Knight of Swords. To ask about Jake, it was impossible not to also ask about Luke. They were twins, and didn't she know it? Her Twins. The volatile changing element of air. The turbulent quarrelsome

Dioscuri warrior twins, that was her boys alright; down to a T. The Dioscuri, never separated from each other, always off on new adventures, breaking up the humdrum of lives. Callous, but brilliant, not allowing themselves to grow old, even though her boys had grown up into delightful men.

There they were on their agitated horse, the horse that barely touched the ground. The horse bearing her boys onward always on a new adventure, thus their company, their work. She would not call it her company, she was getting older, but she did run the finances. Someone needed to run the finances, and there was no one more qualified than herself.

Jane looked at the next card and laughed out loud.

There he was Jake, separate from Luke. The Fool. No surprise at all that he came up in the Mercury position of the spread. Her son, The Fool. Mr. Serious. Mr. Workaholic. Mr. Have No Fun. Callous, all business, her son. He was good at what he did, very very good, and yet her mother's intuition knew that he missed out on some other aspects of life. That is what she asked the Stars about.

The Fool card, leaping into the unknown. That fit Jake, off on a case, placing himself in danger to catch killers, to uncover criminal activities, the one on the street, bringing evil to justice. Then there was his mind, his intuitive sixth sense that aided him like an animal instinct. When Jane had been younger she had the visions too, now she utilized the cards and let the Stars aid and clarify her visions.

The Venus position, romantic relationships, the Judgement card resided. Here she was at last. Here, the new development, she would reveal herself to The Fool. She would magically blend into Jake's life forming a 'larger personality'.

What was that young lady's name again? She couldn't re-member, you're getting older Jane, she told herself. What had her darling Mathew called her? 'Hottie McTotty.' Jane knew that she had to be a sexy number, no one else could touch Jake on that kind of level. Come on already Hottie McTotty, sweep my son off his feet, and bring joy into his life. She would. Jake was in for it, and good for him.

Jake had a hard road ahead of him, because in the Sun position of the spread lay the Seven of Swords card. Jake wasn't good at guile, and he wasn't very tactful. He was going to have to use his wits, rather than strong arming if he was to solve his current case.

It also didn't surprise Jane that in the Mars area of her spread the Eight of Wands appeared. Conflict, Challenge, self-doubt. Catching a serial killer(s) wasn't an easy job. A period of action that fits Jake as well. Next came the Jupiter position and in her reading there sat The Magician.

"It all fits!" The cards were never wrong, it was written in the stars. Good and evil, male and female, dark and light. Love would be possible for Jake, he would see it at last. That brought Jane to the last card in her spread. On the table before her, in the Saturn position, the position requiring constraint or control sat The World.

The World.

The ancient spiralling journey all human beings were on. Achievement and healing and then fresh challenges. Ah yes, The Fool's journey. Her Jake, her boy, now grown into the man he was. And Jane knew that because she was thinking about Jake, that she would be hearing from him soon.

1603 Chicago

He sighed. Mom. He was procrastinating. His favorite person in the universe. He did not want to talk to her right now. Her and her damn cards.

Steeling himself he called their agreed on number, let it ring two times, hung up. Then he waited for a count of twenty and called it again. His hand tightened on the cell phone in anticipation of the third degree.

"Hello Jacob, I hope you have some answers for me." A strong, vibrant voice came through.

Jake smiled. "Mom."

"Jake."

"I need the company turned back on."

Silence.

"I've a few people who need protecting."

Silence. Oh no. When Mom was in this mood she could make an oyster give up its pearl.

"I'm fine Mom. Not working too hard. Matt's fine. I haven't stabbed him in his sleep or beat his pretty face to a pulp."

Silence. Still. Dammit.

"Four murders. Three females and the cop who got too close to the truth. But we are getting somewhere, I promise." Why was she still not saying anything? What did she want from him? This was how she ruled. She never yelled or cried or any of the other ways Moms controlled their kids. No. His Mom let her silence do the talking. She should have been Hitler's right hand for fucksake.

It worked every goddamn time! Jake took a deep breath and shook his head. He wasn't going to crack this time. He was a full grown man.

"No Mom, you can't come home." He stalled.

Nothing.

"Oh for crying out loud. No mother, now is not the time for me to worry about romance!!" Dammit! How did she do that?!!

"So there is a girl!" His mother laughed.

Jake groaned. "Mom, Matt has a big mouth."

"It wasn't your brother, son. It was the cards."

"He shouldn't have...what? The cards?"

"Yes. When you sent Mathew over to the house to get me out of the way I did a reading. There was love all over them. Is she pretty?"

"No Mom, she's disgusting." Jake knew he sounded petulant but he couldn't help it.

"Jake." She said softly. Stinging reprimand.

Jake sighed, capitulating just like he always did. "She's got beauty and moxie, Mom."

"Oh good. Can't have a partner you can push around love. When will I meet her?"

"Hasn't gotten that far yet Ma. We've been busy with a serial slash cop killer."

"Hm. On another note, you should meet Alexander's new flame! Whoo! She's a lovely girl. And guess what? She wants lots of babies!"

"Really? Last I checked Alex was, and I quote: 'Never going to bring a human being into this cesspool we call a world!'"

"I think the love bug makes all things possible Jake."

"Ugh. That's terrifying. I rely on Alex's convictions to help guide me through your silent recriminations"

"When can I come home, son?" She ignored his acerbic tone.

"I'm working on it Mom. Very hard."

"I know you are. I'll have things up and running in twenty minutes."

"Thanks Ma."

"You're welcome. Take care."

"See you soon."

That taken care of, he pressed his key fob and watched as the building came to life. It was a mood booster, to be sure. Like coming home from a prison sentence.

He locked everything up tight, sent the shutters back in place and texted Matt and the other men the news, then made his way to the back room where bunks and lockers stood in neat rows against opposite walls. Employees spent time here, waiting to be briefed or debriefed.

Sometimes they stayed a night here because home was a lonely place or they were getting over jet lag or too much wind-down time at the bar and couldn't drive. No matter the reason, there was never judgement and always an open door or helping hand. It was company policy; treat your people like you're happy they're here.

Chapter 26

1100 Saturday

Zoey read the results. She reread the report. She shut her eyes, and then reopened them. For a third time she read the findings. A partial fingerprint with enough points to make a match. Further the hair follicle from the tattered shirt, made a positive I.D.

Why was she doubting the scientific evidence? Facts were facts. She walked to Kell's desk.

"What's up Boss?"

"Read this," Zoey handed her the results of the first murder.

"Finger print: James Palmer. Hair follicle: James Palmer. Seems cut and dry. He is the killer." Kellesha raised a questioning eyebrow at Zoey.

"I know, one can't dispute the archeological record. The disappointing, unfortunate other fact is that he is a police officer."

Zoey returned to her own desk, and looked at her phone. She couldn't call Victor and tell him. What was this new guy's name again? She scrolled. Well, what the hell? She dialed.

Jake answered with his normal greeting. He must have been in work mode. His voice sounded business, and intense. She thought about his eyes. His hands on her hips. His supportive arm that touched her breast which despite the situation warranting the action, had been electrifying.

"Abero," she said, still thinking about Victor always using her last name. Now that was past tense. Post Mortem. Damn it Victor. For two years you've been that gruff bastard I loved.

"Got results on the first murder. Should we meet?"

"You can't tell me over the phone?" He asked.

"I don't think that would be prudent," Zoey responded as professionally as she could.

"I could go for a gyro."

After he said that Zoey couldn't help herself. "Is that healthy enough for you Detective? Lamb. Onions, peppers, loaded with extra Tzatziki sauce."

"I didn't say I was going to get two desserts with it, Doctor."

"You know that one place?" Zoey asked.

"I know it. I live in Chicago don't I?"

"How long will it take you to get there?"

"Seven days, six hours, five minutes, and four seconds," Corde answered. Zoey could hear from his voice inflection that he was joking. She pictured his smile.

"Funny. See you soon." Zoey hung up.

Putting on her gray coat, she stopped by Kell's desk a second time. The intern looked up, surprised to see her again. Zoey was struck by the Jamaican women's sun kissed bronzed skin. Kell's braids swung around her face, like a beaded curtain opening, and her eyes glinted like rare opulent black pearls.

"Taking an early lunch. Absolute discretion. Zero disclosure to anyone. I don't care if the President walks through that door. Understood?"

Kell saluted.

1110

Jake Corde had his car keys in hand. So much for this being a 'lunch date' work was work. He would bring Matt along. He was a great second set of eyes. He speed dialed his brother.

"Bro?" Matt answered.

"Follow Zoey to the restaurant. Go ahead and introduce yourself and make small talk until I arrive. She has news she doesn't want to divulge over the phone."

"On it," Matt reassured him.

Jake locked down the office building, got in his car and started it. He wasn't that far off on his estimation of time. Traffic this time of day was worse than hellish and it would take him forever to get through it. It wouldn't take him seven days, but it might take an hour.

1130

Zoey was so focused on her course of action that she didn't notice the two sets of eyes following her to the car. Watching her get into her vehicle and buckle up. One friendly and watchful, the other hungry and impatient.

Matt took note of the man in the sweet ride two rows up and four vehicles down. It took guts to drive a Jag in Chicago. Red, and the sun gleamed off the silver jungle cat hood ornament. How much was that dude compensating for? The guy must have his insurance on speed dial. He preferred his Hummer, but sports cars were pretty awesome too.

Matt started his car up and followed Zoey out onto the road. It was a pure habit that had him falling back a few cars so she wouldn't see him. He would introduce himself at the restaurant where she felt safer, hopefully.

He once again noticed the Jaguar as it slid into traffic behind him and made a sharp left onto another street. On a normal day, in a normal life, Matt would have discounted it as coincidence. But today, in this life, his gut told him to pay heed, so he filed the vehicle and it's owner away for future reference.

It was, in fact, one of the things that made Matt so successful at security. He trusted his instincts. He took nothing at face value. Nothing was ever as simple as it seemed.

The Greek place wasn't far from the ME office so Zoey got there in good time. She no more than sat down at a table than a young man slipped into the chair across from her and grinned. She frowned. He looked so familiar that she could only stare, trying to figure it out.

He stuck a big hand out, his night sky eyes shining with the same beautiful smile that curved his full lips. "Hi, I'm Mathew Corde. Most folks call me Matt."

Zoey nodded in recognition and took his hand. "I remember now. I've seen you with Jake."

"Yeah. He called, told me to meet you two here. Guess I was closer. He's 'an old' slowpoke."

Zoey smiled. The younger man was a full on charmer.

Curly dark hair, dark blue, twinkling eyes, double dimples, cleft chin, perfect white teeth and a deep, melodious voice. He was drop dead gorgeous and very sure of himself.

Apparently the waitress thought so too because she brought water over and sat it in front of him along with a menu, her eyes promising all sorts of inviting things. Matt smiled kindly, pushed the items over to Zoey and asked for two more of each, then gave Zoey his full attention. The waitress blinked, turned, and walked away.

"So. Jake." Matt leaned on his forearms and grinned at the woman across from him. Her scar in no way took from her natural loveliness. Her eyes and mouth were instant turn ons, if she weren't Jake's girl. That detracted from her beauty. For sure.

"What about him?" Uh oh, Zoey cringed inwardly. She recognized the glint of matchmaking.

"He's rich." Matt nodded knowingly.

"Didn't ask, don't care." Zoey took a sip of water and picked up the menu, hiding behind it.

"He's an awesome brother. Helped Mom raise the rest of us."

"I bet that was nice for you guys."

"He's a great son."

"So he's a Momma's boy?"

"We all are. She's a great Mom."

"Cool."

"He likes you."

"Aww. That's sweet." She was feeling a little aggravated. He sounded like they were in high school.

"How do you like your ice cream?" He asked out of the blue.

"Uh, frozen?"

Matt laughed. "So does he! What a coincidence!"

Zoey couldn't help it. His laughter was so full of life and joy she had to join in, irritation forgotten. She swatted at him with her menu.

Chapter 27

That's what Jake walked up to. He was surprised to feel a twinge of agitation at his brother. It wasn't jealousy. It wasn't. What did he care that Mathew had managed to put her at ease in moments while she was still slightly stiff and snappy with himself? Why should he mind if he had yet to make her laugh so freely and happily?

He didn't and shouldn't. He pulled out a chair and plunked into it, noticing the immediate silence. He winced inwardly. He was a stick in the mud. A wet blanket. An old fuddy duddy.

Matt watched the play of emotions cross his brother's face as Jake gazed over at Zoey. He grinned. Lord that man had it bad. And Zoey? She was blushing!

He sat back and smirked. Too bad Mom couldn't see this. She would be on cloud nine. It was on her bucket list to see all of her boys in love and married and it sounded like it was all over but the bells.

"Zoey likes her ice cream frozen." Matt ducked as Zoey's spoon came sailing at him. His laughter rang out, turning more than one head.

"What?" Jake frowned. "What are you talking about?" He gaped at Zoey. Did she just throw her spoon?

"Nothing." Zoey giggled, completely unabashed. "He's just being an ass. I hope your other brothers aren't like this. Your poor mother."

Jake glared at his brother and Zoey until they ceased their antics.

"So. A cop." Jake cleared his throat and finally spoke. "That really sucks."

"Yeah." Zoey agreed. "But ninety nine percent marker matches."

They stopped talking long enough for the waitress to take their order then Jake took it up again as soon as the red head could pull herself away from flirting with Matt and walk away. He glowered at his baby brother. Matt smirked and shrugged.

"We have to tell McCarthy of course. My question is do we call him or go to the station?"

"Call. We could see him at my office after lunch if he wants to meet." Zoey offered.

"He's going to want to go arrest the guy." Matt inserted.

"Isn't that the point? What am I missing?" Zoey asked, looking confused.

"Technically, yes, that is the point. But didn't you two have a working theory? What about the skeleton man?"

Jake nodded. "You thinking, stake out the cop? See if he gets a visitor or goes visiting?"

"Hell yeah. I mean, he has to be talking to his partner. Do you think it's only by phone?"

"Could be." Zoey inserted.

"No way. There's person to person contact. Has to be."

"Are you suggesting we don't tell McCarthy for now? What if there's another murder?"

"No. We can't keep it from the investigators. That would put your career in jeopardy." Jake assured her.

Zoey waited for their food to be placed then said, "Well, yes, there's that too. But I'm more concerned with the complete lack of consideration over a new murder victim."

"We wouldn't let it go that far." Matt sighed. "But Jake's right. We can't jeopardize your job. So we tell the detective and see what he says."

The three ate in silence for a bit then Jake glanced over at Matt. "Ma get hold of you?"

"Mhm."

"And?"

"I have Reese, Logan, Lyle and Doobie coming in today." He glanced at his watch. "In a couple of hours actually."

"Doobie? You sure?"

Matt shrugged. "She's damn good and she wants to work."

"Her husband..."

"They're divorced. She couldn't handle the other women."

"Oh, but the fights, controlling, stalking, booze, drugs and gambeling were all fine?"

Matt shook his head. "Of course not. I think it was more a 'last straw that broke the camel's back' kind of thing."

Zoey swung her head from man to man, fascinated. Office gossip. Cool.

"As long as he doesn't appear on one of her posts like the last time."

"Already told her."

"Okay. So, you go back to our place, get those guys briefed. I'll go to Zoey's office." Jake stood, threw some cash on the table and walked away.

Matt moved to follow suit then realized Zoey wasn't budging. The Jake dozer had struck again. He grinned at her stunned look.

"The insensitive bastard just does what he wants. Comes in like a tornado and leaves devastation in his wake."

"I really wanted some dessert." She laughed weakly. "This place makes the best ever Galaktoboureko."

"Sweet Jenny, can you say that ten times real fast?" He chortled. "So order it to go. He'll wait."

"She jerked a thumb at the departing Jake. "He acts like enjoying your food is a mortal sin."

"You're going to have to work out some of these compromises for yourself, you know. I'm not going to be around forever."

That brought her head around, her gaze to his. "What's that supposed to mean?"

But he only smiled and walked away, his physique a replica of the man in front of him.

Chapter 28

1400 Saturday

Beyond irritated didn't begin to touch Jake's mindset. He felt like throttling Matt. Well fuck it, if that little shithead won Zoey over fine. He could have her, that would piss Mom off to no end. If she was wrong. Jake almost wanted to tell Matt to go for it, almost.

He dialed his phone.

"McCarthy," the man answered.

"Sir, Jake Corde here, can you meet with Zoey Abero and I at her office?"

"How soon?"

"As soon as you can get there, we are a good half hour out, pending traffic."

"Give me an hour. I have a short meeting, and then I'll be there."

"See you at the M.E. office," Jake said and hung up. Before he could start his vehicle his phone rang.

"Jake here," Jake identified, recognizing his brother's voice

.

"How is the investigation going?" Alex inquired.

"We are making progress," Jake admitted.

"Good to hear. I got the results of that partial you gave me."

"Great. What's the name?"

"A Mrs. Kathryn Palmer."

"Good job, Alex, I know that was a bugger."

"Anything for you big brother."

"How is Mom?" Jake asked.

"I think you should have been a lawyer, that sounds like a leading question if I've ever heard one," Alex laughed.

"You are supposed to be watching over her. Status report?"

"Don't be so damn serious all the time, Mr. Intensity."

"Alex!"

"Mom is fine. She is getting along famously with Ilaria."

"Good for you."

"Thanks brother."

Jake calmed down slightly. Alex could have that effect on him sometimes. He actually took a few calming breaths.

"You okay?" Alex asked.

"Yes, fine. I'll keep you posted. We will be moving forward quickly from this point," Jake relayed.

"Take care. Don't make any stupid mistakes. Is Matt watching your back?"

"Christ on a stick. Yes, he is very good at what he does. Maybe too good."

"He's a Corde brother."

"No shit Sherlock."

"What's got your panties in a bunch?"

"Alex, keep it up, bullets in the engine block of a corvette means it doesn't drive."

"Don't touch my corvette."

"I won't if you do your job and keep an eye on Mom."

"Don't worry about Mom. I got this. Good luck on the rest of the case."

"Right. Take care." Jake hung up, feeling guilty for being such a grouch with his brother.

Zoey tapped on his window. Dressed in her long grey coat, she looked elegant, professional, and amazing. He rolled down his window and gazed up at her.

"Doctor."

"Detective. It seems that I have identified our killer first," she smiled. Those red lips, startlingly unique eyes, and dark hair made his groin twinge.

"I just got a name for the sedan I saw. Kathryn Palmer. We got our information on the same day, Dr. Abero."

Zoey laughed. Jake unabashedly looked her over again.

"That is still not proof. I have proof."

"Why don't we say that together we found the killer?" Jake suggested.

"I don't know about that… I do know that your brother is a charmer."

"He's single, rich, and an awesome brother."

"He said the same thing about you."

"Oh, and before I forget, he likes his ice cream frozen too," Jake said.

"I haven't met anyone that doesn't like their ice cream frozen yet," a smile played on Zoey's lips.

"Let's go meet McCarthy."

"Let's."

He watched her walk to her car and get in behind the wheel. She had a strong stride, as though daring anyone to get in her way. He liked her personal power.

Chapter 29

His phone going off brought Ian McCarthy's thoughts out of the darkness of death that Victors' murder had him in. He had worked hard to get into homicide and had no intention of bungling it but he couldn't help wondering just how stacked the deck was against him. He had never wanted to gain lead at the cost of a fellow officer's life though.

While he was grateful the transition from Victor as lead detective to himself had been smooth, he wasn't kidding himself. Victor had been an A-list detective, leaving Ian with big shoes to fill and a whole lot of eyes on him while he did it. That made for some uncomfortable moments with Victor's admirers. He had given his struggling marriage a death blow when he came into the department.

As a first generation Irish-American he was proud of the good he was doing in this crazy city. His parents had sacrificed everything to come to the United States fifty years ago. Their gift to him was an American birth certificate and a host of good old fashioned Irish qualities that made him strong both physically and mentally.

"Sergeant McCarthy." He answered curtly.

"Jake Corde here, can you meet Zoey Abero and I at her office?"

Apparently Corde figured he was so well known that he didn't need to identify himself. The abruptness set Ian back a heartbeat. Really? He had gotten the impression that Corde was the type that didn't play well with others. Especially detectives who got their place by default so to speak.

"How soon?" He listened for a second. "Give me an hour..."

Ian had heard plenty about the Corde brothers and their company. They had reputations for being tough, smart, and well connected. It was hinted that not all of their connections were

above board exactly, but the Corde's couldn't be faulted. They got
the job done and nothing illegal had been proven so far.

He realized he was daydreaming. Procrastinating. He had
to meet with the Captain. He had nothing to give the man right
now and that wasn't going to go over very well.

In fact it did not go over well. But worse than that, the
penny pinching bureaucrat wanted to oust Jake Corde. Ian wished
Victor Kingsley had left the secret to his way around the Captain.

On his way out of the building, to his car, and all the way to
the ME's office he fumed over the yelling match he had gotten into
with the Captain. His dad had always said "Start how you mean to
finish," and "You gotta stand up for what you know is right." The
Captain had used words like insubordination and demotion.

Well, what would be, would be. He parked in the nearly
empty parking lot, took a deep breath and hoped like hell these
two had something he could use. The murders were gaining more
and more attention.

The department was buckling under the black eyes the killer was giving them and the Captain was going to shut Ian's career
down if something didn't break soon. If he thought divorce was
bad, what would he do if his life's work went down the tubes?
But the job needed doing. There was a pair of madmen out there
killing, cannibalising and taking body parts. It had to stop, even
if it meant handing the case over to the FBI and flushing his job.
The building was eerily quiet as he used his I.D card to gain entrance. He always got the willies here. Cold cement and gray
paint. Glass and stainless steel.

It was ridiculous to wish for a little bit of welcoming color.
Sunny yellow or something. He couldn't help feeling like the souls
of the dead were wandering these halls and rooms unable to find a
way out.

He finally found Abero and Corde at the end of a long, dim
hallway, through a door with the only real light shining through a
tiny window. He rapped a knuckle on the door and entered when
bid. The smell of fresh coffee welcomed him, along with their
smiles.

He felt the weight of the last two days lift a little. There was something right about this.

1700

Some day off that was Zoey thought, throwing her keys on the table. She hung up her coat. She went into her bedroom and bluetoothed her phone to her speakers. She turned the volume up. Chopin. Just what she needed. Shedding her work clothing, she pulled on her warm pajama pants and a sweater. Much better.

Back in her kitchen she opened her wine fridge. She pulled out a Rutherglen muscat. The Australian sweet red carried a reasonable price tag. She uncorked the bottle and smelled the bouquet. Dried strawberries and toffee. She pulled out a glass and filled it. Then she took a sip of her wine. Glorious.

Turning down her music, she dialed her dad's number.

"Zo. How's my little girl?"

"Frustrated."

"What's his name?"

"Dad. It's work."

"What about it?"

"You know it's confidential."

"Yes, you called me. How can I help?"

"Get a glass of wine, and have a drink with me," Zoey said.

"Twist the old man's arm. Okay. I've got one."

"What are you drinking?"

"I have been waiting for an occasion to try it. Your mother bought me this bottle. It's a Domaine Tempier Bandol Rose."

"Nice."

"Right, My Little Constellation. Now what's on your mind?"

"I just wanted to hear your voice."

"Connerie!"

Zoey burst out laughing. Her Dad had just called 'bullshit' on her in French.

"There might be a man?"

"I better sit down. Are you trying to give me a heart attack."

"Dad. I just don't know..."

"Has he made you laugh?"

"Yes, but he is sort of an ass too."

"Have you slept with him?"

"DAD!"

"Just a question. Although I don't want to admit it, you're not twelve anymore. Okay, you talk, I'll listen."

"His name is Jake Corde. He's a private investigator. Sort of a health nut."

"None of that sounds good."

"I know, that's why I'm frustrated."

"Do you have anything in common?"

"Yes, we both like our ice cream frozen."

"That's a start."

Chapter 30

0100 Sunday

The child in his heart was awake. The city lights of the buildings flashed by as he drove toward the airport. At a little after one A.M. he let himself in the house. In the living room he lit a pumpkin spice candle as a tribute to Katie. He thought it a decent gesture, although it was an atrocious smelling thing.

In his favorite room, he opened the fridge door. She had bought the V8 this week, lucky him. He poured a glass. Katie had made meatloaf for dinner. He helped himself to a large slice. She had made it extremely well. The right amount of barbeque sauce, no overpowering onion, and just the right amount of breadcrumbs to be held together, but not too tightly. He chewed slowly, savoring the flavors.

The last morsel gone, with his gloved hand, he selected one of Katie's chef knives. She had been a good cook. Oh well, there were other chef's out there.

He spent a little while looking at the photographs on the wall for the last time. He passed little Donald's room. Oh, little Donald. Little Donald. Little Donald, he sang in his head. He passed Amy's bedroom, and arrived at the master bedroom. He silently pushed open the door.

The man looked down at plump Katie. Her tits were flabby. Some of the things weak James told him about her, zipped through his mind. Time for the Sanctimonious Harpy to sing her last song. He thought about touching her sleeping body, but resisted. It wasn't easy, but his allotted clock was ticking.

Around and around I go, he thought. It reminded him of a merry-go-around. Now he was on Jame's side of the bed. James snored louder tonight than on previous occasions. Was he ill? Had he over indulged in his beers? Didn't matter. He glanced at the night stand. The green glowing digital clock read 1:47. He placed the kitchen knife on the nightstand. Turned the clock just so. Bending down he put his mouth next to Jame's ear.

"Time to come out and play, my friend...This is what you'll do..."

Jame's eyes opened but he didn't move. The man left the room as many times before. He closed the bedroom door, and moved to Amy's door. He carefully pushed it open.

The perfect little girl's room. He knew the walls were a light pink in color but in the soft glow of the nightlight they took on a rosy hue that pleased his senses. The room was as neat as a pin, the toys lined up on a ledge under the window.

He picked up her stuffed pony, and placed it in his bag. He put a change of her clothes in the bag along with her coloring pad, and markers. Then he zipped up the bag.

The man carried the sleeping four year old out of the house with him.

0232

Once Amy had been safely ensconced in the new bed he had lovingly purchased just for her, he went to watch the tapes. Oh this was going to be so fun. So fun!

He could barely contain his excitement. This would be most gratifying. Pure entertainment. He licked his thin lips, imagining the taste of buttery movie popcorn.

He watched as James sat up as if on cue picking up the knife and walking slowly down the hall to Donald's room. He slashed his son's throat, and crimson arterial blood splattered Donald's robin egg blue wall.

"Do it James. Eat your young!" The watcher screamed at his main monitor screen, spittle spraying onto the glass surface.

As ordered, James gutted his six year old, then bent over the body and began feasting. He ate his son's heart last and left the room dripping with blood. James headed back toward his own bedroom.

The man rewound the recording and watched it again. Then a third time. Third time's the charm. He was so proud of the job he had done. James was the perfect tool. He amended that thought, almost the perfect tool. Then he let the recording continue to play forward.

With blood staining his mouth James kissed Katie. Watching eyes narrowed in disgust as she moaned as if aroused, the hussy! The self righteous Susie Homemaker bitch. He grinned as James threw off the cover and ate out his wife's pussy. Literally. She started screaming, but not with pleasure. With pain and horror.

"That's right James. Eat that cunt!" The man screamed at the image. More spittle splattered his monitor.

"JAMES!"

Faster than anything he pounced on her chest, and with a deft slash of the chef knife cut out her tongue. It wasn't a precision cut, it was meant to do one thing, remove her tongue from the inside of her mouth.

"You will prattle no more." The watcher laughed maniacally.

James slashed a letter X on each of her breasts. He watched as her blood ran in rivulets over her body like rain down a windowpane. Using his bare hands James ripped open his wife's chest cavity and pulled out her liver. Taking a hefty bite. This was what he craved. He ate her liver.

"The liver of an onion." The man watching slapped his knee. "The liver of an onion. Oh that's rich. That's good." He tittered. He slapped his knees, but not with any kind of rhythm. He slapped his right knee a final time and rewound the video. Over and over, at least a dozen times he watched the horrific monster he had created do it's work.

Every time he yelled the same things at the images, and slapped his knees. Marvelous! Just marvelous.

"The liver of an onion. Oh that's rich. That's good." He chortled.

When Katie's body finished spasming in its final death throes, James moved off the bed. He went to the closet, and dressed in his uniform.

The cop walked into the garage, and got into Katie's black sedan. He didn't turn the car on. He drew his Glock-19 service pistol, and placed the barrel against his right temple. He closed his eyes, gritted his teeth, and pulled the trigger.

In the silence following the gunblast, there came a pounding. Pounding and scared screaming. He shut down the cameras, put the computer to 'sleep' and left the room. No sooner did he open the door from the basement than he heard his little prize screaming and pounding on her door in fear.

"Mommy! Mommy! Daddy!"

Oh no, no, no. Can't have my little princess upset. He went through his house to her room. He stood outside the door, but he didn't unlock it.

"Amy, my little princess," he called through the door.

"I want my Mommy," she cried out between sobs.

"Your parents went on vacation. Don't you remember them telling you that. I'm your uncle. If you calm down, I will come in, and then we will get some hot chocolate.

"I don't want hot chocolate. I want my Mommy," Amy demanded angrily.

"Amy, you must calm down," he said more sternly, like a parent would. "We will have no more of this intolerable behavior. I'm going to count to three. You are going to take a deep breath each time I count. Are you ready?"

"I guess so," Amy said.

"One. Two. Three. Now how about some hot chocolate?"

"With marshmallows?"

"Yes, with marshmallows."

Chapter 31

0600 Sunday

Jake, Matt, and Detective McCarthy stood outside the garage gazing in at the black sedan. License JFR 1439. Kathryn Palmer.

Palmer's body still occupied the driver's seat. His head half hanging out of the shattered window, brain matter, bone chips and hair running out of the gape, down the door along with the now drying blood. There were particles of the same mess swimming between the pieces of broken glass on the floor, finding the path of least resistance through the maze.

The three men had chosen to return to the garage after finding the horror inside too much even for seasoned warriors. His own kid for God Sake! It was the worst nightmare brought to stark reality.

McCarthy finally heaved a sigh. "I am officially calling it a murder suicide - missing child/presumed dead, until we find the little girl. That might get the heat off my back for a few days. You guys do what you need to prepare because I think you are right Jake. I doubt this is done." He headed into the house then turned back. "I have a four year old little girl to find. Can you believe this shit? I fucking hate it when kids are involved."

The other members of the task force followed behind him. Matt and Jake watched for a moment then moved off to a quiet corner. There was more Matt wanted to talk about.

"I've got two people watching the crowd and taking pictures. Doobie says there was someone else here last night. She says the footprints were heavier on exit than on entrance."

"The kidnapper carried the little girl." Not a question.

Matt nodded. "He got in a car three blocks over."

"Christ she's good. Tracked him on city streets for three blocks? That's incredible."

Matt grinned. "We need incredible, since your visions seem

to be all wankie."

"Is that a thing? Wankie?"

"It is now. I really don't like this unseen bad guy. He gives me the creeps."

"I know. Could be a woman you know."

Matt shook his head. "None of it feels like a woman."

Jake frowned then sighed. "Ok. What's going after this?" He wanted to know.

"Erik, Burke, Willie and I are going back to the office for some shut eye. Doobie and Logan are finishing up here then Logan is following the Doc to the M.E. Building and watching over her while Doobie is going to the Doc's place to make sure it is safe and stays that way. Lyle and Reese are on the two witnesses for a shift."

"Good." He gave his brother's shoulder a slap. "You are a good man Matt."

"No argument there. Now how about you go get some real rest? Maybe you are a little off because you are not getting enough yoga or something."

Jake grinned. "Yoga? You mean meditation or yogurt?"

"Sure." Matt laughed as he walked away.

Jake shook his head. His brother could be right. But there was no time for rest. This case was not closed and Jake felt like he had seriously failed Victor. He was not going to let this get any more out of hand than it already was. Now add to the murders that a little girl was missing. He needed to stop this fucking monster!

Meditation didn't sound bad though. He was tense all over. It had been days since he had worked out or had a run. Yogurt was out of the question though. No amount of health benefits or fruit could make him put sour milk in his mouth.

What he needed was a certain Zoey Abero massaging his shoulders, her hair tickling his neck as she whispered sexy things in his ear. He shook his head in amusement. Focus Jake, catch the bad guy.

Suddenly he felt the need to stretch. Silently laughing at himself, Jake decided Matt was right. He should try to get a few hours of shut eye. Besides, it would be a good time to catch up on what the other men had observed and what they thought. Maybe some of the film from murder two was developed. He wouldn't mind checking out the crowd.

He gave Matt's plans some thought and couldn't find fault. Of course he couldn't. When he and his brothers had founded Corde Investigations a mere five years ago, the first thing they had done was sit down and worked out employee criteria.

Hi IQ, willing to travel, heavy machinery, any vehicle, multi-talented, willing to work any hours, long times away from home, three or more languages, two forms of hand combat, munitions use, infiltration, ready and able to do whatever it took to do the job. Then there were side talents that made you valuable such as demolitions, communications, computer, pilot, survival, parkour, rock climbing/repelling, and yes, even any form of dance.

Clients were diverse and sometimes the jobs they were hired to do took them all over the world into all types of situations. The Corde brothers were very proud of the crew they had gathered around themselves. It was a beautiful thing.

Decision made, Jake reluctantly re-entered the house and sought out Zoey. She was in the boys room, her face more white than the mask she wore over her mouth and nose. She looked shaken to her core. Everyone in the room did.

Except Kellesha. Always a rock. Jake was impressed by the woman's stoicism and the kindness she maintained while her co-workers looked ready to cry and wretch at any moment.

"Hey Doc." He said quietly. "I'm going to head back to the office for a few hours. You need anything, at all you call me."

He wanted to pick her up and carry her out of this mess. He knew that would be a terrible mistake though. She took pride in her work and her independence. There would be no gratitude for his he-man protective male interference.

Looking up at him with shadowed eyes that had him nearly changing his mind, she nodded once, then went back to work. Three murders and the whole house and garage was a crime scene. Jake knew she was in for a horrendously, painfully, long day. He left her to it. Nothing he could do to help her. Not here anyway.

The guys had nothing interesting to report. No suspicious activity. No strange cars. Willie kept a log of every person Zoey had come into contact with over the time he had been watching over her. It would be useful once there was something to compare it to.

The only pictures they had were of Victor's crime scene. Matt was already working on identifying everyone in the sea of faces. It wasn't a quick process. Jake made a mental note to ask McCarthy if the second murder crime scene photos were available yet.

Breaking up the meeting Jake took a quick shower and fell onto a bunk bed, stretching out. Pulling the blanket over his head he promptly surrendered to the soft cushion of sleep.

Her skin felt like silk under his rough hands. Warm, pliant, she shifted against him and his breath caught somewhere in his chest. She was naked. He was naked.

Her lips found his in the dark, her small hands slid down his chest, her fingers flexing as though kneading his flesh. His breath let go in a gush as those delicate digits delved into the hair just below his navel.

He couldn't help the small buck his hips made as his manhood suddenly grew rock hard in anticipation of her touch. Her teeth grazed his chin, following his jaw to the rigid muscle that ran from ear to collarbone. Goosebumps rose on his skin when her teeth scraped there, her breath hot. Nip, lick, blow. His breath left him again in another painful rush of excitement.

She moved so slowly he was losing his mind. He tried to slide his hands from her arms to anywhere else, just touching other flesh. She caught them in hers, her lips smiling against him. She kissed each rib as she slid her body down his. He felt her nipples brush against him. He surged upward, reaching for more wanting more than anything to touch her breasts.

She laughed softly, ran her tongue down from sternum to naval where she adored him until he was panting.

"Please." He whispered.

Her hair caressed his stomach, her mouth teased his hip

bone, his thigh, his angle. For the love of God!! She was cruel in the best way ever!

Her hands played on his body like children in a jungle gym, touching everywhere, but settling nowhere. She kissed a return path up the other leg. He started trembling.

Her knees planted between his thighs, her beautiful hair falling like a curtain over her shoulders. Her hot fingers wrapped around him, making him moan. He looked down the length of himself just as those red lips parted, the pink tongue flicking out...

Shit! Jake shot up, sweat making his t-shirt cling, his breath fast, erratic. Holy Shit!! He moved to throw off the stifling blanket and realized two horrifying things.

The guys were staring and grinning at him like a bunch of school boys about to witness the best prank ever. And his cock was so stiff there was no way he could hide it if he moved from the cover of the blanket.

He glared at his brother, but gestured at them all. "Get the fuck out of my face."

Mathew's laughter rang through the entire building, joined by three other baritones.

Bastards.

Chapter 32

Monday 0500

At 0500 hours Zoey's alarm went off. She shut it off, and climbed out of bed heading for the shower stall. She turned on the water, and let it run to get warm. She pulled a fluffy peach colored towel out of her cabinet. She turned up her speakers, and put on an upbeat playlist, she needed any help she could get today.

After showering and towel drying, she brushed her teeth. Then she walked into her closet to find the proper attire. The funeral service started at 1400. This would be another long day, not in the sense of a long workday, but a mentally draining day. Victor had been one of the good guys.

Zoey knew all too well that everyone died, but that didn't mean she wasn't human. Victor could have, should have been able to live longer. He should have been allowed to retire, and move somewhere warm and live out the rest of his days enjoying whatever his hobbies other than police work had been.

"I will always remember you, Victor Kingsley," she said to the air.

She began looking at her shoes. Fifty million pairs of shoes. She liked having different shoes to wear. How could men only wear the same pair day after day? How boring! Now though her shoes were overwhelming her, how to pick the right ones?

"Shoes!" Zoey yelled. She walked out of her closet, and into the kitchen. She thought about having a glass of wine just to calm down. 'You can't have a glass of wine at five in the morning.' 'Watch me!' ran the internal dialogue. Zoey opened her wine cooler and started looking. At last she thought better of the idea, lots of professionals attending this funeral the M.E. shouldn't be half cocked. Okay, Zoey, think logically, you are a Doctor. That made her think about Jake Corde always saying 'Doctor.' 'Detective,' she would answer. He needed to do a thorough investigation of her body. Those strong hands with clean fingernails exploring her body, leaving nothing unexplored. She wanted to be touched so bad.

That was loneliness. Waking up in her bed alone everyday. Oh, to have someone lying next to her. The man, with his loud snores and his chest hair. She could ruffle his hair, and nibble on his ears and whisper 'Je veux que tu M'embrasses partout' and then, 'Emmenez-moi avec passion!'

She sat down on the closet floor. Of all the pairs of shoes she owned, only four of them that could not be considered boots were black. She wasn't going to wear the stilettos to the funeral, so now she was down to three. Three pairs to choose from was a much more manageable number, now pants and blazer or dress? Pants and a blazer might look more professional. A dress, more formal. What would Victor have preferred her to wear? Victor would prefer to be alive thank you very much.

"Victor, what am I supposed to wear?"

Victor didn't answer. Zoey slowly stood up.

Zoey picked out a black pair of suit pants, another that she'd had tailored, and the shoes that went with the pants, and laid them out on her bed. She returned to the closet to find a top to go with her slacks. She pushed hangers of clothes aside looking for just the right one.

Grey, maroon, or good old standard black? Where was her black silk top? All the way at the end? There you are she thought as she pulled the hanger off the rod it hung on. She held her shirt up.

"WHAT THE FUCK!"

The blouse was covered in stains. White stains smeared the material. Zoey knew she had only worn the article of clothing once before, and she hadn't spilled anything on it. She more clearly studied the stain. Not bleach, nope, it was an organic substance. There were only a few white colored...That wasn't possible.

Facts are facts. How? What? It didn't make sense...had some pervert...She clutched the hanger until her knuckles turned white to keep holding the hanger so it wouldn't drop to the floor.

Had some creep been in her closet? Someone had been in her closet, there was no other explanation. Zoey shuddered, and forced
her mind to keep her legs from buckling. She was a medical examiner, she would not crumple.

Where are my evidence bags? In the trunk of the car. Still
carrying the shirt, Zoey went out to her car. She managed to open
the trunk, get the evidence bag out, place the semen smeared article of clothing in the bag, and seal it. That will have to be analyzed.

Can't wear that outfit now. Back to square one. Into the
closet again. Suddenly cold, she shivered. The warmest dress it
would be, decision made.

0632

Jake Corde returned from his morning run, and started
the shower. He had worked with Victor for many years. He had
worked with the man for the five years that the agency had been
open, but it went back further than that. Jake had worked with
Victor when he was still on the force. How many years had he
actually known Victor? Eight, ten? Why was that simple answer
elusive?

Towel wrapped around his waist, Jake took time to shave.
He carefully worked the razor. A clean shave, professional, Victor
would have approved. He rinsed off the shaving cream and ran his
hand down his cheek. He felt stubble. Not smooth enough. He
started the whole process a second time. Once satisfied with his
shaving job, Jake began dressing.

He pulled the suit pants on. He tucked his grey dress shirt
into the waist of his pants. Tie, patterned or plain black? Plain,
simple. He put on the vest over his shirt. Pulled the suit coat over
that, and then glanced into the mirror to see the finished product.
He laughed out loud. You better comb your hair Jake, he told himself.

Jake decided to drive his Mustang to the funeral. He hadn't
bought the car to sit in the garage, he bought the car to drive it.
The funeral was at 14:00. Even with traffic he had time to grab a
healthy breakfast.

He opened the door to his car and smelled the interior. His car, not some rental. Jake slid into the seat behind the wheel. He placed the key in the ignition and turned. His car responded with a throaty growl. Low, menacing, he loved it.

Garage door opened, he revved the engine. Jake put the car in gear, and took off. Yes!

1400

The funeral. A proper funeral honoring a fallen officer. The officers in attendance, and there were alot of them, wore their uniforms correctly. Pressed, shined. Jake looked at the flag covered coffin. He would miss the man. He would have to learn to work with this McCarthy guy. If he wasn't fired, it sounded like he was all ready in hot water.

All in attendance saluted the casket before the official ceremony began. Silence. The official ceremony started.

Jake knew how serious of an occasion an officer's funeral was. Serious, fit Jake just fine. Someone decided that Victor would have wanted a bell ceremony. Bells tolling. Mournful.

Jake might have preferred a LODD funeral, but Victor hadn't died while on duty. Jake would have also preferred a 21-Gun Salute to the bells, but he didn't have the authority to make those decisions.

He looked over at Zoey. He didn't regret looking at her, he felt a small twinge of guilt, thinking about her the way he did at a funeral. The dress she wore looked like it was velvet. It fit her perfectly. Perfectly.

Abero. Victor would have called her Abero. Zoey Abero the medical examiner. He couldn't get his dream out of his head. Someday, hopefully. Jake refocused on the proceedings, looking at the casket.

The bagpipes started. Jake clenched his teeth. More mournful than the bells. Sad. Final. A farewell.

Jake looked around at the attendees as the bagpipes played. He knew a few of the officers. The task force members of course. Stephen Abernathy and many other office staff were also among the gathered.

The color guard removed the flag, and handed it to a woman close to Victor's age. A sister, Jake's gut told him.

The pallbearers moved up to the casket. They lifted it, and began carrying it away. Many of the gathered left the official ceremony, Jake walked a respectful distance away from the officers gathering around a police cruiser.

He smelled perfume and shampoo. Jake turned his head. Zoey stood next to him. He nodded at her, and returned his gaze to the cruiser, straining his ears. The dispatcher in the car picked up the radio. The final radio call was placed.

"0803"

"0803 Detective Kingsley?"

"0803 Detective Victor Kingsley has not responded. We thank you for your service. May you rest in Peace."

End of Watch.

Chapter 33

1445

The forlorn ringing of the bells, the bagpipes wailing, the dead leaves rustling across the ground and the chill fall air made the ceremony that much more heart wrenching. The only thing missing was a cold mist so that black umbrellas could lend an air of mystery.

Then the Final Radio call was made.

She stepped up to Jake's side and welcomed the arm he lightly wrapped around her waist and the clean, sweet smelling linen kerchief he handed her as the tears slid down her cheeks. Yet another thing about the man that was strangely at odds with the image he portrayed on a normal day.

"I'll walk you to your car," he said, his hand pressing the small of her back.

Zoey nodded and moved toward her tiny car. "So, as much as it pains me I must admit that you were right. I can't take the time off work, but I should hire someone for protection."

Jake stopped and turned her to face him. "What?"

"I said…"

"I heard your capitulation, now I want to know why?"

Zoey clamped her lips together and started back to her car. She just was not sure if she should tell Jake the whole truth or a complete lie. But the word capitulation irked her no end and made her feel rebellious. She wasn't one to ever surrender. What had been in that Winston Churchill speech, 'We shall never surrender!'

Then she remembered the disgusting substance on her shirt and she couldn't help the shudder that ran through her. This was no time to be stubbornly proud. Someone had been in her closet, masturbated and wiped off on her shirt.

She had an idea of when this had happened. Now she needed time to figure out who. And she needed to be safe. It would take four days at least, but could just as easily be weeks depending

on the method and viability of the sperm for DNA testing.
Even then, it will not give a definitive who without a comparison
so hopefully the police had the culprit in their data bank. It was a
long shot of course. But it was all she had right now.

At her car she abruptly turned to face Jake who skidded to a
halt. She sighed. Her eyes met his, and she grimaced.

"Someone was in my apartment."

Jake frowned. Should he confess?

"I found a shirt that has semen on it."

What the fuck? Jake's heart skipped a beat.

"I'm taking it to the lab after the repast."

"Christ." Jake ran a hand through his hair in an unconscious gesture of concern. "Well, I have a girl who can stay with
you 24/7. She's the best there is."

"A girl?"

"Yes. Her name is Beatrice Dooberman. She is a master at
so many things we'll be here all day if I start listing them. You can
meet her at your place later. I'll have Matt send her there to check
it out. Meanwhile, I will ride with you between now and then."
Zoey nodded. "Ok. Thanks. A woman would be easier to live
with. And explain to my parents."

Jake walked around to the passenger side and opened the
door. "I know you hate asking for help Zoey, but you are doing the
smart thing."

She half smiled at him. "I won't lie. It freaked me out,
finding the shirt hanging in my closet. I was going to wear it."

"I'll be sure to thank him just before I break his neck." Jake
said as he folded himself into her sardine can.

"Thank him?" Her tone was chilly.

"You wore that instead." He grinned pointing at her dress.

"Oh for Pete's sake." Zoey huffed. "Just when I start feeling good will toward you, you say or do something awful and I'm
back to square one!"

They rode in silence to the reception hall where a sea of
blue uniforms and black suits and dresses streamed in and out
the doors. The undulating crowd was stifling and pressing. Like
being under the bedcovers too long.

They no more than stepped through the doors when he put his lips close to her ear and asked, "Do you want refreshments?"

His breath teased the hair that curled there, his scent flowing around her even as his body heat warmed her. She hadn't realized she was cold. Not the cold caused by chilly fall air. No, this was the bone deep cold of too many negative emotions.

Grief because she had worked with Victor for a while and she liked him both as a good cop and a decent guy. Fear because her home had been violated and she wasn't comfortable there any more. Frustration because they should have caught James Palmer before he killed his own child!

Jake cleared the way to the food tables as he practically dragged her along in his wake. When a body wouldn't move right away he said 'excuse me' once then employed elbows. Zoey wasn't sure if she should feel completely flattered that he was determined to see her needs fulfilled or embarrassed that he used such bully tactics to accomplish it.

He had just shoved a bottle of water into her hand and turned to grab a plate when Doctor Abernathy stepped between them, taking her elbow as though to move her. Zoey resisted. She had had enough of being dragged around.

He let go of her and instead leaned down. "Hello Doctor Abero."

"Hello Doctor." She was deliberately loud. He was too close.

"I've been meaning to have a chat with you." He smiled gently, almost fatherly.

"Oh?"

"Yes, of course. I know you and Victor were friends as well as co-workers. I wanted to be sure you were well."

"As well as can be expected, I suppose." She smiled, eyeing Jake who was behind Abernathy, watching.

"And the Palmer house." The doctor shook his head sadly. "I am so very sorry. What a difficult thing to process. I have told everyone involved in the crime scene to feel free to come talk to me. It can be quite cathartic, you know."

"It's my job to work crime scenes." Cathartic to talk to a

shrink? Zoey thought two bottles of Moscato would be a better idea. She had no intention of ever talking to this man for any kind of help. Well, maybe he was just doing his job, but his timing sucked donkey balls.

"Of course it is. But that doesn't mean the horror isn't traumatic enough to affect us. But I won't press. Just please, don't suffer alone."

"I appreciate your sentiment, Doctor Abernathy. Really I do." She nodded and stepped around the well meaning man. Jake handed her a plate of food, gave Abernathy one last look and led the way to a table.

They no more than settled in when McCarthy appeared, dragging a second table up to match theirs. Greg Anderson brought two handfuls of folded chairs and began placing them. Adam Jackson and Jesus Sanches followed with plates of food. Then suddenly women and children appeared. Jackson and Sanches made introductions.

What had started out as a twosome ended up as an even dozen with no extra room around the table. Zoey was touched to her soul by the symbolism. The task force, showing its unity, even at such a sad event. And though the case would be closed officially tomorrow, today a gauntlet had been thrown down. Not even death will divide them.

Many eyes looked them over. Only two were narrowed in anger. A small smile lifted the thin lips at the corner. Very well. Challenge accepted.

Chapter 34

When Doobie met them at Zoey's apartment's garage, her demeanor was casually professional, but iceberg chill and space-time continuum distant. Zoey was a little dubious of Jake's earlier assessment of the woman as Doobie turned out to be a mousey looking female of indeterminate age with such a scarred soul it shone out of her deep green eyes like hellfire.

The strangest thing about her was that she was unremarkable in a way Zoey was hard pressed to describe. She exuded the stereotypical runaway that you deliberately didn't look too closely at because you didn't want to know the truth that your eyes would see. She wore a tree bark brown turtleneck sweater, dark jeans ending in frayed bottoms that rested on top of nondescript hiking boots. Her hair was so many shades of brown it looked dirty and her expression was the exact amount of mutinous Zoey had seen on troubled teens.

"Thank you for taking the time to stay with me." Zoey said, feeling like somehow she was being judged by standards she didn't comprehend.

Doobie shrugged then said, "It's what I do. Did Jake tell you what to expect?"

"You are going to stay with me and watch over my apartment because it was broken into recently."

Doobie scowled at Jake who had the grace to look shamefaced. "Coward." She accused him.

Turning back to Zoey she sighed. "It's a little more complicated than that. But let's get to your apartment. She gestured for Zoey to follow her. I changed the security system to one that Corde Investigations controls and monitors. One of Matt's inventions and it is top of the line. There is a new lock set with a silent alarm. Only the matching key will shut the silent alarm off. It has a chip that turns the alarm on when you lock the door and off when you unlock it. It cannot be copied because the chip is specially formatted with that alarm. It is another system that Matt created and it is the best I have ever seen."

The elevator doors swooshed shut and Doobie continued. "I will give you the passcode to your new alarm once we get inside. I think we need to go over the rules. I won't force myself on someone who is unaware of the situation, proper."

Zoey felt uneasiness creep up her spine and she glanced at Jake who smiled sideways and winked in an ineffectual attempt at reassurance. Obviously he hadn't told her everything about this bodyguard stuff. She had a sinking suspicion she was going to regret confiding anything.

"First let me assure you," Doobie continued as they left the elevator and she walked them to Zoey's door. Unlocking it she ushered them inside and quickly disarmed the alarm. "Perverts who invade your home and masturbate on your clothes are not good people. They are not going to stop until they have lived out their fantasies, whatever those may be. They escalate fairly quickly and it always ends badly for the victim.

I have the tools, the training, and the meanness necessary to stop him. But only if you cooperate to the nth. I will not do this if you don't truly want to save your life. I think it is too much of a coincidence that at the same time as a serial killer makes an appearance and your cop friend is murdered, you suddenly acquire a stalker who is so far along in his neurosis that he is invading your home. It's connected, no doubt in my mind. So tell me Doctor Abero, do you want to survive this full on Autumn Nightmare?"

"Of course." Zoey said impatiently, going to her kitchen. She needed a drink. Maybe even five or six. But she would start with one glass and see where things went from there.

Doobie waited for her to flop onto the couch and hike her feet up onto the coffee table. Jake tore his eyes away from the amount of thigh being displayed. He walked over to the first bay of windows and began closing the drapes.

"So. The rules. No exceptions.

One: No more open drapes that allow someone from neighboring buildings a full view of your home and the people in it."

Zoey loved the morning sunshine and the view. Already she was hating the restrictions and that was only number one.

"Two: No more organized planner. Besides going to work at the same time every day, there will be no written or acknowledged set plans. You do not let 'your people' know what your movements are going to be beyond the next ten minutes."

Holy crap. That was insane. How does one do anything without a planner? Did she mean the calendar on Zoey's phone? Well, she wasn't going to ask the woman and bring attention to it, that was for sure.

"Three: No more jogging. Get a gym system for the corner of your apartment or get a gym membership where the situation can be monitored and controlled."

Well, that wasn't so bad. It was the excuse she needed to buy that awesome new bike thing, megatron or something or other. Do-able.

"Four: I am with you at all times. Here, I can be outside the bathroom but all other times we are Siamese Twins. In necessary crowds such as crime scenes there will be two or three of us."

"I am sure I would be perfectly safe at a crime scene." Zoey commented dryly.

"Do you want to bet your life on it? Have you ever really looked at the crowds a murder draws in? Can you be sure you would be able to pick your possible murderer out of that sea of faces?"

Zoey felt a little defensive; the questions were fired at her so quickly.

"Oookaaay." More wine. Yep. She brought the bottle back to the couch where she sat the glass on the end table and tipped the bottle, deciding to stop pretending she wasn't going to get shit-faced. Oh Victor, you will be missed.

"Five: Limit crowded areas except crime scenes if you insist on working. This includes restaurants, cinema's, concerts, ballet, opera, whatever you love to do that involves more than five people in your immediate area. The less we have to watch, the quicker we find the threat."

Sweet Jesus. "I eat out more than I do in." Zoey protested.

"Not anymore. As it happens I am a good cook, so we won't worry about feeding you. Better that all of your food is prepared by known, trusted hands anyway."

"What does that mean?"

"We don't know your stalker's subtype. If he is 'Resentful', then he might seek revenge for some perceived wrong and poison your food."

Zoey tilted her head sideways and raised her eyebrows. "Subtype? Really?" She asked in droll disbelief.

"Really. Rule six: No entering a room that has not been checked first. I always check ahead of you. Always."

Zoey nodded reluctantly.

"Seven: No more unmonitored calls. I listen in on all of your calls. Dead serious. No joke. No exceptions."

"No. Absolutely not. What the hell? Bad enough you have to be in the same room as me all the time, but to listen to my calls?"

"Let me give you an example. Your office calls. Your right hand, what's her name...Kellesha. It's her. She tells you she has found something you need to see right away. She doesn't want to tell you over the phone, she's worried about secrecy. You rush to see what she has found. Once in the building you find her sitting at gunpoint, her fingers and toes crushed and bleeding. She has been tortured to get you to come here alone. Now he not only has her, he has you too. Fact: he is not going to let either of you live. Period. He cannot be reasoned with or cajoled, or begged or bribed.

Get it in your head. These guys are driven by sex or causing pain, more often than not, both. He isn't going to play nice. He doesn't want your money or your car. I have not determined what subtype he is exactly but I am leaning toward Intimacy or Preda-tor. I have questions I can ask you to determine that, but I want to make sure we are on the set course I know to be successful and right."

"He's a pervert for sure; not a killer." Zoey argued.

"You're lying and you know it. You would not have told Jake about it, or considered a bodyguard if you didn't feel this was more than a mere pervert." The bodyguard called her out. Then without warning she grabbed the waist of her shirt and in one smooth motion pulled the turtleneck up and over her head.

What was revealed was such a sad testament to the woman's inner turmoil. Scars. Everywhere. Burn scars, knife scars, whip scars. Long, short, thin, thick. Some faded, some still dark pink. "This was all done by a subtype 'Rejected' but he was also a 'Predator.' There are no words to convey the depth of terror and horror that I lived with at his hands. What did I do to call this upon myself? I divorced him.

Then, I stupidly believed I could 'talk him down' from his rage. I was so damn sure that he wouldn't seriously hurt our child or me. He loved us right? He hunted me down like an animal. Then, like a damn idiot, I met and married another one just like him. It didn't take me long to end that shit. Now, don't you dare tell me I don't know what I'm talking about."

Zoey swallowed and nodded. She turned her eyes to Jake who was studying the carpet at his feet, perhaps for the hole he felt should open at any moment. She looked back at Doobie and sighed.

Waving the wine bottle around like a flag bearer she capitulated gracelessly. "Fine. But I am not fucking calling you Doobie. I feel like I'm on the set of that pothead movie where the two guys just want a burger. I wouldn't mind a burger either, now that you mention it."

1932

Three went in, one came out. Every time he thought he fixed a problem, Corde created another. Seriously, he should have had James take out Corde instead of Victor, but the Detective had been so close. He had panicked.

But time was running out for him. When he had planned this venture he had known that he was limited in how long he could take to reach his goal. He could only keep the body parts viable for so long. Assembly became more and more difficult with each passing day.

He needed to set his latest experiment in motion. This one

wasn't controlled by hypnotism and suggestion. This new one had a real hunger for killing and inflicting pain. He hadn't needed to break down any inhibitions or preconceived ideas about the value of human life.

He had great hopes for this one's efficacy.

Chapter 35

2200 Monday

Nothing, if not efficient. If there was a list of tasks to be done, they would get done, checked off the list. The list existed, it contained four items, with the forth item being saved for last. With the other three items the order in which they were done, didn't matter.

Now to find the targets. The specifics. That was key. Just the right women. The correct specimens. Vibrant life that would be taken from them.

The taking of human life was the greatest pleasure. Power. Snuffing out the spark. Taking away thoughts, memories, because in the end, on the deathbed, one didn't think about how much money they had made during their lifetime, one thought about spending more time with the people they loved. That was taken away from them too. That was power.

Hunting for just the right target specimens wasn't just some willy nilly task. Correct proportions were important, and Chicago was vast. What was the approximate population of Chicago? A little over two million? Hunting females at least cut the number roughly in half. Which was still much too large a number, but there were narrowing variables.

Ages were important. The targets could not be on the extremities of age, not younger than fifteen, and not over forty-five. This narrowed the gap a little, but still locating three perfect women in that thirty year age range was no small task. Where were the best possible hunting grounds?

Despite the fact that one of the previous murders had taken place at a college, that didn't seem like a bad place to start hunting. No candidates under fifteen, and very few above forty five. Now which university? You had to ask the right questions to get the correct answers.

For now the closest college would do. Tools packed in the

car, laptop in the passenger seat, and phone/camera in hand, it was time to start reconnaissance. The thrill. Hunting.

Parking at the campus tavern seemed like the thing to do. Might as well start there. The place's name wasn't familiar, a weird word like Gandalf's, or Gimli's, or some such. It didn't matter. The interior was dimly lit, and resembled an Irish Pub, if an Irish pub contained a milieu of students, pool tables, dart boards, air hockey, and multiple T.V.'s. The establishment thrived, it teemed with humanity. Oh, the possibilities.

"Do you have Red Stripe?"

"You must be new. We're a brew pub. Would you like to try something similar?"

"When in Rome. That is the saying, right?"

"Caesar, beware the Ides of March. Let me get you a few samples to try," the bartender turned to his work. Three small sample glasses were placed on the bar.

"This one is our equivalent of Bud Light, but tastes better, more flavor, we call it Arwen. Next is our Irish red, like Smithwicks, named Smaug. And last, if you're feeling bold, is our Habanero porter aptly named Mount Doom."

They weren't Red Stripe, but they weren't half bad. Bud Light, no matter what it was named, tasted like lightly hopped water. The red left an undesirable aftertaste.

"I'll go with Mount Doom."

"Coming up."

The beer arrived. After paying and adding a generous tip, it was time to get to work. Scanning. Scanning. She might do? Oh no, that one was much better. Very nice. Camera activated. Snap, snap, snap. Time to introduce yourself.

"Hey."

"Hey."

"What are you drinking?"

"Arwen."

"That is what I want to switch to, this is way too spicy for me. Let me get you another one."

"Here you go. I'm new. May I join you?"

The student closed her book. She gestured at the empty

chair. What a specimen.

"Thanks. What are you reading?"

"It is so boring. English is not my thing. Need to get the general credits out of the way."

"Don't we all. English isn't my thing either, I'm a science nut."

"Cool. I actually am here to study veterinary science."

"Admirable. What's your name?"

"Regina."

"Regina, I'm Blake."

"I love that name. So what are you studying? No, wait, let me guess." Regina purses her lips and narrows her eyes. "Law!"

"Nice try. I'm studying to be a nurse. Working on human anatomy at the moment."

Regina smiled a crooked smile, "Human anatomy huh? That sounds interesting. You must be super smart."

"It's a fascinating subject. I don't know about being smart," Blake raised the beer and took a gulp.

"Awe, come on. Don't sell yourself short. I think brains are hot." She winked.

"Tell me more about yourself."

"Well, what do you want to know? What you see is what you get really. I like hiking and cross country skiing. I enjoy beer, vodka, and good food. I have a couple of brothers and a sister and we get together once a week for lunch or Sunday dinner or whatever. I have a thing for sexy lips like yours," her throaty laugh was as inviting as her words.

"Do you live on campus in the dorms, or do you have an apartment nearby?" Blake asked.

"Sorority house, actually. There are six of us girls, just off campus."

"Do you like living with your sisters?"

"Of course! They are a great bunch. It's a big house and we throw weekend parties all the time. I love college."

"Excuse me for a quick second. I need to use the bathroom, and I'll bring us another beer."

"Are you trying to get me drunk? Shame on you." She

laughed, "But go ahead, I will wait for a minute or two."

"I'm sure a sorority girl like you can drink me under the table." Blake walked toward the bathrooms. Halfway there, turned, smiled at Reginia and took some more photos. Exiting the restroom Blake got them each another knock off Bud Light, and returned to the table.

"Hm. Thank you. Do you live on campus? You look like the type to have an apartment."

"Yes, I'm in the apartments right off campus. The neighbors are pretty loud, hard to study there. I spend a lot of time in the library."

"Studying! So how long does it take to get your RN?"

"I'm trying to decide if I want to take the fast track, and go through the summer or not?"

"Don't waste your summer! There are plenty of online courses you can take during the regular year as well as the full class schedule. They earn you the credits you need in the dummy subjects, like a writing course. It's crazy how many unrelated classes you have to take to satisfy the graduating requirements."

"I'll have to explore that option. I don't want to waste my summer if I don't have to. You mentioned food. What is your favorite?"

"I will not give the obvious answer." She giggled. "I love seafood."

"I see food, I eat it," Blake laughed. "But in all seriousness I love seafood too. Succulent, smothered in hot dripping butter. Juices all over your fingers," Blake winked.

Regina smiled slyly and wiggled around on her seat. "I like how you describe things Blake."

"Would it be too bold of me to suggest we exchange phone numbers, so we can text?"

"Yes, but, that's ok. I think I would like to get to know you better," Regina answered, looking a little more nervous than earlier.

"There is so much about you I want to know better too. Here is my number," Blake held out the phone showing the contact information. "I'll leave the ball in your court, as they say."

"Perfect! Thank you. I appreciate your thoughtfulness. I think you will be hearing from me soon." She stood up, stuffed her book into her oversized purse and smiled down at Blake. "By the way, what is your sign?"

"I look forward to hearing from you. I'm a Taurus."

Blake watched Regina walk away. That went well. Time to find number two.

Chapter 36

0500 Tuesday

At 0500 Zoey woke up. She could not go for a run, the rules said so. She spent a little over an hour researching exercise equipment on her phone. 0623, shower time. She put a hand in to check the water temperature. Almost. She checked it again, yup, that was right.

She stepped under the hot water. She wanted to go back in time, and not tell Jake she needed protection. But there was no going back in time. Only forward movement. Now she had a fucking baby sitter at age twenty-seven. Good job on that one Zoey! Maybe she could tell her dad she was into women now, and see if he laughed.

Another day off, and once again she didn't know what to do with herself when she wasn't working. She grabbed the loofa, soaped it up, and began washing herself. Neck, throat, breasts, and down to her toes.

Once that was complete, she applied shampoo to her hair. That could sit for a hot second. She picked up her pink razor and slowly shaved her legs. Her smooth, athletic, legs. Once her legs were done, she shaved her armpits. She would not embrace that old French stereotype, thank you very much. She carefully shaved her lady parts.

When she finished shaving, she rinsed the shampoo out of her hair, and conditioned. Shower complete, she stepped out of the shower and towelled dry. She walked into the kitchen to start coffee, and there was her watch-dog. Oh shit, someone else here, she had better get dressed, coffee could wait.

"Don't you ever sleep? She asked the bodyguard, turning back toward her bedroom.

"Not much," Doobie answered.

Zoey hurriedly pulled on a pair of black panties, and matching bra. Then she covered up with a pair of blue jeans, an old t-shirt, and a sweater. Dressed, she returned to her kitchen and opened the wine fridge. She studied her choices and selected a bottle of Low Hanging Fruit White Zinfandel. A California wine it tasted like juicy watermelon and ripe raspberries with a refreshing finish. She poured some in her large glass.

"Do you always drink this early in the morning?" Doobie asked.

"Are you my mother?" Zoey shot back.

"Just need to know my clients," Doobie answered.

"Most mornings I have coffee. But today is a day off. You won't let me go for a run. I'm a little frustrated already," Zoey blurted.

"Small price to pay to stay alive," Doobie said.

The woman had a point there. Zoey took a sip of her wine, and walked to her bookcase. She studied her small collection of special books. The ones not related to medical science. She pulled down two. Both of them were favorites from her childhood. The first, The Herald of Shadow, an amazing fantasy. A tale of the Skaaron people battling the evil planet eating monster. She especially loved the way the author described a fall festival Specnock which meant specters of the night. The festival honored the ancestors and generally was celebrated with a silent meal, face painting, bobbing for apples, and a large bonfire.

The second was a thin book of poetry titled Spring Souls. Love poems. Zoey couldn't give two fucks if other people thought it silly, she liked it. The book had received terrible reviews but her father had read her the poems in both French and English when she was a little girl and they had stuck with her. Zoey embraced the romance of the author's language in both languages. Books in hand, she curled up on her chair and began reading. She took a sip of the White Zin, and flipped to one of her favorite poems.

"I am just me, says he says he, as he shows me so much more to see to see. His heart is gracious and kind, his eyes are windows to his brilliant mind. I am just me says he says he. I wish you could see what I see, when I see what you truly are."

Zoey giggled. She should read it to Jake. She took another sip of wine.

There was the real debate, did she call him or not? Did she call Jake Corde to see him, not in a professional capacity? People met at work all the time and hooked up right? Right! But that didn't mean she was going to be one of those people. What was wrong with being one of those people? They were happy. They weren't alone.

To call or not to call. 'To be or not to be,' and here she sat like Hamlet, not doing anything. Hamlet, Zoey, she told herself, the world is going to go on around you while you sit and do nothing. People are going to die. People are going to fall in love. People are going to go grocery shopping. People are going to do laundry. People are going to have sex. And what are you going to do? Sit here reading a book you've read a thousand times?

Zoey took another sip of wine. She shouldn't call him now. She wanted to call him though. Wanted to hear his voice, even if he said the wrong thing. Damn. Better have another glass of wine.

She crossed to the kitchen, and poured a second glass. It was really good wine. She wasn't sure that she tasted raspberries, but it was still an amazing wine. She might have to buy her dad a bottle.

Chaos. Her mind felt like a crime scene with cars parked all over the place. Alright Zoey, order the chaos. That meant cleaning. Did she really want to clean on her day off? The answer was a resounding no. Then there was Doobie, but she would not call her that.

If she had a girlfriend, the girlfriend would tell her to call Jake, maybe even goad her into it. That same girlfriend might then try to steal her man. 'Her man', that was a laugh. Jake Corde certainly wasn't 'her man'. Not yet anyway. Maybe she should put on a skimpy dress, flash some leg, anything to detract from her scar. Fucking scar!

She kept thinking about Jake. His intense hazel eyes, with a kindness behind them. His smell. His manness. Was that even a word? Zoey laughed out loud. Did she want him? She would be lying if she said no. But no, she couldn't call him, not with her scar, her disfigurement. and not while her bodyguard would screen the call.

That is why she worked. Fucking days off, why couldn't she just go into work anyway, get her mind off Jake Corde. She could do something mindless like watch T.V., but she was reserving that in case the day got even worse.

Here you sit Hamlet/Zoey doing nothing, and the world goes on. She picked up her phone, you only live once right? Then she put down her phone again. Why was this so difficult? Because it was a matter of the heart, it wasn't scientific. It was not fact, it was ambiguous, amorphous, shifting like clouds. If the clouds moved, could you see the stars?

Could you sail through the clouds, into the outer beyond known as space, known as love. Oh, her dad would be laughing at her right now, 'I'm a demigod sent to earth to seduce your mother.' And her mother, what would she say? Most likely something like, don't jump, take things slow.

Zoey didn't want to take things slow. She wanted to jump. She needed to do something, she needed to move.

"I'm going out," she told Doobie. She put on her long grey coat.

"Where do you need to go, that is so important?" Doobie asked.

"Maybe I want to see my boyfriend," Zoey said.

"Jake checked, you don't have one."

"Fuck Jake! And Fuck you too!"

"You hired me, remember. You are not going to take a random, directionless walk. That is a good way to get killed," Doobie said.

"You're right," Zoey sighed and took off her coat.

Zoey stood in her kitchen. Her mother said things like 'when in doubt, eat.' Maybe A huge piece of apple crisp, with vanilla ice cream, and gobs of caramel. Ice cream! Jake Corde liked his ice cream frozen. Okay, one point for Matt Corde.

One day she might call either of those brothers, and not for work, but not when her calls were being screened.. Right now, there was her assigned watch-dog. She needed to give herself credit for being intelligent, she wanted to stay alive. That phone call would have to wait for another day.

Right now she thought food was in order.

"What are you making for breakfast?" Zoey asked.

Chapter 37

1000 Tuesday

The day was bright, sunlight illuminated the campus sidewalks. A rare blue sky unobstructed with clouds. A warm breeze rustled the leaves that were changing colors in the Windy City.

This was the perfect time to check out the girls as they took their daily runs or just walked around campus. Too warm for sweats and jackets. Great for shorts and t-shirts. Had to love sweaty t's.

There, a fine specimen. The jogger's ass filled out the tight grey running pants just right. That wasn't her best feature though. She had great posture, her best feature was that spine that was clearly delineated by the sweat that dampened the yellow t-shirt she wore. Every vertebrae could be counted. Yes, that spine.

Phone working again as camera, click. Click. Click. That done, Blake started jogging. There would be no losing this one.

It became fairly obvious that jogging was more the target's thing than Blake's as air wheezed in and out of lungs that just did not want to do this for much longer. Better bring things to an end soon. One must always be aware of one's shortcomings, mustn't one.

Blake put on a burst of speed to catch the attractive brunette. That spine, just perfect. Once they were side by side, Blake turned on a smile.

"I'm new, do you know where a drinking fountain is?"

A sideways glance from the woman and a grimace. "Nope. I bring my water." She gestured to the bottle hanging at her waist. Quick as a Gizelle she turned onto an offshoot path between buildings and picked up speed.

Glancing around Blake reached into a nearby bush and broke off a dead stick about the size of a golf club. Perfect. The girl just needed to be slowed down a bit. A fall wouldn't do too much harm.

Grimacing at aching calves the stalker took off running again in a huge last burst of speed, came within ten feet, took a chance and whipped the stick at the runner's feet. Weather by luck or Zion, the damn thing did as hoped. It tangled her up and knocked her to her knees.

Quickly, with death like force Blake delivered an elbow to the runner's temple rendering her unconscious. That done, Blake carried the woman back to the vehicle. Duct tape did a fine job of stifling and binding.

A quick look around found them still alone. It was divine intervention for sure because the campus should be crawling with people. Heart racing with adrenaline, or maybe all that fucking running, Blake got in behind the wheel and took two seconds to think about where to take this woman. Obviously the order of collection had changed. It looked like the spine was first, Regina would have to wait.

The best laid plans of mice and men always changed. Originally Blake was just going to mark the victims, and kill them all in the same night, but that was fine. Maybe one at a time would produce even more pleasure. The power of taking another's life. Now where to drive?

But the excitement of kidnapping was a serious adrenaline rush. So maybe it would serve to whet the appetite for the main event! But where?

A sly grin slowly spread over full lips. Hmmm. What about the morgue? How hard would it be to sneak an unconscious woman in there? Just wait for the night.

All the tools to do the job right were there. Even the equipment needed to preserve the spine. Exhilaration made Blake's lungs pump harder, breath coming in gasps now. So close to an orgasm, just thinking about the extraction.

0600 Wednesday

Flashing red and blue lights welcomed Zoey in the ME parking lot as she arrived at work the next morning. What the hell was going on? She eased into her usual spot, shut the car off and prepared to exit the vehicle.

A hand on her wrist stopped her. "Hold one second. A cop is coming over. Let him speak first. We need to know what is happening." Doobie was sitting on the edge of her seat, her right hand down, out of sight. Her eyes were narrowed and tight, moving back and forth, taking in everything.

Suddenly Zoey felt the rightness of having this woman with her. Like when she was with Jake, there was an air of calm watchfulness. A sense that all would be well. It was a very reassuring feeling.

McCarthy leaned down to look in the open window. "Hey Doctor Abero."

"Lieutenant McCarthy"

He sighed. "I know it's your job and all, but this seems pretty personal, being in your place of work and all. Your girl is pretty upset."

"You might want to start from the beginning, officer." Doobie said softly.

"That Kellesha girl. She came in to work and found a body all laid out on one of the tables. Spine removed, nice and neat like."

"Thank you. Ian. Give me a moment," Zoey said, then turned to Doobie. "You ready? I have to get in there. Crime scene to process and all that. Besides, it sounds like Kellesha is stressed. She doesn't get stressed."

"I will walk with you to the morgue then leave you to calm your friend. I need to look around and ask some questions." Doobie was out and around the car in an instant, practically pushing McCarthy out of the way.

McCarthy followed them to the autopsy room, but stopped at the door. Doobie stepped ahead, did her room sweep then nodded to Zoey. "Call me if you need me, I will be close." She told the doctor.

Zoey stepped in and her eyes immediately found Kellesha sitting at the desk, her head down on folded arms. "Oh Kell, are you ok?"

Kellesha looked up, her beautiful brown eyes bloodshot and

frightened. "Right here in our morgue Doctor Abero," she whispered.

Zoey put a hand on her shoulder and knelt next to her chair. "I know. I know it's terrifying. And I am so very sorry you had to come into this. Do you need some time off? Maybe you should call that Doctor Abernathy?"

Kellesha teared up, sniffled. "I don't know. I feel like I should work, but look at my hands!" She held out the wildly shaking appendages. "I just don't know if I can calm down."

"Call Abernathy. Have him prescribe you something. Come back tomorrow. I can do this one without you."

Kellesha sniffled. "I am so sorry. I never fall apart like this. I can't imagine what's happening to me."

"This one is too close to home. It's fine. We will be alright today. Go take care of yourself. I insist you talk to Abernathy and do not return until he clears you." Zoey helped the silently weeping girl to her feet and led her to the door.

"Is there anyone who can take her to the precinct to talk to Abernathy then get her home safe?" Zoey asked Detective McCarthy.

"Absolutely." He led Kellesha toward the exit.

Doobie appeared from around the corner and Zoey almost grinned. She hated that name but damned if she could think of a better one. The woman did not look like a Beatrice at all.

"Hey, guess what?"

Zoey raised her brows in question as she re-entered the autopsy room and walked over to the sink. She would first treat the room as a crime scene and then as a morgue. First gather exterior evidence.

"The cameras were off. Like shut right off, computers and all. Not a single alarm was on either. The guards are my next move. Are you ok here alone?"

"No, I am going to need McCarthy to clear at least one of my techs to help me."

Doobie did a thumbs up and moved to leave. "Anything else you need, you just holler Doc, I'm here for the duration."

Chapter 38

0600 Wednesday

Jake stood just inside little Amy Palmer's bedroom door, letting his eyes wander over the pink walls and fluffy soft stuffed toys. Back and forth, every square inch was covered before he stepped inside and walked to the center of the room. Six steps. Turning in a circle slowly he examined the room again.

Friendly, comfortable. A happy room made up just for a four year old girl. It was hard to reconcile James Palmer as the father of such a child, much less one with this contented feeling room. No doubt that was Katie Palmer's mother's touch.

His eyes fell on the line-up of stuffed toys. A white kitty, a black puppy. A teddy bear with big brown eyes. A giraffe, an elephant. His eyes slid back to the unicorn, then the giraffe. An empty spot.

He looked under the bed. Nothing. Slowly he looked around again. Turning he went out to the hallway. Sure enough, there was Amy in a family photo hugging a white pony with a rainbow colored mane.

"Hey." Matt said from the end of the hall that led into the living room. "Look what I found."

Jake frowned. "What the hell are you doing here?"

Matt rolled his eyes. "That again? I fah low ed you" the smart ass sounded out. "That isn't what's important. Look what I found." He held up a round plastic object with a glass window.

"Is that a..."

"Nanny Cam." Matt finished succinctly. He was so dramatic.

"Is it chipped?"

"No, wired. Direct feed."

"Now isn't that interesting? What are the chances there are more?"

"I'd say pretty good since this one was in the garage."

"Let's get looking then."

After two hours of searching they found a total of ten of the little cameras. Matt was in seventh heaven. He examined each one with an intensity that would have made a woman blush.

"How long will it take to find the source?" Jake asked his brother.

"Wow." Matt gave a bark of laughter. "Thanks for the vote of confidence."

Jake just stared at him.

"I honestly don't know. I've never had to trace to a remote location. Usually there is a room where a computer is being fed the images from nanny cams. If these are hooked to a phone and the phone is off, it could take months to trace it. If it's a computer, not too long, half a day or so, depending on firewalls."

"Better get busy. Get hold of Mom, see if she can help you."

"How is she going to help me?"

"I don't know Matt, Inspiration maybe. Motivation? Just make shit happen fast. We have a little girl out there somewhere and I think those cameras have the answers."

Jake went back into Amy's room and sat on the small bed. The bedding had been bagged and tagged and hauled away to the lab for forensics to go over. The bare bed made the room feel lonely somehow, abandoned.

Slowing his breathing he closed his eyes. There had to be something in this room that could tell him where she was. The smallest detail to give him hope.

When they came, the visions were so violent Jake fell back, his hands going to his head as though trying to keep it from flying apart. Black gloved fingers gently pushed a blonde curl off the pink cheek of a sleeping cherub. Long fingers.

Those same hands stuffing clothes into a pink backpack. Black shoes with soft soles. Narrow shoulders covered with a jacket, no longer. A trench coat? Really?

"Come on. Give me a face. A face." Jake whispered. "A clue. Something. Anything."

A sound pierced through the string of visions and suddenly

they were gone and Jake was left with a headache and more questions than answers. He cursed himself for leaving his phone on. Then he saw Doobie's name and felt his heart skip. He answered gruffly.

"Doctor Abero and I got to work this morning and guess what?"

What the hell was it with these people? Was he a game show contestant or something?

"Okay, I'll play your game. What?"

"Someone broke in. You better get down here."

"Matt!" Jake bellowed on his way out of the house.

He found Zoey bent over the body, her little helpers everywhere. "I can't leave you alone for a hot second Dr. Abero." He teased to cover the relief he knew was clearly written all over his face. He was getting way too worried about this woman.

"Indeed." She gestured at the corpse without looking up. "Have a look."

"Son of a bitch," he whistled. "That's the best damn filet job I have ever seen."

"Yea. The killer used my tools. Mine! Jake, to kill."

"Your…, wait, what?" Had he heard that right?

"You heard me. He cut her spine out, or at least began the process, while she was still alive. "I am fairly certain she died about a quarter of the way through the job. The pain would have been excruciating."

Feeling a little green around the gills Jake stared at Zoey's mask tie until he got his anger under control. This job never ceased to surprise him in so many bad ways. "How did he do that? Did she fight at all?"

"I just finished the evidence sweep and was getting ready to do the autopsy. I haven't turned her over. I can't say I've seen any defensive wounds as of yet. I can call with my final report."

"No. I will hang. I want to talk to McCarthy anyway. I'll check on your progress periodically. One question…"

"No." She said, reading him quite accurately. "This one is different. I'll explain later. Detective McCarthy said he was going to stick around for a while as well. Bring him back here in a couple of hours."

Jake nodded. It wasn't James Palmer but it seemed too strange of a coincidence for it to be a completely separate situation. Two body part trophy takers? He supposed there could be a copy-cat killer. Shit, why did everything have to be such a mess? He was so caught up in his thoughts that Doobie startled him enough to make him jerk a little. She stared hard at him a Moment, a little smile curling one corner of her mouth. He leaned against the wall and stared back.

She finally filled him in on everything she had found then moved to a corner where she had a full view of both exits and the entire room. She would stand exactly there for as long as Abero was present. It never failed to impress him how much endurance such a small package contained.

Chapter 39

Well that had been fun. And rewarding. So rewarding. The screams echoed loudly around the sterile room, fulfilling in a way that couldn't easily be explained or described.

No mess to clean up, either. Extra bonus. The autopsy table was designed with a drain so the blood had just flowed right out. The brilliance of the idea was a satisfying boost to Blake's ego.

Too bad the others would have to die elsewhere. Maybe at the shipyard in one of those big containers. Perhaps a satanic ritual in a cemetery. Change things up a bit.

It was a little strange to collect body parts. Added a touch of danger to it actually, the threat of being caught seemed stronger somehow. But it wasn't for Blake to decide. That was a favor to the man who made it all possible.

Blake had already chosen one lovely lady. Now they needed one more. The hunt had lost its appeal after the near disaster at the college. How no one had seen was beyond amazing. Best not be that brazen again.

What about that know-it-all doctor? Yes! Why the hell not Zoey Abero? The way she had comforted the lab rat, as though some sort of mother figure.

How ironic if she were splayed out on one of her own autopsy tables? No. Can't do that, no matter how great it would be. But wait, there was another spot that would be perfect!

Decision made, Blake drove away from the Medical Examiner's building feeling quite accomplished.

Chapter 40

0530 Thursday

Jake pulled out a Quest protein bar, and started chewing it as he ran. The protein bar advertised itself as tasting like chocolate and peanut butter, Jake didn't think it tasted like either one, not really, but it would do. Unconsciously he slowed his pace, and realizing that he could eat and run at the same time he increased his pace again to the one he'd achieved moments ago.

Running hard, pushing himself. His legs burned, and his breathing attested his pace. Sweat plastered his t-shirt to his chest, and the perspiration darkened the fabric of his outer sweatshirt. Move it! He coached himself.

As he ran many thoughts zipped through his mind. How to cut business costs? Did they pay too much for electricity? Could they use another, cheaper service? What about internet service, could that cost be lowered? He'd put Matt on that. Let him do the research.

Matt really should take that little waitress out. Matt with his curly brown hair, women had to find him attractive, and his addictive smile. In addition to his good looks, he was one of the kindest, best people Jake knew. Not that he didn't also piss Jake off, they were brothers. Matt should take the waitress out, she deserved to be introduced to a Corde brother. Jake needed to give Matt shit for being shy.

Cutting company costs, just part of business. Business was business. The company turned a profit, a decent profit, but if they decreased overhead, they could increase their profit margin. Not to mention new accounts. Finances and Matt made him think of Mom.

He loved his mother more than anything. Why did he need to worry and procrastinate before he called her? Because, a Mom never stopped being a Mom, never stopped fretting about, and wanting the best for her children. Therein lay the answer, ev-

ery time he called her, he felt like he was ten years old again. So
be it, he would never stop being her son either. But now that
he knew the answer, he would call with the knowledge that he
wasn't a little boy anymore.

Next his brain went to the case. He needed to stop these
killers. He had a gut feeling that the one who manipulated Palmer
still lived in the shadows. He would find the son of a bitch, even if
the police department severed his services as a consultant at this
point. He would bring the criminal in, and the police department
would continue to utilize the Corde brothers' services in the future.

A blonde ran by. He turned his head and watched her ass
bounce. She wasn't as hot as Zoey. Zoey, smoking hot, super intelligent. Oh fuck, now he was comparing. No woman could even
touch Zoey. Maybe he should invite the M.E. for a morning run.
Innocent enough, and then he could look at her. Your intentions
are not noble Mr. Corde, he told himself. Fuck you, he answered
himself. He wanted her, so what?

Work, women! Better finish this run, he had work to do. A
quick glance left at the next intersection and Jake put on a burst
of speed to cross over. He would take this street down a block
and return to the office a different route than the one he had just
taken.

The sweat trickled down his spine in spite of the cool
fall air. The sound of his running shoes slapping the pavement
mingled with his rhythmic breathing. In through the nose, out
through the mouth. Small puffs of white accompanied each ex-
hale. Chilly indeed.

Always when he ran Jake felt hypersensitive to his surroundings. The temperature, yes, but more than that. He could
assimilate the smells, like the bakery, the coffee shop, gasoline,
and if the wind was just right, even Lake Michigan. The sounds
around him too, birds chirping, squirrels chittering, vehicles rev-
ving.

It was this hypersensitivity that saved his life. The instinct
to duck off the bike path and onto the sidewalk. Not a moment
too soon as a motorcycle sped by and a square tire iron glanced off

his shoulder.

The power of the attack knocked him into a blue mailbox, stunning him for a heartbeat. His entire left side burst into pain and his arm went limp and painfully numb, like he had lain on it all night and it had gone to sleep. Pins and needles. Nails and ice picks, more like.

Forcing the pain back he caught himself up and dashed into the street for a view of the disappearing motorcycle. Son of a bitch. No plate. Well of course not. Stupid to think it would be that simple.

That he was meant to die was in no way questionable. If he had ignored the sound of the approaching bike he would have suffered a crushed skull. There was no doubt in his mind that it was connected to the investigation that had just been closed.

It was not pleasurable to know that he had been right. He would not be crowing 'I told you so' to the team. They were being targeted. Victor, Zoey's stalker, now this.

He pulled his phone out and called Matt then McCarthy. It wasn't easy with all of the people now surrounding him, asking him questions left and right, offering help to the hospital or help making calls. If he wasn't in so much pain, he would have felt warmed by the outpouring of care by these strangers. There were a few good people left in the world, but being in pain dimmed that fact.

His third call was to Doobie. He kept it short and sweet. "Keep her in until I get there."

McCarthy could warn the other members of the team. It didn't seem unreasonable to think they might also be in danger. They should take precautions with their families. The world wasn't as kind as it once was.

After giving a somber McCarthy a report on the scene Matt took him to the emergency room. Several hours later he walked out with his left arm in a sling, a prescription for some decent but not awe inspiring pain killers and a hairline fracture in his scapula.

Lucky for him it hadn't been a bigger weapon like a bat. Lucky for him it had been a glancing blow and he was muscular.

He didn't feel lucky. He felt angry.

His first stop was Zoey's. He hoped this would finally get her to understand the true danger of their situation. Maybe she would see the sense in having Doobie there for protection and stop chafing so much.

Chapter 41

1400

    Matt was driving. Fucking arm. At least he was alive, Jake told himself, considering the alternative was dead. Of course if he had to ride with Matt and his electronic shit music he was going to finish the job the motorcyclist had failed.

    On the bright side, Zoey hadn't been her reserved self. She had shamelessly teased him about his arm. Had she maybe even been flirting with him? No, that didn't make sense. Maybe it made sense, women were always a ball of contradictions. Whatever the case, she had been fun, vibrant, full of life.

    The woman had even agreed with him that having Doobie stay with her for her protection was a sound thing. Her wording, 'It's a prudent arrangement.'

    Time to get back to work, Jake put his mind back into the blackness of the case. What was he missing? He knew he was missing something. Damn it Jake, think!

    Where had he missed a critical clue? It had to be at the Palmer house. His visions started in the little girl's room and then they were interrupted. Back into the darkness, he needed to return to that room.

    "Matt, back to the Palmer house."

    "Again. I thought maybe it was lunch time," Matt grinned.

    "Lunch can wait, we are working on a case. Right now it is a losing battle. We can't make any more mistakes. We are not going to lose the war."

    "Can't you hear my stomach? It sounds like a monster truck show."

    "What did you say?" Jake feigned hard of hearing.

    "I said…"

    "I heard you. Since when have you thought with your stomach? Could it be since meeting a certain little waitress with pink hair? By the way, I think you're chicken shit. Shy Little Matt, can't ask the waitress out? You need to find out if she cooks, take care of that stomach of yours."

"I'll drive there right now!"

"No you won't! Palmer house, go."

"I am. Calm down. See, you see Zoey and you're all tied in knots. Mom's cards are always right."

Jake growled, turned the radio volume up violently. The thump, thump of drums and the electronic dub-step filled the small car, rattling the windows. Anything was better than Matt going on and on about Mom and her omniscient Tarot cards.

Thankfully it didn't take very long to reach the Palmer house. Jake practically fell out of the car in his haste to escape. His body from brain to toes felt the beat of excessive drums. He was pretty sure he had acquired tinnitus in the twenty minute ride.

The bedroom seemed so small when both men stood looking down at Amy Palmer's little furniture. The silence stretched on, neither man willing to put voice to their thoughts. Jane Corde had always said, "Don't give evil a foothold by throwing negativity into the universe."

Jake finally took his jacket off, hung it on the headboard and stretched out on the mattress. The springs creaked in protest. A child's bed wasn't usually built to withstand one hundred and eighty pounds of muscled man.

Cradling his arm Jake stared up at the white ceiling. If he ever had a little girl he would build her a princess bed with a canopy and flowing curtains. He would put soft white string lights all around so there were no scary shadows.

The thought no more than flickered through his mind than the images came hard and fast, almost violent. A red Jaguar. A door that opens to stairs going down. Two huge oak trees standing sentry at the mouth of a long driveway. A man's hand brushing a little girl's pink cheek.

As quickly as they came the visions were gone, leaving Jake feeling sluggish and hollow. So goddamn vague! What the hell good was two oak trees? How many houses had basement steps? Slowly he sat up. He could hear Matt's voice out in the hallway, muted by the closed door. Snatching up his jacket he opened the door and stepped out. He waited for Matt to get off his phone then moved toward the front door.

"While you were napping McCarthy was being officially signed into his new post, some of the trace evidence from the second murder came in and the motorcycle used in the attack against you was found between two port-a-potties at a construction site down by the beach."

Jake grinned. "Jeez. A guy can't close his eyes for five minutes? Let me guess, all the trace was Palmers, the bike was stolen, and McCarthy wants to see me because his boss wants me to back off and let the police handle the missing little girl?"

"That's why you are the master detective my brother. Your turn."

Jake shook his head. "Nothing so easy. Oak trees, basement steps, a red car and a man's hand. I think the hand was brushing hair off Amy Palmer's cheek."

"Could have been her dad." Matt said.

"Could." Jake agreed.

"Can we go eat now? I'm so hungry my stomach thinks my throat's been cut." Matt complained.

Chapter 42

1800

Zoey started her Renault. An early night. She put on Schubert's piano Sonata No. 19 in C Minor, D. 958. If Doobie didn't like it, the woman would just have to deal. Driver picks the music, passenger shuts their cakehole.

"Were you flirting with Jake?" Doobie asked.

"Me? Flirt? Do I look like I flirt? I'm a medical doctor, I don't flirt. And if I flirted it would not be with Mr. Serious Detective Jake Corde."

"Bullshit! You were flirting."

"What do you want to eat?" Zoey asked.

"You are asking me?" Doobie asked.

"No, I was asking the Ghost-cat I have in the passenger seat," Zoey laughed.

"Why are you asking me?" Doobie needed to know.

"You're the boss. You want to make something, or am I buying us something? I need to eat. I'm starving, and nobody wants Little Zoey Abero hangry."

"What are you in the mood for?"

"Food. Tiramisu. A man slathered in caramel and spilled whiskey." They both laughed.

"I'll make us steak, mushroom, shrimp, and onion Kabobs that ought to fulfill your order," Doobie said.

"Sold to the French woman's stomach," Zoey said thinking about what wine would pair with kabobs.

1900

The meeting had been very informative. Blake smiled a small smile. So much can be learned when one takes the time to watch and listen to the nuances in another person's voice and actions.

Blake recalled every word of the conversation from earlier.

The secrets he had no idea he had given up. Ammo, just in case things went south. Leverage.

"No! Absolutely not. Zoey Abero is not to be touched. She is mine to kill. Find another."

Well, well, well, what was this? The guy had a soft spot for Dr. Abero? Given, it was a soft spot with a catch. Zoey Abero was going to die. Probably horribly. But with love?

"Actually, I just had a great idea. Do the Regina girl, then the doctor's new roommate. She can be your final one. That will give me the room I need to catch Zoey and finish my project."

Blake glanced at the basement door, spine tingling with unease. This guy was too damn weird. Who kept body parts like that? And with the intention of building his own monster? A modern day, female Frankenstein? NO. Too, too off the charts crazy.

Did he really think he could animate it? Or did he just want a half flesh, half bones body to...to what? It made Blakes' skin crawl. The killing was fun, entertaining. Blake got that. The rest? Not at all.

It was time to go shopping for some supplies. A mood had to be set because, while it was disappointing that the Doc was not going to be Blake's to kill, Regina was and Blake wanted to make things perfect for the occasion.

Blake set up the apartment with painstaking precision. Everything must be set just right. Everything in its place. All precautions in place.

The project was nearly complete. It looked like the set for a pornographic film. The plastic covered the floor. The armchair sat on top of the plastic in the middle of the room, for sexual activities. Sitting in the chair was a bottle of baby oil for slippery naked bodies on the sheet of plastic with more sexual activity. Candles were set around the room on end tables. Two large beer steins and a bottle opener were strategically placed on the coffee table.

Perfect.

Blake placed a duffle bag filled with tools in the corner. One could never have too many tools. Need good tools to do the job properly.

2100

Blake's phone pinged indicating a text message.

"This is Regina from the other day. I could use a study break. What are you doing?" Blush emoji.

Flawless timing, Blake thought.

"Hi Regina. I must admit that I've been waiting for you to get a hold of me. I'm not doing much. Laundry doesn't count, does it?"

"Laundry definitely does not count. Wanna meet at Gimli's?"

"Are you buying?"

"Maybe?"

"Tease. Anything is better than laundry. But you are two-hundred and ten percent better. Maybe that percentage is even a little low? See you in a few."

"See you there."

Blush emoji.

Blake was keyed up. Tonight was cranium night. Blake meticulously packed the car, with everything that might possibly be used. Better to have too much equipment, than not have something. One needed the right tools. The same set of tools were in the duffel bag in the corner. Blake double checked the supplies. Everything in place. Time to dress for success. Once dressed properly, Blake got into the car, started it up and headed toward the weird named bar.

Inside the campus tavern Blake ordered two Arwens and then scanned the place for Regina. She sat at a table oblivious to the world around her. She was engrossed with her phone. Blake walked over, and set the beers down. Regina looked up and smiled a radiant smile.

"Hi. Umm, I thought you wanted me to buy the round," she said.

"You can get the next round," Blake offered.

"Oh, I will," Regina confirmed.

"May I sit?" Blake asked.

"No, I want you to stand there all day," Regina giggled.

Blake took a seat and looked Regina over. Yup, Cranium night! Such a specimen.

"Your hair looks great," Blake opened.

"Really?" Regina asked.

"Really. Five-hundred percent better than laundry. Your lips look very kissable too," Blake complimented. Regina blushed, and tossed her hair with her hands.

"A girls gotta do what a girls gotta do."

Blake raised an Arwen. Regina lifted hers in suit.

"To you," Blake toasted. They clinked beers and drank.

Chapter 43

It was easy to get Regina to leave the bar. She was eager to follow Blake out to the parking lot. Blake felt the excitement building in her.

This was going to be a wild night. The stage had been set with every intention of taking the time to bathe in the power and euphoria. Everything would go without a hitch, of this Blake was sure. A mild sedative in Regina's drink had made her malleable, even agreeable.

Blake escorted Regina to the car, and drove her to the apartment. Inside, two Red Stripes were procured from the fridge. The beers were opened with the bottle opener on the coffee table. The candles were lit, and Spotify played Frank Sinatra.

"That's a lot of plastic Blake." Regina said with a slight slur.

"I know baby, but I want to slather you with oil so bad it makes my hands shake and I just bought the furniture, can you forgive me this once?"

"I'll forgive you. Are we gonna play naked Twister? Are you going to kiss me already?" Regina asked, a little unsteady on her feet. Blake caught her, and led her to the chair.

"First the chair. There are so many things I want to do to you baby. The oil can wait. Place your hands on the arms, like that, yes.

Now hang on tight love, we are going to play a game. If you let go of the chair, I stop. You look so amazing. Let me help you out of your top."

Stripping Regina out of her entire outfit was easy. The girl didn't even notice when Blake used a knife to cut the side of the skirt to make it slide off a little easier. Regina's skin was soft and warm and smelled of lavender.

Blake's gut tightened in sexual response. Arousal, desire, no stopping it. The heightened sense of the moment, adrenaline flooding the body.

Those feelings were only the tip of the iceberg though, under the water a massive chunk of ice lurked ready to surface like a leviathan. That was the thrill, the power of taking another human's life.

First though, some fun, some pleasure. If the girl had to die, at least she would die satisfied in a most primal way. Blake bent down and took a rich pink nipple between sharp white teeth and pulled.

The sound of Regina's gasp was all the encouragement Blake needed to turn it up a notch. From one breast to another a path was drawn in hot kisses and laving tongue. Blake was no fool. The ascendency that sexual energy could raise a soul was mind bending.

Blake licked upward, running the tongue along the hollow of Regina's throat, and kissed her. Her lips trembled and eagerly returned the kiss. Regina's hands wrapped around Blake's body attempting to dislodge clothing.

Blake slapped the hands away. "No, no, don't forget the rules."

"But I want you naked too!" Regina protested.

Blake smiled at the woman then pulled her back into a good position. "You just get comfy, Baby, I'm going to lick you till you scream for mercy. This is going to kill you."

"Yes please. Please." Regina gasped as Blake sat down and pulled Regina's bottom to the edge of the chair. She cried out when Blake put tongue to work drawing across her quivering woman's core with quick, raspy licks.

Blake continued to work. Up and down the sides of the woman's pleasure center, and teasing the tip of it with flicks of the tongue. Regina's body responded with uncontrollable bucks, and she moaned like a wolf romancing the moon.

At the peak of Regina's orgasm, Blake, in a movement so fast Regina didn't stand a chance to fight back, flipped the chair to its back, taped Regina's hands and feet to the piece of furniture and stood over her smiling down. The bound girl looked up myopically. Blake put a finger to mouth and made a shushing sound. "Don't worry Baby, I'm not done. I just wanted to make it a little more interesting. Comfy?"

"Wh, what are you going to do next?" Regina whispered. "This will be a night you will never forget Baby," Blake said. Tape again, this time over the suddenly nervous girl's mouth. Out of the duffel bag came the circular bone saw. It's blade glimmered in the candle light.

"Now go ahead and scream all you want Baby, I want to feel it all the way to my toes." The now struggling girl was told. Blake stripped out of her clothes, stuffing them into the duffel bag. Down on knees, naked bottom resting on Regina's face, Blake watched the look of horror come in Regina's eyes. Holding the woman's head between her thighs, both hands brought into view. If she hadn't already been suffocating in Blakes' crotch, the terror might have taken the breath from her lungs.

Blake began to quiver with excitement, admiring the blade of the bone saw. The room grew hot, the sweat trickled down Blake's body, running over Regina, to the plastic beneath. Blake smiled in pleasure. Regina did have the perfect cranium.

She had the perfect scream too, Blake soon discovered. Through the tape it rose above the whine of the saw and the crunch-grind as bone was bit into. The orgasm was building in Blake's nether regions, spinning ever closer as the blade spun on the saw bit.

Pretty red hair tangled around the saw blade then tore out of the scalp as torque proved stronger than flesh. It was so beautiful, the screams of both the victim and saw, the smell of body waste as Regina's organs let go. A precision cut all the way around that perfect skull.

Blake watched as the blood fanned out, a crimson spray of mist formed artwork on the plastic. The orgasm struck with ferocity, taking Blakes breath even as Regina's scream died on her last. Both victim and murderer in tandem.

Blake felt the blood trail down from arms to thighs to plastic. So much blood. That is what the plastic was for, to catch the blood. Blake looked at the splatter pattern. Such artwork. And held the masterpiece in hand, the perfect cranium.

Somehow it felt like that was the door prize. The real prize was the gift Regina had imparted without even knowing it. The release.

Chapter 44

0500, Friday

McCarthy let his thoughts range out for a moment as he got his system ready for the shock of what he was told he would see. A body in the cemetery, satanic ritual. What by all that's holy does that mean? A few candles and an upside down pentagram?

Daylight had not graced Chicago with its presence yet, but the harsh glare of flood lights clearly marked the location Mc-Carthy headed toward. Satanic ritual? It couldn't be, this was modern day Chicago. Well it could be? What was the definition of a Satanic ritual anyway? It could have been teenagers that got carried away playing that old Dungeons and Dragons game too. Maybe it was a sick love triangle that failed out of jealousy. These seemed more feasible ideas.

McCarthy gave a snort of amusement. He was never very good this early in the morning. His flights of fancy were ridiculous at best. Maybe it was a million different things, but the one thing it was, was a murder. A crime scene, and after he had taken a cursory look he would call the Medical Examiner.

He slowed for Detective Anderson as the rookie came hurrying over. He liked the kid. Steady and dependable with a good head on his shoulders. Just what a good cop was supposed to be.

"Morning Lieutenant. The body was discovered by the groundskeeper after someone called him about the broken gate. Apparently a car nearly hit someone as it came out about three hours ago," Anderson brought McCarthy up to speed.

"That would have been about 0230?"

"Correct, Sir."

"Show me what we got," McCarthy instructed the kid.

"Right this way. She's sprawled out in the center of a bunch of candles..."

"Yes, yes. Satanic pentagram. Just show me."

"Well, right over here."

Sure enough, in spite of his silent prayer to the contrary, there she was. Naked as the day she was born. Beautiful girl, shapely, young. At the five points were black candles, melted, no longer burning. One for each foot and hand and the top of the head.

The missing top part of her skull. McCarthy heaved a great sigh of frustration. He was going to have to wake up the Captain. The case just reopened and became seriously complicated.

Calling the Captain wasn't his idea of fun, he would rather crawl around in a pit of vipers. That could wait for a little. He looked at the dead girl. He shook his head, he needed a cup of coffee.

McCarthy walked back over to the corpse. He pulled out his cell phone. He scrolled down the contacts. Captain. C came before D. Dr. Abero. He hit send. The phone rang once, twice.

Three cups later, thanks to Anderson's little coffee run, and a little better lighting gave him far too much to see. He made a judgement call and dialled Jake Corde's number. Ian was fairly certain he knew what was going on here but decided to wait for Dr. Abero to confirm a few things before jumping to any conclusions.

The key to good police work was to not form an opinion until you were sure you had all of the information, and don't voice that opinion until you had seen every alternative to its conclusion, leaving only the one you held. He was also fairly certain he didn't really want to know the truth. Everything would be so much easier if this was teenagers going too far with a stupid game.

Steeling himself he placed the call to the Captain. Whatever the repercussions, the case needed to be reopened. This was the same case, and he felt that they would need to continue Jake Corde's services, even though the penny pinchers didn't want to pay for outside sources.

"I specifically told you…" the captain ranted and raved for a solid minute. Ian held the phone away from his ear. It didn't matter if this cost him his job. He had made the right decision and he would stand behind it. A man had to take a stance and dig in his heels. It was how he stayed a man.

"Sorry boss," he finally interrupted the barrage of angry demands. "I already called him. I want him on this with me. You can of course fire me, that is your prerogative. For now however, I have a job to do."

"Prerogative. McCarthy, you are on thin ice. Why don't you high tail it back to the station."

"Sir?"

"You heard me. I did not stutter."

"On my way," McCarthy ended the call. He turned to Zoey. "Dr. Abero, tell Jake Corde that I believe in him, and I believe in our task force. I believe in them so much that I may lose my job over it. I will stand my ground that Jake works this case. I'll be in touch with you."

Ian climbed into his car and headed to the station ready to do battle. Come hell or high water this was the last goddamn time he left a fucking crime scene because of politics. The Captain was going to cave or pull him off the case but this argument was over today.

His large frame would have broken the glass in the doors if not for the air pumps that prevented them from slamming, as he stormed into the station. He didn't even notice Dr. Abernathy sitting on the couch in the Captain's office as he walked right in without bothering to knock.

"Let me tell you something right now Cap. I'm done explaining myself to you on this subject. You harassed the fuck out of Vincent and I'll be damned if you pull that stunt with me. Yes you are my boss, but I am good at what I do and you better back off and let me do it. This isn't the only precinct in Chicago or the only police force in the States. Get past your ego, your dollar signs and your promotions and let's do some goddamn good in this city for once!"

"McCarthy, have a seat."

Chapter 45

0620 Friday

Jake and Matt walked the aisle between headstones. The main driveway was only ten or so grave sites from where Zoey knelt in the grass and leaves. Fallen leaves, now turned brown, littering the ground like age spots. Fallen leaves, fallen bodies. Next to her another figure was working with what appeared to be a sandbox shovel and rake.

It seemed an odd place to commit a murder when the cemetery's back end was deep in the surrounding woods. Many, many better places for concealment and privacy. Was she meant to be found quickly?

He took note of the number of people on the site and frowned slightly. Anderson and the other men on the task force were here, huddled together like nestlings. It had been McCarthy who had called him, so where was the Lieutenant?

"Matt, go find out where McCarthy is, will ya?"

"He had to go." Zoey spoke. "Said something about believing in everything and took off. He did not sound very happy. Hello Matt, how's it going?" Zoey didn't bother looking up from her examination. "You should check this out Jake."

Jake squatted down next to the doctor giving a whistle of surprise. "Whaaaaat? The skull is gone."

"Technically just the cranium bone and hair. The rest of the skull is there."

"How is that distinction relevant?"

"He already has the mandible. Now the cranium. The upper jaw up to the forehead is here." She gestured to the point just above the eyebrows. " I can't help wondering why he didn't take the whole skull in the first place. Either way, there isn't much left before he has his entire body."

"Shit. So you think it is the same case, just a new perpetrator."

"I do, yes. McCarthy does too. The guy behind the scene has found himself a new killer to get his parts for him."

Jake leaned over a little for a better view of the hole. "Where are her brains?"

"They fell out." Zoey pointed to where a forensic nerd was squatting next to her.

"That's just freaking wrong." He rasped.

"It probably happened when she was dumped."

"Have you gotten any visions yet?"

"No, but there is a reason for that, I believe." Now she meets his eyes. "This isn't the scene of the murder. It's staged. Very nicely, except for that," she points to the guy next to her again, "but staged."

"What brings you to that conclusion?"

"No blood for one. There would have been blood everywhere with this kind of death. Even with no flow, in the autopsy room, when we remove the cranium there is a spray of blood and bone chips."

"Okaaay. Nuff with the details doc."

She shrugged. "Don't ask questions you don't want the answer to. The other reason I believe this was not done here is because the cut was made with a stryker saw. Do you see an electrical outlet around here anywhere? The killer would have had to haul a generator along with the saw. Rather ungainly.

The third reason I think it was done elsewhere is her ankles, wrists and mouth were all taped recently, but there is no tape here. See the strain marks where she fought the bindings? Look at the back of the ankles, no marks. Now look at the wrists, again a gape where the tape didn't touch flesh. She was taped to a chair. See one here?"

"Damn Dr. Abero, your brilliance is going to make me lose my head!" Matt spoke from above.

Jake and Zoey both looked up. Jake with annoyance. Zoey with a grin.

"Why thank you baby Corde. At least when you speak your brains don't spill out." She winked.

"No, but you're so sexy in that full body suit, if you stand up, I might lose my mind." Matt air smooched at her.

"Oh, this old thing?" Zoey gestured at the white uniform from hoodie to booties, laying on the southern drawl. "Why honey, I just threw on the first thing I came across. My mind wasn't in it."

"Alright you two. Christ. Have some reverence." Jake growled. "What else can you tell me Doctor Abero?"

"That you're a fuddy duddy?" Doobie said from a few feet away.

Zoey stifled a laugh and put herself back into work mode. "One final thing at this time. I'm pretty sure the girl was still alive when the cutting began."

"What the hell? How do you know that? How long would a person live through that?"

"I really don't know. I suspect. Autopsy will reveal the truth. And as to your last question, actually, it depends on too many variables. I would think they would pass out fairly quickly, but that's a guess. I can find out once I'm back at the lab and can consult with other examiners. I've never seen this kind of thing before. I admittedly feel ignorant to some extent." Zoey nodded to the technicians and walked away, pulling off her gloves and mask.

"It seems to me that the body part guy has found himself someone with more sophistication than James Palmer. More knowledge of anatomy and the tools needed to surgically remove specific parts." Zoey said as they drew further from the corpse and forensic team. "I hate the fact that this guy is loose. He is just as responsible as the ones killing for him."

"I agree with you Zoey." Jake lifted his hands in a defensive position. He took note of Matt's grin as he leaned against a tree some feet behind Zoey's back.

Doobie stood out of earshot to the left. Jake could feel her vibrating energy from here. She was anxious. He understood that feeling. They were exposed here, wide open for attack. These outdoor settings made good bodyguards supremely nervous.

"Sorry." Zoey apologized for her angry tone. "My sugar is too low, I haven't had food yet this morning. I will let you know the results of my findings once I get the body back to the morgue and perform an autopsy." Zoey's voice brought his attention back to her face.

"I know you will. And I know you are chafing at the bit to get rid of your shadow. I very much appreciate the level of co-operation you are exerting. Now, I think Matt and I need to find McCarthy and get some stuff tidied up. I had a vision yesterday. Remember I told you I was going back to Palmers?"

"Yes. Was it helpful?"

"No, not one little bit. Yet. Who knows in an hour or a day or a month?"

"God don't let this hang on that long. I can't wait to get back to my normal humdrum heart attacks and strokes."

"I feel you Doc." Jake sighed.

"In my dreams." Zoey whispered as she walked back toward the body.

"What was that?" Jake was sure he had heard wrong. He was tired of this woman tying him up in knots.

"In your dreams, Jake Corde, in your dreams." She just kept right on walking.

Chapter 46

2100 Friday

Long days were something she was quite used to. Long days without Kellesha to help was a different story altogether. The pre-med student had been doing her internship with Zoey for two years now and they had established a working pattern that ran like a well oiled machine.

Mais, c'est la vie. There was nothing she could do about it. Kellesha had not taken a murder in their sanctuary well at all. She needed a couple of days.

For once Zoey was grateful for Bea Dooberman's presence. The bodyguard was a very good driver and Zoey had no problem relinquishing control of her car. She leaned her head back on the seat rest, closed her eyes, and let the purr of the Renault lull her into a catnap.

It made the trip home seem instantaneous. The down side was that now she felt lethargic. That was ok though. A hot shower and soft bed was moments away.

Groggily she followed her roommate to her door and into the apartment. She looked over at the kitchen longingly but chose shower and bed. Hopefully the killer took a rest because Zoey was exhausted from the last two weeks. Aside from the normal daily activity this serial killing was mind numbingly draining.

The shower was as amazing as Zoey had hoped. She stood under the spray and just let the hot water beat on her shoulders and run down her body to the drain. It did not take her worries with it, but there was a loosening of tight muscles. A soothing quality nothing else compared to.

Her head still ached a little, she realized. And she was hungry. A glass of wine sounded wonderful. But once dry and in flannel jammies she fell onto the queen sized mattress, unwilling to walk the twenty or so steps to the kitchen. Sleep claimed her quickly.

0005

It seemed like ten minutes but was actually three hours later Zoey woke to the sound of her phone. She rolled over and pulled a pillow over her head. It worked. The persistent annoyance stopped.

No more did a sigh of relief pass her lips than Bea Dooberman was yanking the pillow off her head. "Get up NOW." She whispered harshly.

"What the hell?"

"Shut up!" The woman hissed. "Matt called. Someone is trying to break in. They jimmied the lock."

"Oh shit!" Zoey leaped from the bed, then came up close to but not touching her bodyguard's back.

Doobie leaned back, turned her head, "Steady your breathing Doc."

Lord, wasn't that easier said than done. Adrenaline swamped her system, blood pumped through veins by a heart that was cranking 180 bpm. Slowing her breathing didn't seem very important right now but if Bea said do it, then she would do it.

Inhale through the nose, out through the mouth, count to ten. That was when she realized how quiet Doobie's breathing was compared to her own rasping, throaty exhales. Terrific, she was a beacon in the dark.

Dark. Pitch black actually. All of the drapes were pulled. The clock on the stove was out. The guest bathroom night light was off. Doobie had worked fast.

Finally she felt the bodyguard move out the bedroom door, to the right. Bookcase against wall. Couch five feet out from there. She was gently pulled down to the floor behind the large piece of furniture.

The interminable waiting was nerve wracking to say the least. Zoey was about to say something when suddenly there was a high pitched siren sound that pierced the ears. She felt Doobie move.

In an instant the lights came on and Zoey heard yelling. Jumping to her feet she ran to escape the very loud alarm as much as it was to catch her bodyguard who was pelting for the front door. Bea Dooberman stopped at the alarm box, punched in a sequence, then stared hard out the door for a moment, before closing it.

"They ran." She huffed, sounding angry the intruder hadn't stayed to play.

Zoey nodded. "Why didn't you follow?"

Bea frowned. "Could have been a ploy to get you alone. I told you, I won't leave your side willingly until this is done or I am dead."

Ten minutes later a loud banging on the door alerted them to Jake's and Matt's arrival, followed a few moments after by McCarthy. Zoey was touched by everyone's concern. But she was more irritated. For a quiet living girl this was too damn much attention.

"So," she finally broke into the many conversations happening around her. "Now that the gang's all here, I want to thank Matt for the amazing security. Those alarms obviously work." Matt grinned at her. "My pleasure. Can't have the world renowned Zoey Abero in danger, now can we?"

"What do we know?" She asked.

"Actually, almost nothing." He grimaced. "The perp approached your door wearing a ski mask and heavy clothing at 0004. The key alarm went off a few seconds later."

"When can we get the camera footage from the building?" She asked.

A moment of uncomfortable silence, Jake coughed a little. "Well, we already have it. We tapped the building's feed when Doobie came to stay. There is a camera at the far end of the hall." Jake admitted.

Zoey nodded, turned on her heel and went into her bedroom, shutting the door firmly behind her. This shit better end soon or she was going to end up behind bars with the killer. She climbed into bed, pulled the covers over her head and shut out the world.

It meant working harder to solve this case. She would have to ride the lab for results quicker. Study the reports harder.
All serial killers had a pattern didn't they? Sure they did. The dif-

ference here was there were two serial killers led by a manipulator or leader. That kind of thing changed the dynamics a bit.

0045

Jake watched the door close and fought the urge to follow her. She had looked haggard and afraid and angry. He wanted to comfort her. He was fairly sure she would not accept his overtures.

So, he turned to Doobie. "Great job tonight Dooberman."

"She did good too. Followed my orders, didn't bitch. She's smart. But she's near the end of her tether boss. She hates my intrusion in her home. Hates the circumstances. Hates not feeling safe."

"I know." Jake rubbed his forehead. "Is everyone on the same page?" He looked around at the three others. They responded with nods.

"I doubt he'll stop, even after this setback." Doobie spoke up. "If he can't get her here, he will figure out another way. He wants her."

"M.E. parking lot?" Matt asked.

"That or the parking garage here. Only two places other than a crime scene."

"Too many people at crime scenes. Let's put two men in each of the two parking places for the hours she will be working. I won't even bother asking her to stay home. We know where that will lead."

"I sure wish we had more to go on." McCarthy shook his head sadly.

"Me too. Just keep an eye and ear out for a red Jaguar. That's the best I have right now."

"What did you say?" Matt asked.

"That's the best I've got. Oh, red Jaguar."

"Why didn't you say something sooner?"

"I did."

"No you said red car. I didn't make the connection. There was a red Jag in the M.E. parking lot the other day when I was taking my turn at keeping an eye on the Doc. The guy was just sitting there watching her leave."

McCarthy cleared his throat.

"What?" Jake asked him.

"I don't know. It's a nag in the back of my head. I'll have to get back with you on it. You guys all do your thing. We will get together with the task force in the morning and try to make sense of it all."

"Alright. Well, Matt's going to camp here on the couch for the rest of the night. I will be at the office if you need anything." He should stay, he knew, but he wouldn't be able to stop himself from checking on her, there in her bedroom.   Not a good idea.

Chapter 47

0530

Blake cursed soundly all the way back to the house. What a botched fucking effort that had been! A goddamn shit show on every level. Almost getting caught had definitely not been part of the plan.

Whose brilliant idea had that insane alarm system been? That was a no-brainer. It had Corde Investigations written all over it. Probably their idea of a joke. Ha Ha. Very not funny guys. The alarm had not been the usual silent type. Ten seconds after entering the apartment the equivalent of a microphone too close to a speaker had sounded. The screeching siren had nearly burst Blake's eardrums.

In fact they were still ringing. No, wait, that was the phone. "Yes?"

"Well?"

"A very loud alarm system. Probably woke up the whole building, if not the entire neighborhood. Pretty sure the cameras got me. Don't worry though, I was disguised. They won't even be able to tell gender.

I don't think the apartment is going to be a viable place to catch the bodyguard off her game. That leaves the garage, the Medical Examiners parking lot, where there are cameras every-where, plus they added a couple more rent-a-cops since the body was found there, and the road between the two. I spent enough time watching to know there are plenty of places a team could take the two on the road."

"No, no more people involved. Just you."

"Things are escalating too fast. We need to slow down a bit, take stock of what's happening around us. What are the cops doing? It's going to be really hard to get them at the same time. I have no doubt Corde is going to double the doctor's guards after this."

"Just get it done, both of them." The voice was pretty close to the same decibel as the alarm had been. "We are out of time. Tonight or you will spend the rest of your miserable life in mortal agony inflicted by your own hand."

Blake cursed again, hanging up the phone. Bastard. Nothing like not giving a shit about your flunkies. Head pounding, ears ringing, Blake went over the options again.

Things were looking more and more bleak for the future. It was almost a sure thing Blake was not going to come out of this on top. What could be done to rectify this situation? To change the odds?

0532

Well, this morning had been a setback, true enough. But he had faith in Blakes ability to adapt and overcome. He hung up the phone and wandered down the hallway to the back of the house. It was a much travelled path as the basement was his favorite room in the rambling old mansion.

The lock responded with a quiet snick as he turned the key. Twenty four steps down. It was quite a few, he knew and the reason was impossible to discern. The staircase had been there when he bought the place. The light barely managed to illuminate the steps and the base.

At the bottom there was another light toggle. This one cast bright relief over a room straight out of a horror film. Things no man should have in his possession floated in jars of liquid along three walls.

A larger glass vat sat in the back of the room. A naked woman, missing her legs and part of her pelvis rested on a pedestal of sorts, her body frozen, her eyes staring. A fissure snaked along her lower jaw. Closer examination revealed several such cracks all over the body. She was falling apart. In a ritual months in the making he walked to her and placed a hand against the glass.

She had been beautiful once. Her skin; smooth, soft and warm. She had been strong both in body and mind too. So vivacious and alive.

A lone tear tracked down his gaunt cheek as the memories flooded in. Her in a long trained white wedding dress all frothy with lace. The veil as he lifted it away to reveal full, red lips, ready with a smile and a kiss.

Unconsciously he rubbed his breast bone. The memories always brought pain there. But he didn't try to stop them. It was all he had of her right now. The memories.

The vacations they had taken! Her, posing in front of the leaning tower of Piza as though she were holding it up. What a prankster she was.

And the time she had come home from the store with pink and cream cloth and paint. She was planning a child's bedroom. Curtains, throw rugs, wall paper. The whole shebang. That was why little Amy had a room to come to. Lily had gotten it ready years ago.

Then tragedy. She had become exceedingly lethargic, thirsty, and weak. Diabetes. They had tried everything except the diet. She loved her food.

She had cut her foot one day, put a bandaid on it and went about her usual everyday life. It became infected so quickly she hadn't realized it until it was too late. First the toe, then the foot, then the leg.

That was when he made his decision. He would find a way to save her. He was a highly intelligent man. He would give his wife her life back.

It took longer than he had thought. She lost part of her pelvis and hip. He finally just brought her home. She had been resting in the nitrogen for a couple of months now.

There hadn't been any choice. She would have continued to rot away while he did his research. He would have lost her forever.

He had worked out what needed to happen, then set Palmer to work. The original intention had been to just grab a body and do the organ switch. However, the test run with Palmer had been a little more destructive than planned. Somehow he couldn't quite get Palmer to make a smooth kill.

So he switched gears, he was no medical doctor but body

parts were body parts and once they were all assembled it would be fine. If Palmer was going to destroy when he killed, then he would have to make due. It did no good to cry over spilled milk. He knew there was a time limit on the validity of body parts once removed from the flow of blood so that put more stress on the situation. But he was close now. So very close.

He was confident that soon he would have everything he needed to give his beautiful Lily Beth a second chance. To give them both a second chance. He had even found them a daughter to adore and spoil.

He just needed to get all of the parts ready, assemble them, then thaw her out and put her organs in place. The last piece would be her brain. That wonderful, most important part that was his lovely Lily.

He took a deep breath, wiped the tears from his face and gave the glass a last, loving caress. It was time to get the equipment ready and the blood for transfusions. His Lily was going to need a little blood no doubt.

The light snapped off as he tapped the switch. The room disappeared in blessed darkness once again, where it belonged. His steps were measured and steady as he ascended.

As he passed the pink door he heard little Amy inside the room crying her eyes out. He might have to employ a sedative again. She had not been as receptive as he had thought she would be.

He couldn't imagine wanting James and Katie for parents but the little girl was having some issues with homesickness. It was unfortunate but not tragic. She would get over it as soon as his Lily showed the little girl how wonderful life with them as her parents would be.

It was going to be a truly beautiful thing to behold, their little family. Maybe they would get Amy a kitten. Yes. Girls liked kittens, didn't they?

He congratulated himself on having the brilliance to deal with all of life's little upsets.

Chapter 48

0510 Saturday

Jake pushed himself harder. His muscles were already screaming, but they could take more. Sweat poured down his neck. Faster. Now think, get inside this killer's head? Where would he strike next? Zoey said he didn't need many more body parts. Jake was no expert on anatomy, but arms and pelvis, and the other bones of the skull were needed depending on what the twisted fuck might already have.

Need to stop this nightmare. Jake reviewed the case in his head. He knew that Matt and McCarthy were working on it, how many red Jaguars in the Chicago area? Why didn't his vision allow him to see the plate? It didn't work that way. Sometimes he wanted to be able to bring parts of the visions into sharper focus. That would be something, if he could hone the visions to see more specific details.

 The task force meeting was at 0745, Jake figured that McCarthy set the meeting at a three quarter hour as an incitement tool for everyone to remember when it was, verus it being on the half hour or whole hour. Jake's frustration level had not dropped, it continued to rise. He wanted to chase this killer on foot, catch him, and beat the shit out of him to the point of death and then bring him to the police.

Jake finished his run, and took a shower. He took his time shaving, making sure the razor didn't miss any facial hair. Next Jake dressed in one of his professional suits. He liked this suit, it had been a gift from Alex. Slate gray with green pinstripes. Alex said something like Jake needed all the help he could get. Fuck you very much, Alex! Of the brothers Alex was the clothes horse, and this suit would bring out Jake's eyes.

In truth, Jake had always admired Alex's dress sense. His brother made each day's circumstances a stage. How many jurors were women/men made his suit choice change, dates, casual or formal, where was he taking the girl? Was he having dinner with just Mom or the whole family? Alex dressed the way he lived, big, beautiful, strong.

That was what Jake envied and admired. His brothers were all special in their own way, but Alex was a whole new level. Jake always felt like a smudge on the nose next to Alex, in the looks department.

Jake sat down at his desk, and turned on the computer. He started hunting for information. One site was looking for red Jaguar owners, even though Matt could do it faster, he was still running his own search. He had another search engine running criminal psychology, and a third and forth site researching classical music and wines; not that Zoey enjoyed those things, maybe Jake Corde could learn something? There wasn't time for this right now. As he shut down a few windows, glancing, he saw the icons for running the business. Jake hated running the business, that is what Luke did. Luke had the mind for it. He needed to call his brother, he dialed the number.

Luke could see patterns that would make up a whole. He was a visionary, and he ran the business like he was solving a jigsaw puzzle, he just saw where the pieces fit and placed them correctly. He had a nose for investing that kept a continuous income feeding the company. Jake found it amazing and comforting that his brother ran that aspect of the company, but it was also boring. Luke himself wasn't boring, just the work. Luke had a firm handshake, and a manly laugh. Luke liked fishing, and smoking cigars. Jake wondered how Peggy put up with that. So unhealthy and foul.

"What's the good news?" Luke answered.

"I wish I had some. Luke, you didn't hear me say this, but I need you. I can't do my job and effectively run the business," Jake admitted.

"You stubborn mule. It just so happens that I can do most of my job, right here, from my phone," Luke said. Jake could picture his brother grinning like a jackass. Jake didn't normally ask for help, but Jake also was smart enough to let others utilize the skills they excelled at in those areas.

"Will Peggy be pissed?"

"Peggy is itching to get back to work even more than I am.
I was hoping you would have said, 'all wrapped up, come home.'
How is that little number you're hot on?"

"Shut up! All of you, really? I am going to kill Matt."

"Matt does have a big mouth, but he is so cute. Besides
he is my brother too, if anyone is going to kill him, it's going to
be me. Do you know what he did? The brilliant little shit, set up
a whole new security system around our company computers. I
couldn't even access my own shit. Had to call him and get a new
passcode."

"That is why Matt is our security nerd." They both
laughed. "Okay I need to get to the police station. I'll call you
soon with good news. If you could..."

"I got you Bro," Luke said.

"Smoke a big cigar." That was a relief, now Jake could stop
worrying about that stuff, and devote himself to what he did best,
investigating and action.

"Catch the killers. I miss my own bed."

"Copy that." They hung up.

0637

Zoey studied her reflection in the mirror. Just no erasing
the unsightly scar. Just when she tried to make herself look good.
She had already reapplied her makeup three times to get the right
shading on her cheeks and eyelashes. Fucking scar. There was
no point in makeup, no amount of it would cover her blemish. No
amount of normal makeup anyway, she could use stage makeup.
Zoey laughed, what use was trying to look good? Was she trying to
impress Jake? If she answered that question honestly the answer
was yes.

Zoey brushed her teeth and turned to her closet. She
shuddered thinking about the pervert using her shirt. Eww! She
should bring all of her clothes to the dry cleaners, just for peace of
mind. She put dry cleaners on her mental to-do list; wondering if
they still charged by the pound to do a 'wash and fold?'

What to wear? Did that matter either? It is not like Jake

hadn't seen her in that white suit Matt pointed out. She was a medical examiner and that meant that most of the time she wore the white suit, or a lab coat with other protective gear. But she was a human being too, what if she wanted to be viewed as something different than an astronaut?

Matt, who had mentioned her white astronaut suit was cute, but he was not Jake. What was it about Jake Corde anyway? Arrogant ass! Arrogant ass with a nice ass, and eyes like liquid peridot.

"Merde!"

Zoey decided to dress the way she wanted anyway. You only live once. She put on her non-funeral black dress and looked at herself in the mirror. It was a great dress. It showed enough cleavage to distract any male with a pulse, and it covered her ass, but left a little to the imagination. Just enough to tantalize. It made her hair, eyes, and lips pop. She smiled looking at her hair, eyes, and lips. If those features weren't enough the man wasn't worth his salt anyway.

She picked out the black shoes with the criss crossed straps. Yes. The right shoes to complete the outfit. Time to go to work. They needed to wrap this case up, so she could get rid of Bea, and get back to drinking wine in peace. She needed to be able to run in the morning, getting exercise equipment inside the apartment wasn't going to happen.

"You look ravishing. Are you going to a task force meeting or the club?" Doobie asked.

"The meeting sounded boring, I'm going to the club."

"I'd wear that shit all the time if I looked like you."

"Thanks, I guess," Zoey said thinking again of her scar.

1345 Florence, Italy

"How is it?" Ilaria asked.

"Have I told you today what a great cook you are?" Alex said.

"Stop it, we are eating lunch with your mother."

"I can't compliment your cooking?"

"That's not what I meant, and you know it," Ilaria flashed

Alex a mischievous look.

"You have truly surpassed yourself, Ilaria. These are the best meatballs I've ever tasted. And I've tasted a plethora of meatballs. The noodles, the sauce, wow just wow," Jane Corde said.

"Can't take the Italian out of me," Ilaria beamed.

Chapter 49

McCarthy paced. The I.T. tech finished setting up the computer. Nobody had arrived yet, they better not be late. One more cup of coffee. He poured one, and waited for the task force to assemble.

Greg Anderson, Adam Jackson, and Jesus Sanchez all entered the room. Anderson looked ragged. McCarthy made the mental note that he'd pulled an all night shift, best not to ride him about anything unrelated to the case.

On the other hand, Adam Jackson looked like a lighthouse. A shining beacon of hope in the darkness of Chicago crime. The homicide man had more than illustrated his skills. McCarthy hoped he would continue his diligence. They needed all the help they could get, and fast. Yesterday Fast!

Sanchez didn't look tired or wide awake. He looked stoic. They needed that too. Backbone and resolve. They were going to put these murderers behind bars.

Where in the hell were Abero and Corde?

0740

McCarthy watched with an impatient eye as each of the task force members filed in, grabbed coffee and found seats. The Captain and Doctor Abernathy entered and sat next to each other. McCarthy grimaced. He really wasn't sure why those two were such good friends all of a sudden.

He still burned with anger over the fiasco yesterday. Why had the Captain insisted on him coming in to give a report right then? And in front of Doctor Abernathy which was unheard of.

A small smile curled his lips when a thought occurred. Jake Corde would be arriving soon and it would be very interesting to see the Captain's reaction. He had been adamant that Jake be removed from the case and Ian had dug in his heels like a true Irishman.

Speak of the devil. Jake strode into the room like he owned it. The man had the assuredness of a King. It was an enviable trait.

He glanced over at Captain Easton and felt satisfaction as the man watched Jake eagerly welcomed by the men where he squeezed in between Anderson and Sanchez. McCarthy himself felt it was good to see the men all getting along with each other like they had been friends forever.

Finally the last member strolled in, her shadows hard on her heels, and sexy heels they were too. McCarthy felt his eyebrows shoot up to his hairline as the good doctor poured herself a cup of coffee and sashayed to the front of the room, settling into a chair next to Dr. Abernathy.

Her guards stayed behind, taking up spots on either side of the door. Even though Matt was a gregarious man, somehow, coupled with Bea Dooberman on guard duty, he looked intimidating. McCarthy wondered if all of the Corde brothers had that air of steely strength about them.

His eyes returned to Zoey Abero, to make sure she was ready and realized she was not nearly as confident as Jake Corde. The pink in her cheeks spread over her face and down her neck as all eyes took in the short, tight, black number she wore. Hardly work attire, but none of the men would complain. Ever.

To end her discomfort Ian McCarthy cleared his throat and turned on the display panel. Pictures of the victims came up as well as James Palmer and his family. It was a gruesome sight for so early in the day but Ian wanted no one to forget the serious nature of the situation.

"I'm going to begin by recapping what we know absolutely. I may point to someone who has thoughts that might fill in the recap a little. Then we will have a discussion about suspicions. After that, how we are going to end this nightmare." He tapped the tablet in his hand and a new picture came up.

"Scene one. Two hairs found and teeth impressions connected this murder to James Palmer. No witnesses. The victim's lower jaw was torn off and taken. Some organs were consumed on the spot."

The next photo came up. "This one had witnesses placing James Palmer at the site around the time of death. Thanks to Jake and Zoey that timeline was narrowed to a half an hour window, making it possible to also tie James Palmer's personal vehicle in the alley a block away. It is curious as to why both his patrol car and his personal car were near the scene but Sanchez has a theory."   He nodded.

Sanchez grinned sheepishly. "Uh, well, uh, we have established there had to be two people involved in the case. Palmer and someone behind the scene. I think the second sick bastard is a voyeur and smart enough to make sure only Palmer was tied to the crime even as he himself was present. He wanted to be there but couldn't ride in the cop car, that would be too visible.

Plus the timeline would be suspicious if Palmer was away from his patrol car for too long. Also taking into consideration the mess he must have made on himself with the viciousness of the attack, he would need to clean up. So he went in Palmer's personal vehicle, with a change of clothes and a clean up kit.

That way he could watch, collect the body parts, and give Palmer a better chance of avoiding discovery."

Jake whistled. "Nice, Sanchez. That's smart thinking. It would have been perfect too, if not for my witness."

Jesus Sanchez beamed like a kid at the praise. Jackson clapped him on the back in congratulations. McCarthy nodded approval.

"The legs were taken from the victim and what organs could be found had all been half eaten or bitten into. Again, dental impressions helped in identifying Palmer as the killer."

He tapped the tablet again and the display changed. "Victim three is the most mysterious and to me, horrible. Her sternum and ribs were taken. Bite marks again. Most of the possible evidence was compromised by the nature of the area where the corpse was found. A dog walker found her when the six dogs she was caring for dragged her over and basically destroyed anything that might have been viable."

A fourth photo. "Here is where we lost Palmer and gained a new killer. Different M.O. except still taking body parts. This guy is talented with tools. Cutting tools to be exact. The spine was removed precisely. In a minute Doctor Abero will expound.

For now let's go to the last murder. The cemetery. Dr. Abero's report was as I suspected. This body was dumped here. A cursory attempt at masking the fact. There is almost no evidence. I doubt we will ever find the original crime scene, but keep your eyes and ears open anyway. Again, a power tool was used."

He nodded to Zoey and she stood up. "It is my opinion that our new killer is a doctor or a student of medicine. There is intimate knowledge of the human body and the use of surgical instruments. The spine of victim four was precise. The ablation was perfect and the excision almost as good as my own work.

I also believe this guy is keeping his victims alive as long as possible. Their suffering is part of his ritual. There were restraint marks on the last victim and drugs in both women.

Additionally, he is cleaning up his crime. The lab was almost sterile when the body was found. She had been washed and neatly covered. All evidence washed down the drain. The last girl was bloody, but otherwise nothing to give a clue.

As for the man or woman behind the scenes. The idea, man. It is my considered theory that this one is building a body of sorts. I don't believe he knows what he is doing because the body parts are different in proportion and won't fit together well.

I cannot see any other reason for the taking of trophy body parts except fetishes but for me, that does not fit either. Normally a fetish is for one particular thing or another not randomly grabbed. But Doctor Abernathy would be a better authority on that."

Everyone looked at the psychologist with questioning eyes.

"I can certainly study up on it. I could not hazard a guess right now. Dr. Abero is accurate in her assessment but perhaps if I look a little deeper I can find something. More evidence would be nice."

McCarthy grunted. "The very lack of evidence is, in a way, telling. In the lab, the cameras were off. No obvious break-in. Whoever the killer is, they are familiar with and have access to the Medical Examiners building. And this one is smart. A thinker." He shut the display off.

"Okay, let's talk." He took a sip of coffee, a breath, "The common denominator is age. All of the victims are between the ages of twenty two and twenty five. But, there are outside clues that are not positively connected to the murders.

Detective Kingsley was killed by Palmer. Why? What did he know or see or both? And how did they find out what he knew? Had Palmer gotten his hands on reports or something like that?

Also, Dr. Abero is being stalked. Someone broke into her apartment sometime around Victor's funeral and another attempt was made just last night." There were angry murmurs around the room. "Luckily Jake had installed two new alarm systems and this time the stalker was scared off. But it begs the question; Is this coincidence? If not, then what do they think Abero knows? What is the purpose of attacking her?"

He gestured around the room. "Does anyone want to add?"

"The guy could be driving a red Jaguar." Jake spoke up.

"That should be easy to find." Detective Jackson said. "How many red Jags can there be in Chicago?"

McCarthy grinned. "Exactly my thought. We are going to run it through our database today. I believe the Corde brothers are on it as well."

"And what about the little girl?" Anderson asked. "Anything new on that?"

McCarthy shook his head sadly. "No. Not yet. But we won't give up."

The room grew quiet for a moment then McCarthy shrugged. "What do we have going on to find this asshat and his little freak helper?"

"This is where I take my leave." Zoey stood up. "I have work to get to. Gentlemen, please excuse me."

There was a scrape of chairs as all six of the seated men stood to attention. Zoey nodded to them in general and walked, head high, out of the room. No doubt she felt every single eye that followed her too.

Chapter 50

0930

They were late. Zoey hated being late. She practically ran into the building, barely containing herself long enough for Bea Dooberman to get in first and look around.

When they walked into the morgue they discovered the room bright and cool. Kellesha was already there. Dressed in her lab coat, the graduate was halfway through the morning preparations. Of course she was. The day was supposed to start at 0900.

Doobie immediately went to the chair in the corner and set up her post for the day. She would move only when Zoey did. They had a pattern set in the short amount of time Doobie had been her bodyguard. It worked for them.

"Kellesha! You were supposed to take a week off. Are you sure you are ready to be back?"

"Really Dr. Abero, I'm fine. I hate missing work," Kellesha assured Zoey, not pausing in her work.

Zoey hesitated, feeling like she should urge the woman to go home, then nodded. She understood the need to work. It was therapeutic in its own right. "Ok. I can't pretend I didn't miss you. However, if you need to stop, just speak up."

"I will. I promise." Kellesha finally looked over at the doctor and smiled. "Now, there are three from a fire coming in. I put out an extra mask for you, Miss Dooberman. The smell can be quite unbearable."

Doobie nodded. She knew what burnt bodies smelled like. One didn't work in war zones without learning a few unsavory smells. While a whiff of charred flesh was not entirely unpleasant, over time, like however many hours an autopsy three times would take, the invasive scent would indeed become quite unbearable. She would be grateful for the mask.

Zoey walked to her locker and pulled out her go bag. She was grateful for the extra set of clothes she kept there. There was no way she could work in heels and this tight ass bandaid called a dress.

Unwilling to analyze why she had worn the thing in the first place she carried the bag to the restroom and changed quickly. Red linen shirt that was cool, absorbent and wouldn't bunch up under her coat. Loose black slacks that did not pinch or constrict and glory of glories, black low heeled shoes with gel inserts. God bless gel.

Over the ensemble she wore her lab coat. Now she was ready for business. She returned the bag to her locker and moved to her computer. Time to log in, check emails and reports and get paperwork ready for the new arrivals.

She heard the buzz that indicated the techs were on their way down with their cargo. A few seconds later the door swooshed open just as she was putting on her last glove. Taking charge she instructed the two men which victims went into the cooler and which went on the table.

In short order one was in a refrigerated drawer and two occupied the autopsy tables. The work force was divided up and Kellesha took one table and tech and Zoey got the other. It was the most efficient way to make sure things run smoothly while the three techs acquired the experience needed to move on with their own education.

The room grew quiet for a moment, then Zoey pulled her recorder down and began speaking into it. "October 27th of the year 2014. Time is 1000. My name is Doctor Zoey Abero. I am assisted by Doug Engstrom. We are beginning with the first burn victim brought in to us. On the other table is Kellesha Clarke assisted by Holt Rimera. We are all working on cleaning up the debris still attached to the victims."

Zoey had no more than finished her last syllable when a crash brought everyone's attention to Bea Dooberman's convulsing body.

"Oh my God! Doobie!" Zoey ran over to her thrashing body-guard. Through the mask the woman's eyes were wild and rolling and she was foaming at the mouth. The foam was tinged red from a bloody tongue and lips where Doobie's sharp teeth tore the flesh.

"Christ! Kellesha, call 911!" She yelled. "Doug! Holt! Help me get this mask off of her!"

"I wouldn't do that if I were you, Doctor." Kellesha said quietly. "I'm no expert on toxins but I doubt she inhaled the whole container of Sarin, no matter how small it is."

Zoey fell back on her hind quarters. "Jesus, Kellesha, why?"

"Blake. It's Blake. Kellesha is gone. Probably forever. As for why, well, I need her arms."

Zoey felt the blood drain out of her face. Her body went cold with shock. So many things came together at once that her vision went blank for a moment.

She cast about in her mind for some solid thought. Anything to calm her. Anything to take her mind off Bea dead on the floor at her feet.

Matt! Matt was doing a sweep of the building, talking to people. How long before he made his way down here? Did Kellesha know about him?

Stall, she had to stall. "I guess I don't understand what you mean. Where is Kellesha?"

Blake rolled her eyes. "Stupid, meaningless questions. You get on my nerves so badly Dr. Abero. Always so kind and generous. As though you are the one doing the world a favor. You don't deserve the prestige of this position.

As for Kellesha, well, she is lost." Blake tapped her forehead. "She was too weak to cope with the truth. I have always been her protector. Now, I am the one the world has to deal with. Lucky you." She smiled that brilliant white smile. It didn't seem so beautifully friendly any more.

She gestured at the two men with the gun. "You two, push this one off here and put that bodyguard up. I have things to do and very little time to do it."

Apparently losing patience, Blake reached out a hand and gave the body the two men were trying to move gently, a hard shove. They yelped and jumped away. Not once did Blake's eyes move to the victim as it tumbled to the floor.

But Zoey's did. She watched in horror as the flesh busted

open and the jaw detached. It was a desecration beyond contemplation. A body was never, ever treated so callously.

Stunned, she didn't realize Blake/Kellesha had moved until her hand tangled in Zoey's hair. "Get the fuck up. Now, while I watch, you remove her arms."

Zoey glanced at the door again, which only served to make Blake laugh. "Give it up Doc. No one is coming to your rescue. Even if they do, I will deal with them as easily as I did your little protection detail. Let's get this done. Then you and I are going for a ride."

"A ride?"

"Stop with the questions! Ah yes, thank you boys. I won't be needing your services any longer." Blake pulled the trigger. Two pops. Two bullet holes. Two dead men.

Zoey couldn't help the scream, or the tears that quickly followed. "Oh my God Kellesha! What are you doing? They were innocent!."

"Men are born tainted by evil. I am doing what I have to. Can't have witnesses, can I?"

"Kellesha! Please! This isn't you!" Zoey tried again.

"Of course not. Didn't I just tell you that?" The woman laughed. "My name is Blake. Say it. Blake."

"Blake." Zoey obeyed, moving slowly toward the table. "It looks like we have a standoff situation here."

"How do you figure that Doctor Abero? I have a gun."

"Yes. Yes you do. And I have had enough. You will have to use that gun on me because I am not going to cut Bea apart for you and your sick fetish."

"My fetish? No, not mine. Do you really think I'm crazy? Wow Doctor. I'm hurt. That's a disgusting thing. But I can tell you it isn't a fetish. He is building a body for his dead wife. Pretty sick huh? And, worse, he truly believes he is going to animate her or something. Like Frankenstein."

"He who?" Zoey asked as casually as she could manage.

"Uh, no. You will find out soon enough. We are going to his place after this job is complete. You are the last one. He wants you for himself."

"Sorry. I'm not cutting Beatrice Dooberman up, and I am not going anywhere with you." Zoey smiled. Her heart was beating so hard she was sure it was echoing around the room enough for the other woman to hear it.

"I don't know what makes you so sure I can't make you do what I want, but you had better get over it quickly. My goodwill is nowhere near as fine as Kellesha's was."

Zoey grinned. "He will never let you get away." She nodded at Matt who suddenly slammed his fist into the door.

"Zoey!"

Blake spun around, her right hand following the rest of her just slow enough that Zoey took her chance. She plunged the autopsy scalpel into Blake's wrist, causing the hand to convulse and go useless. It was easy enough to wrench the gun out of the woman's immobile hand.

Just as easily and without giving it a single thought or a moment's hesitation she emptied the remaining bullets into the killer's torso. She stood there watching Blake fall to her knees, then her face. No emotion touched her heart. Maybe later there would be something, but right then, she was icy cold right down to the marrow in her bones.

Chapter 51

0845

Jake fidgeted. He stared at his computer screen, and thought about taking the Mustang for a drive. Watching Zoey exit the meeting room definitely was a highlight to his day. Damn that woman knew how to dress. What a woman!

Jake's phone rang. He answered without looking at who called.

"Hello."

"Jake it's Alex." Alex greeted.

"How's Mom?"

"She's fine, but that's not why I'm calling," there was excitement in Alex's voice. "I have something for you."

"What have you got?" Jake asked.

"There are exactly two candy apple red Jaguars in Chicago!" Alex said.

"The rest of the family is right to call you a genius," Jake complimented.

"I got addresses, but no names, my sources would not release them, if they even have them," Alex continued.

"You do?" Jake raised an eyebrow, "Are they fake?"

"Ye of little faith," Alex clucked.

"Sorry, I know better than to question your sources."

"Got a pen?"

"Go," Jake said, and furiously wrote down the addresses. "Thanks, Alex. I'm gonna tell Luke to give you a raise."

"You do that, and you're welcome, as always." Alex hung up.

Jake dialed his phone.

"Yo," Burke answered.

"Burke, I need you and Erik here A.S.A.P. Get here faster than that. Wear battle gear."

Jake put on his Kevlar vest. Then he checked his gun. It

was loaded, safety on. Jake ran down to the basement and re-trieved Matt's drone. He checked the battery pack. He also picked up the tablet that showed the video feed, then he ran back upstairs.

Burke and Erick waltzed in.

"We're going on a mission. I got addresses for two Jaguar owners," Jake announced.

"How did you get addresses?" Erik asked.

"My brother Alex has contacts. Are you ready?"

"Born ready," Burke said.

Jake waved his hand and the three of them headed out the door. Jake dialed Doobie.

"Yo!" Doobie answered.

"Everything good?"

"You didn't hire me for nothing," Doobie answered. Good old Doobie, Jake thought.

"Stay vigilant. I don't want anything happening to that black dress," Jake said.

"Yes boss. I K N O W you don't," Doobie laughed.

"Later," Jake hung up. Finally Jake felt like he was in his own element. Time for action.

"Equipment check," Jake called. Everyone checked the oth-er's vests.

"Weapons check," Jake called. They checked their guns.

"Burke, can we take your Hummer?"

"I didn't buy it to sit in the garage," Burke said.

"Let's roll!" Jake headed for the door.

They arrived in the correct neighborhood. Four blocks away from the residence they parked and Erik sent up the drone. Erik worked his controls while Jake watched the video feed. Burke kept watch on their immediate surroundings.

There were no guard dogs. There were video cameras, but they were just standard home security, nothing out of the ordinary. Jake didn't see any signs of life in the house from what the drone revealed.

"You guys ready?" Jake asked Burke and Erik.

"Let's do it!" Erik said.

"Erik, can you hack the garage door?" Jake asked.

"My pleasure. You, going to give me anything hard to do today?" Erik grinned. Burke drove the few remaining blocks toward the residence going the speed limit. They parked opposite the house. Erik's fingers flew over his keyboard.

"Done!" Erik announced as the garage door started opening. Jake was already opening his door.

As a tight well coordinated unit the three men entered the garage. The Jag sat there. A second vehicle was missing.

"Look at that thing!" Burke whistled.

"Stay focused," Jake said. "Burke, Erik take the second floor. We are looking for any egress to a basement. Go!" They entered the house and began searching. Jake wanted no stone left unturned and everyone knew it.

Jake moved quickly and cautiously. Immaculate stainless appliances. Not much cooking was done in the residence. The kitchen was clear. No doors that might lead to a cellar. Jake moved to the living room.

The room, a variable home theatre. There were two chairs that might have been stolen from the local cinema, but they were better quality than the newest movie theatre seats, which were quite amazing nowadays. At the far end of the room nearly the entire wall was the T.V. screen.

Jake moved to the next room. This room didn't surprise him. Clearly it wasn't used much. There was a sliding glass door leading out to a deck. Which again, didn't see use. The houses' occupant didn't sit on the deck.

"Upstairs clear," Erik called.

"Let's move out," Jake yelled. The three men exited the garage, and climbed back in the Blue Hummer H2. Erik worked his computer and the garage door closed.

Jake looked at the house, slightly disappointed. That is when it hit him, there were not any oak trees.

"This isn't the right place," he announced.

"That was a bust," Erik said.

"That was covering all our bases. Burke, take us toward the next address. Erik when we get close, take up the drone, and look for oak trees." Jake said.

Chapter 52

0930

They had refueled Burke's Vehicle. Everyone chugged an energy drink of choice and now they neared the destination. Burke and Erik had devoured some sort of greasy gas station breakfast burritos. How those two could even think of eating at a time like this Jake couldn't begin to fathom. It didn't matter. A happy team made a functioning team. That is what they needed right now, efficiency. They couldn't afford any mistakes. Mistakes got people killed.

"You know breaking and entering is illegal, right?" Erik asked.

"Then you are just as guilty as I am. I couldn't hack a garage door open. But that is what we have Alex for," Jake responded looking at the passing houses.

"Oh, that's what he's for," Burke laughed, pulling over to the shoulder.

"You're learning," Jake grinned.

"Erik..." Jake didn't even finish his sentence.

"On it boss," Erik stepped out of the vehicle to get the drone in the air.

"Fly in from the front," Jake said.

Jake intensely watched the video feed as Erik navigated the drone toward the residence. The black and white feed was blurry, but served its purpose. Sure enough there were the two oak trees from the vision. One on each side of the driveway. In his mind Jake replayed the vision, the red Jag pulling into the driveway between those two oaks. Jake took a breath, held it, and let it out.

"Bingo," he told his team. Jake returned his eyes to the video feed. The lawn was clear of leaves, a service must clean it daily. There was a two car garage. That meant the Jag, and another car. Burke and Erik crowded around the little screen too, like three kids watching a video game. This was no game.

"Erik, do a fly by," Jake said. They continued watching, but the drone flight revealed very little of use. They couldn't get a good look inside the house.

"So much for determining if anyone is home," Burke commented.

"Captain Obvious," Erik jabbed.

"Focus," Jake hushed them. Erik retrieved the drone and stowed it. Tension radiated through the three men, it could be felt like a heavy blanket.

"Plan of action?" Burke asked.

"Same as last time. I'm on point. Burke next, Erik, watch our six," Jake answered. Burke put the vehicle in gear. Erik started tapping on this laptop. They pulled adjacent to the house, and Burke parked.

Jake looked at the oak trees in the real world. Okay you son of a bitch, you're going down, he mentally told the killer. You've done more than enough damage in this world, I'm gonna take you out of it. Adrenaline coursed through Jake's body.

"Done," Erik said as the garage door started ascending.

"Go time!"

As a unit they exited the Hummer and ran for the garage. Two cars were parked inside. One the Jag, and a tan Volvo.

"Some winter-beater," Burke commented about the second sixty thousand dollar car.

Jake listened at the door leading into the house. He couldn't hear a television or music, but that didn't mean the house was unoccupied. Two cars in the garage said otherwise. He drew his .45. Taking a breath he twisted the door knob, pushed inward, and entered the residence.

Ignoring the kitchen Jake headed down the hall. He opened the first door he came to. A master bedroom. The room appeared to have a woman's touch. The bed was made with multiple pillows placed precisely in matching colors. Two bedside tables sat on either side of the head of the bed. Both tables had lamps. One had a book on it, the other a vase of fresh flowers. The room was unoccupied.

Jake continued down the hall to the second door. Locked.

Time was of the essence, he kicked it in. A scream of terror. Huddled next to a bed, clutching a stuffed pony, a little girl shivered . Amy Palmer!

Jake stood where he was for a Moment, thinking. He pulled out his fake police badge and held it up for the little girl to see. "Hi sugar. Are you Amy Palmer?"

She sobbed, stuck her thumb in her mouth and, tears streaking her cheeks, reluctantly nodded, her eyes on the badge. It was a symbol she recognized. Something that represented the familiar safety of home.

Jake smiled, "I work with your dad. He is out searching for you. Do you want us to take you to him?"

Amy nodded.

"Well then, sweetie, will you let Erik take you out to our car while we find the bad guy?"

She stood up, sniffled, and, refusing to remove her thumb from her mouth, wiped her face with the stuffed pony. She trusted that badge. The policeman had nice eyes, wide open and smiling. She took a hesitant step forward then froze as another man squatted to her level.

"Hey, I'm Erik." He practically whispered. "I have a little girl just like you! She loves Minnie Mouse and Dora. How about you?"

"Peppa." She finally spoke around her thumb, leaning hesitantly closer to Erik. His voice was so soft she could barely hear him. He had nice eyes too. And a crooked bottom tooth. And a pretty earring.

"Peppa? What? That little pig? Do you have Peppa toys?" Erik scooped the little girl up, talking about cartoons and toys. He walked steadily but slowly, so as not to jostle or frighten Amy. Jake watched for a second, seeing a new side to Erik. He shook his head. One never really knew.

Once they exited Jake continued down the hallway. A laundry room, a bathroom. Where are you fuckface?

Jake opened the last door in the hall. A staircase led down. Without hesitation Jake descended 24 steps. He entered a realm of horror, the lair of the monster.

To his right, the room resembled Matt's office, and a movie theatre combined into one. There were three huge t.v. screens set up in a panorama. A black leather recliner sat a few feet away from the screens. Frozen on the screens were three twisted, confirming stills.

One depicted James Palmer on top of his wife with a bloody knife in his hands. The second showed James feasting on his son Donald. On the final screen, blood and brains splattered around the shattered sedan window. James Palmer's demise, at the instruction of the demented.

Jake tore his vision from the screens to the rest of the room in front of him. At the far end of the room, a tall man in a grey suit stood with his back to Jake staring at something in front of him. The man seemed unaware of Jake's presence. Jake's ears heard the man speaking softly.

"Very soon my darling. My lovely. My Lily. Your arms and pelvis are on their way. I'll have you in my arms tonight."
Three steps forward. Jake stopped and positioned himself. A shooter's stance. This was a fight. Jake wasn't known for fighting fair, he was known for winning the fight.

Jake aimed his .45. His weapon was just an extension of himself. Mentally he traced the trajectory of his bullet. He took a breath, exhaled, and pulled the trigger.

The shot of a master marksman. The bullet blasted through the back of the man's right kneecap. The man toppled to the ground landing on his remaining left knee. Jake moved forward, closing the gap between them, standing over his target.

In agony the man twisted to face Jake. Thin lips, an extraordinary belt buckle. Stephen Abernathy.

"Jake Corde," Stephen said coldly.

"That one's for me," Jake said, indicating Stephen's shattered right knee cap.

"Should have killed you earlier," Stephen spat.

Jake pointed his gun at Abernathy's left lung. He didn't care what the monster had to say. He squeezed the trigger. The bullet ripped through its target. Blood sprayed out Aberneth's back. The crimson mist coated the thing erected behind the monster.

"You bastard!" Abernathy wheezed through the hole in his lung.

"I'm supposed to turn you into the police, but," Jake deadpanned.

"You're ruining my plan. I must...but what?"

You must die, Jake thought. Ending your plan is long overdue. Time to end your life, you psychopathic scum.

"That one's for Amy Palmer, fuckface," Jake said, indicating the deflated lung. "Did you smear your filth on one of Zoey's shirts?" Jake asked, directing his .45 at the aberration's head.

Abernathy laughed, spewing blood over his sharp chin. "You should have seen her lovely hands working herself over...You should have..."

Jaked pulled the trigger.

Brains and skull fragments exploded from the exit wound.

"That one is for Zoey."

Chapter 53

1100

"Goddamn it Jake! Have you got any idea of the shitstorm you just created? Do you care? Are you aware of the full definition of consultant? You know it doesn't secretly stand for police officers right?

How am I going to make the Captain believe this wasn't premeditated murder? You know you just handed him a gold card don't you? He's never wanted you on this case and now he has the ammo needed to put your ass in jail!

Victor told me about you. He told me you were like the Lone fucking Ranger! He said exactly that! Watch Corde, he's a helluva investigator but he's a cowboy with guns. And I ignored him. Couldn't believe it. I should have listened to Kingsley.

You better have a good explanation for Kevlar vests, a drone and goddamn guns like you're some weekend fucking warriors having a balling time in the U.P. You know flying drones over residences is illegal? But that's the least of your transgressions my friend.

Jesus Christ! It's like a Goddamn Hollywood movie or something! You didn't even bother to call and let us know you had addresses! If that doesn't scream pre-fucking-meditated I don't know what does! Shit, what a mess!" Ian McCarthy had bypassed angry and pissed off and shot right into spitting, red-faced, livid.

He shoved a hand through his thick hair in a gesture that was a sure sign of his frustration. Took two steps away from Jake, turned and retraced his steps. It was obvious he was just getting his breath for a fresh tirade.

"We saved the girl." Jake pointed out imprudently.

"Oh no you didn't just speak to me. Are you kidding me right now McClane? That's where you want to take this? How about you do yourself a favor and shut your pie hole until you have your attorney present?"

Jake shrugged. "Then arrest us. But calm the hell down

before you have an aneurism or some shit. I did what I thought was best. I won't apologize."

Just then his phone went off. Caller I.D. said "little shit". "What Matt?"

"You need to be here yesterday. Doobie's dead, Zoey shot Kellesha."

"Wait, what? Where?"

"The M.E.'s office."

"Is Zoey hurt?"

"I would have led with that if she weren't. Fuck Jake, just get here." Matt hung up.

Jake put his phone away, "Something went down at the morgue McCarthy."

McCarthy checked his phone, cursed, and gestured to his car. "When you make it rain, you do it right," he said to Jake.

"How are both incidents my fault?"

"I'm sure the connection will become clear." McCarthy said as he got in behind the wheel.

Jake climbed in and buckled up before turning to the detective. "You give me too much credit."

"We'll see. Are you going to fill me in or do I have to call one of the guys on scene?"

Jake shrugged. "Death and destruction from the sounds of it. Look, I'm barely holding onto sanity here. Can you step on it? You drive slower than my grandmother's pet sloth."

"I swear to God I am going to shoot you." Ian growled. Jake turned his head to hide the worried frown. Matt had sounded desperate. Doobie dead? How? Zoey shot Kellesha? When did Zoey acquire a gun?

It took an eternity to reach the M.E.'s office from the suburbs. Jake was on his phone most of that time. Matt didn't answer right away so Jake called Willy and Lyle and told them to get over there. Finally he got through to his brother and some of the details got cleared up.

Kellesha was the newest killer. She poisoned Doobie somehow and shot two technicians. Zoey stabbed the woman, got the gun away from her and shot her dead. The police on the scene agreed to wait for McCarthy before arresting Zoey.

Zoey was on the phone with the two dead lab techs families. No, she didn't want to talk on the phone. Matt mumbled something about more questions from the attending police and hung up.

At long last Ian pulled into the parking lot at thirty miles an hour, Jake jerking on the door handle all the while. Mc Carthy grabbed his arm and yelled at him to knock it off. "You damn idiot. What are you going to do, tuck and roll? Well I hate to tell you Mr. Wick, but the door won't unlock until the car is in park."

Matt met them in the hallway, accepting Jake's hug with a sigh. He stepped back and shook his head. "She's in there." He pointed at Zoey's closed office door.

"You ok?"

"No. Jesus Jake. Doobie's dead." Matt's voice cracked. "I was upstairs chatting it up with the guards while she lay in the autopsy room dying."

"Bro." Jake rasped out around the lump in his throat. That wasn't the kind of guilt talk would fix. Time and family was needed. "Call Alex, Luke, bring them home."

Matt nodded, swallowing hard. "You should know, she's barely holding it together in there. But she was great. Didn't freeze up or anything, kept Kellesha talking until the chance opened up. That's a woman worthy of the Corde name Jake."

Jake's crooked smile flashed once then disappeared. He left his brother's side and moved down the hallway. How was he going to explain why he hadn't been here for her AGAIN? Looked like he and Matt had a few demons in common.

After a sharp knock he opened the door and stepped in. The first thing he saw was Zoey, head down, as she spoke softly into the phone. A soft cough alerted him to the female police officer standing right next to him.

Jake jumped. "Uh, you can go."

Her eyebrows went up. "I'm not leaving her alone with anyone."

Jake frowned. "I'm Jake Corde."

The officer nodded. Stayed put.

Zoey must have finished her call because her voice barely cut through the short distance to them, "It's okay, Officer Afton. He's part of the task force."

The officer hesitated then nodded. "Alright Miss Abero. I will be right outside the door if you need anything."

Jake stood silently for a heartbeat until Zoey's tear filled eyes met his. He was devastated by the heartache in the golden depths. He went to her, spun her chair to face him and fell to his knees, pulling her close to him.

"Oh Jake, Doobie..." She whispered brokenly, wrapping her arms around him, soaking up his warmth.

"I know my love. I know. It's not your fault." He rocked her gently back and forth.

She sobbed for a moment then pulled back, grabbed a tissue from the box. "How the hell did I miss it Jake? Kellesha! And she kept calling herself, Blake. What's that about? She killed them all. Doobie, Doug, Holt! Poor Holt's babies! How did I miss it?"

Jake squeezed her shoulders. "We all missed it. Do you know who the guy behind the scenes was? Abernathy!"

Zoey sucked in a shocked breath then nodded. "Of course. That explains so much."

"I have a theory." Jake stood up, pulled her out of her chair, picked her up and walked over to the couch. He sat down, snuggling her close. "Wanna hear it?"

Her hair brushed his chin as she nodded against his shoulder. He caught her scent and closed his eyes. It was sensory overload for him.

"Jake?" Her voice jerked him back to the room.

"I think things happened so damn fast we didn't have time to catch up. I've never seen a serial killer much less two and both doing the bidding of a psycho. Too fast. Kellesha seemed so normal, kind even. I liked her. Plus she's had this job for a few years now. Why start killing now? Why would we suspect her at all? It will be days before we can piece it all together. Weeks maybe."

"Is McCarthy questioning Abernathy?"

"Uh, no." Snap. "I, uh, I killed the nutbag."

"Oh." She sniffled. "So we both killed people today."

"No sweet, sweet woman, not people. We killed the worst evil I've ever seen today. We did what had to be done. You had to survive."

She was quiet for a Moment then sighed. "Can you take me home Jake?"

"Absolutely. Just rest for a few minutes while I talk to Matt and McCarthy and I will get you out of here." He stood up then lay her on the couch. Gently he tucked a throw pillow under her head, kissed her cheek and left the room.

Half an hour later after promising McCarthy they weren't going to blow town, getting Willy to make a few phone calls, sending Lyle off on an errand, he had her safely ensconced in her car and they were speeding through the city. He couldn't keep from glancing over at her from time to time. She looked so vulnerable. It was a painful sight, his feisty woman so sad and subdued.

Her head rested back, eyes closed, mouth slightly open. Her pale cheeks were streaked with tear tracks, her makeup long gone. Every now and then a small hiccup shook her frame followed by a sigh. He doubted she was sleeping, but he let her get what peace she could.

Chapter 54

Only when they arrived at their destination did Jake gently touch her shoulder. "Hey beautiful, we're here."

Her eyes opened. She frowned. "Where's here?"

"A hotel. I sent someone to clean up your place, grab you some clothes. I thought a quiet night away from reminders would do you good. And only three people know where we are. You, me and Willy.

Tomorrow we will face the world together. This afternoon and tonight, you can decompress, grieve in peace. The room has a hot tub, a fireplace, all night room service and an in suite mini bar."

Zoey forced a small smile. "A hot toddy sounds great. Just, minus the water, lemon and honey. Double the whiskey and add some ice."

"You got it babe. Tonight's yours. You want to get stupid drunk and puke in the bath tub, I will hold your hair."

"I bet." Zoey gave him a raised eyebrow.

"Scout's honor." Jake held up both hands, proclaiming his innocence. The valet handed him the ticket for the car. "I will be at your beck and call, no strings attached."

"Why?"

Jake took her elbow in his hand and gazed down into her shining eyes. What the hell, time to be honest. "Because I am head over heels for you Zoey Abero and it breaks my heart to see you so hurt. I can't fix it, but I can make sure you have whatever you need to help you process and begin to heal."

He stopped only long enough to grab the key from the concierge, then lead a stunned Zoey to the elevators. Her silence the entire ride up was nerve wracking, but Jake was determined not to push her for a response. This was not going to be about him.

The room was beautifully appointed in creams, tans and greens. The balcony showed a breathtaking vista of Lake Michigan. The master bedroom did indeed have a hot tub as well as a fully stocked bathroom.

"Are you hungry?"

"No." She said from the mini bar.

She hadn't been kidding. Three fingers of brown liquid over two ice cubes. Alrighty then. He steeled himself for several hours of drunken tears and retching. Such was love.

A knock heralded Willy with two small suitcases in hand and the news that Burke and Erik were let go. For now. Also, Jake's family were on their way home.

Jake thanked his employee and carried the bigger of the two suitcases into the master suite. The other went to the second bedroom, across the living room. He didn't like being that far from her but figured, for looks, the case could rest on the bed in there and he would take the couch once she passed out.

"Thank you." Zoey said from her position by the balcony doors. She had pulled a curtain aside and was looking out.

"You are welcome." Jake stepped toward her, stopped. No pushing. "Do you want to talk?"

She shook her head. "No. I know it is only like two in the afternoon but I think I am going to take a shower and try for a nap."

"That's fine. I'll be right here if you change your mind or need me."

"I appreciate that." She refilled her tumbler and went to the bedroom, shutting the door behind her.

Jake decided a shower wouldn't be a bad thing. He unpacked the one change of clothes and the few toiletries and grimaced. He hoped like hell Willy had done a better job with Zoey's stuff.

He was toweling off when his phone rang. Tossing the towel onto the bed he dug into the discarded jeans. Just as he retrieved the phone, the ringing stopped.

He rechecked it. Luke. Call back or not? He wouldn't stop. Call back then.

"Hey bro. I was in the shower."

"Oh. Sorry. So bittersweet news huh?'"

"Yes. Matt needs family. He was pretty fond of Doobie."

"Yes. That's why I called, actually. We got an early flight. Should be home by supper time tomorrow."

"Cool. Have a safe flight."

"Right. You okay?"

"I will be. Just preoccupied right now."

"Gotcha. Okay, see you tomorrow."

Jake finished drying his hair, donned the clean t-shirt and jeans and returned to the main room. He was hungry. Where was the room service menu? He ordered yogurt, a salad, and baked salmon. Simple, healthy. He had been slacking lately. Energy drinks. Those things were poisonous.

After the food arrived Jake turned the television on to a music channel for some soft Mozart. Not really his cup of tea but he guessed Zoey would appreciate it. And this was about Zoey, not Jake.

He placed the used dishes on the tray and pushed it into the hallway. What now? He couldn't help thinking about McCarthy and the task force. Should he be there with them?

No. The job was done. They could figure out the details. He was needed here, even if only as a presence.

Jake settled prone on the couch and considered the cable guide. Movies. Did he want a movie? A sitcom? Stick with the music?

"Jake."

It was barely loud enough to be heard over the music, but it shot him to his feet like a red-hot poker. He spun to face her, lost his footing and fell flat on his face. Gathering what little dignity he had left he stood up, brushed his hands together, looked over at her.

His knee's wobbled, his gut shivered and his manhood tightened so fast he lost his breath. Standing there in a forest green silk and lace teddy that revealed a great deal of breast and limbs, was a vision straight out of his dreams. He sucked air into his lungs.

"Jesus Zoey, y…you need to cover up." He could barely get the words out.

She shifted nervously from one slender foot to the other. "Did you mean it Jake? Before? Outside I mean?"

Jake blinked. "Uh, yes. Of course. I would never lie to you about that kind of thing Zoey."

"Would you...could you...I want you to make love to me Jake. I want to forget the world." She met his gaze.

"No Zoey. Not like this. I can't take advantage of you like this. Please, just go back in and lay down. Or at least get a housecoat or something."

Zoey stood straight, her chin up, her shoulders back. One slender hand moved up her body. Jake swallowed, but his mouth was cotton dry. He watched in hungry fascination as trim, efficient fingers slid under a strap and moved it down her gracile arm.

More creamy breast was revealed. The other hand treated the second strap the same way. Jake died a little inside as the silk slowly slid down over firm flesh, past lovely dark nipples, hard and inviting, to catch just a tantalizing bit on flared hips. By the grace of God he held himself still.

He wanted her more than anything else in his entire life, but this had to be in her hands. At least at first. If she didn't change her mind, and continued on in this vein then he would eventually take over. And he would love her like no one ever had.

She stepped out of the pool of silk at her feet and moved softly toward him. "Are you going to make me beg Jake? Is that how a man who professes love treats his woman?"

Jake cleared his throat. "I think I am the one begging here. Christ you are so fucking hot Zoey. Please, I am trying to be a gentleman. I have never been one and I think it's the hardest thing I've ever done."

She smiled shyly. "I don't want a gentleman right now Jake. I want a man. I want you, just the way you are. Make me beg Jake."

Her hand slid from his chest down, over his clenching belly to the hard ridge pushing at his jeans. He jerked. His breath hissed out of him.

Fast as a blink he picked her naked body up into his arms and carried her to the hot tub. Sitting her on the edge he turned it on. He stripped his shirt off, shucked his jeans. He couldn't help feeling gratified, just a little as her eyes widened and her cheeks flushed.

He knelt in front of her and took her face in his large hands. Slowly he traced her features with his fingers, pushing her hair back, his touch soft. He bent forward and feathered kisses in a trail that chased his touch.

She sighed, leaned in.

Jake let his lips follow her jawline to those beautiful pouty lips. "I've wanted to really kiss you for so, so long. A lifetime." He said softly.

Putting action to words he pressed his lips to hers, suckled on the bottom one, nibbled the top. His mouth invited her tongue to join his. They danced first in his mouth, then in hers.

Several long moments later he pulled away, kissing her down her neck to her cleft. He gave his tongue free reign of first one luscious bud then the other, reveling in the moans each lick and sip elicited from her. His hands ran over her back and arms, no pressure, just lightly petting, loving.

He pulled away, reached around her, and tested the bubbling water. Perfect. Lowering her in he followed. Jake knelt in front of the nearest stream of bubbles. Carefully he pulled her around so that her soft bottom nestled against his lower belly, his hard member pressing against her.

"Last chance, baby."

"Do it Jake. Please."

Jake wrapped an arm around her and lifted her onto his thick manhood, gently lowering her until he was fully sheathed. He felt his muscles shaking with the effort he was exerting. Slow, slow. You are not a teenager. Take this slow. Control. Her pleasure first. God she was so hot.

He moved forward on his knees until the stream of water was a constant pressure on Zoey's woman hood. She moaned. Jake slid his hands up and cupped each breast, working the nipples. He began moving under her.

Zoey fell forward, hanging onto the edge of the hot tub. It was too much. There was no build up, no tingling sensation, she just exploded. The orgasm hit her so hard she cried out, panting, bucking.

Jake smiled. "There you go baby. Now, let's get another one out of you before we move this party to the bed."

He spun around, sat on the seat and turned her to face him. "Hang on sweet love, we will do this one together, yes?"

She nodded, still panting. Jake lifted her onto him again, holding her hips as he pumped into her over and over again, rubbing her mound over his pelvis on each downward stroke. His blood was roaring in his ears, his breath rasped, his muscles screamed.

Zoey cried out. "Oh Jake!"

He felt her convulse around him and he let go, losing his mind in that moment to the joy of having her, of hearing her cries of pleasure.

At last he carried her out of the water to the bed where he laid her gently among the pillows, pulling one down to shove under her hips. He wasn't done making her beg. He gazed down at her beautiful womanhood.

"I love you too Jake." She said clearly, her gaze direct and hot.

Jake Corde looked at his destiny with a resigned, crooked smile.

Goddamn Mom and her tarot cards.

Epilogue

Jane Corde shuffled her cards. She placed the deck on the table in front of her, and closed her eyes. She cleared her mind, and asked the stars her question. With her eyes still closed she flipped the cards, placing them in the planetary spread.

Moon. Mercury. Venus. Sun. Mars. Jupiter. Saturn.

Jane opened her eyes and focused on the cards before her. The answer to her question. Tears silently streamed down her cheeks.

"Oh, This, is not good."

About the Authors

John Opskar graduated from Western Michigan University. He enjoys a good cigar and a great book.

Janet Lintemuth grew up in Michigan, married her high school sweetheart and went on to graduate from Davenport University. She has been happily telling stories since the ripe old age of eight.

www.ingramcontent.com/pod-product-compliance
Lightning Source LLC
Chambersburg PA
CBHW070455200726
48293CB00007B/2208